T0149303

INN-BY-THE-BYE
STORIES - 5

William Flewelling

authorHOUSE®

AuthorHouse™
1663 Liberty Drive
Bloomington, IN 47403
www.authorhouse.com
Phone: 1 (800) 839-8640

Published by AuthorHouse 02/25/2016

ISBN: 978-1-5049-8238-2 (sc)
ISBN: 978-1-5049-8237-5 (e)

Print information available on the last page.

Also By This Author

Poetry

Time Grown Lively
From My Corner Seat
Enticing My Delight
The Arthur Poems
From Recurrent Yesterdays
In Silhouette
To Silent Disappearance
Teasing The Soul
Allowing The Heart To Contemplate
As Lace Along The Wood
To Trace Familiarity
The Matt Poems
Elaborating Life
The Buoyancy Of Unsuspected Joy

Devotional

Some Reflective Prayers
Reflective Prayers: A Second Collection
A Third Collection Of Reflective Prayers
For Your Quiet Meditation

Directions Of A Pastoral Lifetime

Part I: Pastoral Notes, Letters To Anna, Occasional Pamphlets
Part II: Psalm Meditations, Regula Vitae
Part III: Elders' Studies
Part IV: Studies
Part V: The Song Of Songs: An Attraction

Inn-by-the-Bye Stories
vols. 1, 2, 3, 4

Exegetical Works

From The Catholic Epistles: Bible Studies
Paul's Letter To The Romans: A Bible Study
all published by AuthorHouse.com

Contents

CCI 1

CCII 5

CCIII 9

CCIV 13

CCV 17

CCVI 21

CCVII 25

CCVIII 29

CCIX 33

CCX 37

CCXI 41

CCXII 45

CCXIII 49

CCXIV 53

CCXV 57

CCXVI 61

CCXVII 65

CCXVIII 69

CCXIX 73

CCXX 77

CCXXI 81

CCXXII 85

CCXXIII 89

CCXXIV 93

CCXXV 97

CCXXVI 101

CCXXVII 105

CCXXVIII 109

CCXXIX 113

CCXXX..117

CCXXXI 121

CCXXXII.. 125

CCXXXIII 129

CCXXIV 133

CCXXXV... 137

CCXXXVI 141

CCXXXVII...145

CCXXXVIII 149

CCXXXIX 153

CCXL..157

CCXLI 161

CCXLII...165

CCXLIII..169

CCXLIV..173

CCXLV.. 177

CCXLVI..181

CCXLVII...185

CCXLVIII 189

CCXLIX..193

CCL...197

Appendix: Texts For The Stories... 201

Foreword

Revisiting these stories once again brings up a great deal of emotion. I commented to a friend that on some of them I found myself weeping; on others, it is more of a gentle smile. I go looking to see what the scriptural text behind the story was, and often nod at the still unexpected twists of my engagement by those texts.

In my opinion, the stories have become richer than the earlier ones were. Perhaps I could have skipped the first year or so – except that those stories began to introduce my characters and to open up the geography of Hyperbia for me, and for my readers, I felt. So, it would seem, I convince myself once again that the early stories when I was more in a learning mode myself – basic learning – provide a framework for the unfolding of the more nuanced reflections that do indeed presume the character development that has gone before.

This is my fifth run of these Inn-by-the-Bye stories, a total of 50 to a run. By the time I finish, there will be a twenty third issue, that of the last twenty six stories but also including the earlier dabbling that provided an acquaintance in my own mind with the emerging possibilities – preliminary sketches at the sense of Hyperbia and of some of these characters and their strangely chosen names.

I hope that the acquaintance with Carymba and Missus Carney, Mother Hougarry and Thyruid and Marthuida, and the rest of the rounding list of characters become your friends, too.

William Flewelling

CCI

'Why do you have to leave *now*? This is a lovely evening now, but my bones say it will storm over night.'

'You are just too full of worries, Mather Hougarry"! You know very well that I am one who just goes because I must. We have gone through this same discussion many times before.'

'I know. But there is always hope that you will listen to reason *some* time!'

Carymba stepped off the porch of the Hidden Cabin. 'I must be going now' she said finally.

With a sigh, Mother Hougarry saw her step away. 'Oh … you must take a snack! You might get hungry.' The look back said a silent 'No'. 'Well, here, take this rain parka, just to keep you dry when the storm comes tonight.' The slicker hung in her hands, untaken.

Mother Hougarry watched her young friend, whom she had largely raised, trudge off into the dusk. The syncopated gait went down the hill, bobbing along, weaving the way between the mammoth tree trunks. Carymba vanished, then reappeared beyond another tree, barely visible in the deepening grey of dusk. Mother Hougarry had learned long ago just where to watch, and how long it would be before the last sighting had eclipsed and it would be time to retreat to her rocking chair, or even inside for the night. She always waited longer than she could see before deciding to give up and retreat for the night. This night was no different. Carymba had long left her view, and the shadows of evening had long faded into a pervasive black before Mother Hougarry sighed and left the porch post against which she had been leaning; her shuffling steps drew her into the unlit cabin, there to find by habit the light for her window.

Carymba's parting steps carried her down the slope and on to the tree-root steps to the Valley Road. She paused there as if to sniff the wind. All was peaceful to the eye and ear. Mother Hougarry's storms were far away as uncounted stars peeped coolly down upon the waiting waif. Setting her jaw resolutely and nodding her head with assurance, she spun on her heel and headed toward the Fields. The lurking trees overshadowed her with broad, leaf-heavy limbs whispering in the cool bare breeze of early night time. As she would pass along, the leafy barriers would bar the star spangled sky from view; though leaving the path no darker than before, the trees denied her the companionship of the clear sky's offered host. Her steady pace pulled her to the 'Y' and then out to the Fields. She angled down toward Mary's Flower Shop.

One light still flickered in Mary's window upstairs as Carymba moved toward her Flower Shop. A quick grin of recognition flashed across Carymba's face as she hurried her limping step onward. The night felt warm to her, under the press of her stiff-paced walk. She found herself at Mary's door, knocking and then gathering her breath as her heart pounded inside her chest. Running hands through her now-moist hair, she peeled it away from her cheeks and pulled it back to dangle in clinging locks behind her ears. There was no noise within; she knocked again and waited while her breath gathered and her body settled. Smiling to herself, she decided she must have been walking harder than she had supposed. Somehow sensing that a listening ear was on the other side of the door, she spoke: 'Mary ... this is Carymba ... I need to speak with you ...'.

The door creaked open onto the night; Carymba stood impatiently ready for Mary to be ready. A low light flickered across the room, throwing dancing shadows all about. Mary's face looked at her from the shadow of her head, her hair frazzled enough to catch the lamp light into an aurora around her face. Carymba blinked; the way the light fell made vision difficult for her. The fuzzy feet were clear, as were the skinny legs sticking between the slippers and the knee-length gown. The lamp showed the bare arms hanging at Mary's side. 'Oh. Are you ready for bed already" Is it that late?' 'Yes. You are right on both counts. What do you need to talk about at *this* hour?'

Having heard Carymba's word, Mary stood with her hands on her hips, her elbows pointed outward diamond shaped against the stubbornly insistent lamp. 'You want me to go?' 'Yes'. '*There!?*' 'Yes'. '*NOW?!*' 'That is right' returned Carymba quite innocently. She certainly went about at almost any time, in almost any weather, with no real regard for anything but what was needed. Simply put, that was Carymba's normal way. Mary stared at her: 'But Carymba, it is night out there!' Carymba looked wide-eyed back at her friend. 'And it is time for some people to sleep'. Carymba looked puzzled at her defense. 'I am not dressed to go out' Mary declared with a finality which presumed that it would answer *every* objection. Realizing Mary had finished her fragmented speech, Carymba asked: 'Are you ready to go now? or do you need to turn off your lights first?' Mary almost exploded: 'Didn't you hear me?!' 'Sure, I heard you. But I need you now'. Mary dropped her hands to her side, and her jaw hung open. 'Thanks, Mary' smiled Carymba. 'I knew you would help me ... only, hurry please!'

Mary watched her friend turn and hobble off, turning left and then down the graveled run-off in the corner of the Fields. She muttered to herself: *she* was not going anywhere. Not now. Maybe in the morning. Ha! Maybe next week. Stomping upstairs, she turned into her room and began to pull some real clothes onto herself before stomping back down the stairs, turning off the lights, and throwing herself through the door, into the night. Turning right, she headed for the 'Y' and then on to the Valley Road, muttering every hurried step of the way, her empty hands pumping with her paces under the winking stars.

Carymba skid down the gravel wash-way, nearly tumbling farther than she wished. She managed to catch herself on the narrow walk which she then followed by guess up to the unlit door. Breathing deeply and setting her jaw again, she rapped upon the door. A shuffling sound came from inside; she could hear the confusion which her rapping made. She concentrated on her rap, making it sound as authoritative as she could. Oddly, she reflected on the knocks in Apopar, and shuddered. *That* was not her intent. Shortly, in the weak light given by the hand-held lamp, she saw Guerric, barefoot, in need of a shirt and blinking. 'Sorry about the hour, but I need your help.' 'Oh?' asked Guerric seriously, his curiosity tugged. 'Yes. Down the Beach, near the Great River ... out behind Mahara's old territory ... I need you there tonight. Bring Mahara, but nothing else.'

'Can I dress first?' he asked, curling his toes. 'I imagine. But do hurry. And travel light. I will see you there as the moon comes up'.

Carymba left. Guerric watched her exaggerated hobble rush down the path and, faintly seen, climb up onto the Commons. Yawning and stretching, he turned to dress. 'You are going, then' said Mahara matter-of-factly. 'Yes'. 'I will come, too'. Soon dressed, he reached for his tool box. Mahara noticed his habitual reach. 'Didn't she say to come light, with no extras?' 'This isn't extra!' he reacted, surprised. Pausing, he added: 'But she did say nothing, didn't she?' Nodding to himself, he set the box down again and left, Mahara leading the way to the Commons, and then beyond, toward the Valley Road and on to the Beach and the Sea Road.

As the moon was about to rise, the wind stirred and the clouds hurried over and the storms began. Mother Hougarry rose to look out her window and wonder what was happening with Carymba this night.

21 July 1985

CCII

The brassware shone appreciatively to Thyruid, responding to his daily polishing work. This morning, more than most mornings, Thyruid was mistily absorbed in the brass work. The Inn-by-the-Bye lay quiet in the early hours. Marthuida had not yet reached her kitchen; but then, Thyruid had risen early this morning, earlier than usual. The Sun was not up, so the curtains served only to filter starlight from the Dining Room. The lamp – he had lit but one when he had first wandered into the Dining Room from his room behind the paneled wall – burned low, casting its soft light shyly into the room. When the lamp-glow met the newly polished brass, then it became bold and warm and softened the Innkeeper's heart. Patiently, he re-stuffed his polish rag into his polish pot, pulled it out and began to rub the trim ware. Having been polished the day before, the trim was barely tarnished. Thyruid knew that, but had long loved to see the brass-glow respond to the polishing action. The brass never failed him; when he rubbed the compound on, then off and buffed it all with care, the glow came in response to his effort and the lamp's teasing. At least in his eyes, the glow became deeper each day; one has to see that maturing of brass under caring hands to appreciate it all.

Misty-minded, Thyruid poured his energy into the brass. He had not slept real well; the weather had been muggy the day before, a closeness which had clung in the Inn until the cool of the night changed it into a clamminess which clung all the more. Outside a sheet, he was chilly and damp; beneath a sheet, he steamed. He had risen in surrender to all that while Marthuida slept simply. He recalled having looked back to her as he slipped out of the room – with just a tinge of jealousy. Now, there came that, for him, simple pleasure of coaxing more gleam out of the brass.

5

Intently, Thyruid worked. There was half a night to spend, so he need not hurry. As a result, he gave miniscule attention to each detail of each piece of trim. The idea never occurred to him that he normally would not spend so much time, nor so much energy, nor so much attention – nor so much polish – on the polishing chore. Other days were not this day. Now, nothing pressed him to another chore, another role. The work pushed back from him the damp chill he had suffered. Beads of sweat rose on his brow, then congregated to run off and drip away; he didn't notice, for his thoughts were all brought close upon his favorite pastime.

Only after he was fully satisfied with one piece did the Innkeeper move to another. The close carefulness took time, time marked by unseen stars overhead as they marched their way across the night sky. The close carefulness also let time pass unnoticed in the regular snapping motion of the polishing cloth moving across the brass, raising a deeper glow to the fine glance of Thyruid's inspecting eye. Absorbed in intrigue over the corners of the trim, Thyruid did not notice the gradual greying around the curtained windows.

Marthuida, long asleep while Thyruid attended his pet chore, stirred with the pre-dawn greying of the sky. Stirring, she became aware that Thyruid was up – and had been for a while. Wondering, she sat up and felt the cool damp; nodding, she rose and dressed for the day. Slipping out the door, she silently saw Thyruid bent over, inspecting his on-going polish work. Smiling with a hint of a smirk, she closed the paneled door softly and moved into her kitchen. As for Thyruid, he never imagined she had left her comfortable sleep; he still had a ways to go in order to finish his chore, so the night must still be fairly young. Suddenly he noticed a drop of sweat cascade from his nose. Surprised, he realized he was warmer now; the thought of taking a nap before Marthuida rose crossed his mind. Stretching his back a moment, he shook his head with a scowl: no, he would finish first; there would be time then. He plunged his polish rag into his polish pot and moved to the next piece with jaw set in readiness.

In her kitchen, Marthuida was busy stealthily arranging herself for the day. The biscuit dough would need to be made ready, and the coffee pot begun. The oven was started and she paused to pin a straying lock of hair back into tidy place. The big teakettle was set on the stove, near the back to warm but not yet to come to boil. The tea-drinkers wouldn't be around for a little while yet; the coffee-favorers seemed to rise first. Besides, Thyruid preferred coffee, and he had been up and working for some time. Frowning momentarily, she wondered just *how* long. With a shrug, she decided the time did not matter; but when he thought about it, he would be hungry. Breakfast would be a nice surprise about them. Her face spread out all around as she smiled over *that* thought. Her hands plunged into the floury tasks of readying breakfast for the two of them, and later for their usual company … and whoever else might decide to 'drop in'.

Her work in a momentary lull while the oven and stove did their part of the labor, Marthuida peaked through her swinging door, being careful not to move the door out too far lest the hinge squeak (it squeaked only on the swing into the Dining Room, not on the reverse swing into the kitchen). Thyruid, she saw, was stretching as he looked over his work – stretching as if to ease some sort of kink. The diversion did not last long: nodding approval after one last wipe or rub, Thyruid moved to his last piece of trim and began what Marthuida could tell was a painstaking process. She had some time left; with a twinkle, she eased the door shut and gleefully checked the preparations. The coffee was almost ready; her nose knew that was true. The biscuits for two were nearly done. The tray! Yes … it too was prepared: two plates, two mugs, the butter, the jam all set out in readiness with the other necessary utensils.

The biscuits done, the tray prepared, the coffee poured: Marthuida marched out of the kitchen and took the breakfast past the counter they usually used and took a table, just like customers or guests would do. She set the breakfast out for them and sat down. She had not worried about the squeak, and the hinge squeaked; but Thyruid did not notice. She half-pouted. Thyruid still did not notice as the biscuits began to cool. Instead he seemed singularly engrossed in some minute corner of the last piece of brassware. She wondered that he hadn't tired of the polishing for today. She wondered if there were something wrong with his nose, for the aroma of biscuit certainly was noticeable in the air. She frowned at the whole thing and began to reach for her own, still hot, biscuit: no reason for *two* cold breakfasts, she decided for herself.

Thyruid straightened; Marthuida paused and looked his way expectantly, her hands suspended over her biscuit. He backed away and stretched around, loosening himself for another day. The thought of breakfast entered his mind as he crammed the cloth into his pot. His nose twitched: biscuit smell! He frowned at the notion in the middle of the night. He even yawned. Marthuida set her hands on her lap just before Thyruid turned around. She tried to suppress a grin, unsuccessfully, and then said: 'Wouldn't you like a bite to eat? Suddenly tired, he sighed and nodded.

Over steaming opened biscuits, the butter and the jam melting into waiting crumbs, Thyruid paused: 'Thanks'.

25 August 1985

CCIII

Drizzle dribbled off the roof of the porch of the Inn-by-the-Bye as Thyruid stood and watched. He had closed the door behind him and stood now looking through the line of drips from the roof into the slow and casual near-rain which more floated than fell into the awaiting Commons. The grass slumped under the weight of the water. The paths were slick in clay-mud, pocked with puddles marred with ringlets from a zillion drops of drizzle. The Innkeeper folded his arms across his belt, his sleeves rolled up, as was his custom; his apron was only slightly dirty from his morning's chores; his face hung round and somber as he watched the sky slump toward the Ground. Now should be high noon, with a late Summer Sun high in the sky. But the Sun went hiding today, and the sky had been slithering lower and lower since what was supposed to have been dawn. The sky kept coming down, trying (or so he imagined) to catch up with the drizzle which wept away. The Great Rock was growing misty now, as the sky reached it. The Leaferites' Hill was visible only in the lowest parts. Tops of trees were lost, swallowed by the lazy sky.

Thyruid sighed a whimpering sigh. This day was not supposed to be so damp. He was discouraged, for he had planned a party on the Commons, to gather everyone together and surprise Marthuida. He had even arranged for everybody to bring a dish so as to give Marthuida a day off, a relief and a surprise. But now, the sky was slumping downward like the canvas on a circus tent when the poles are lowered and the ropes grow slack. Only this sky was merely wet. He looked toward the Great Rock; the sky had devoured it from his sight; he snorted in dismay and gradually drummed his fingers on his arms, like a drummer tapping the pace for a wake. His dream and his plan and his surprise were all becoming entombed in fog. All the furrows on his tired face plunged into the contours of frown as the drizzle dripped as a fringe upon the fog which obscured now even the puddles in the yellow mud-slick paths.

The door opened behind him; Marthuida stepped out. 'The fog is chilling, Thyruid. Why not come in? I have made some lunch for us. This weather does not look promising for much company today. Clyde and Geoffrey went out earlier; they may be back later, if they don't get lost in that soup!' Thyruid turned to her, and smiled at her soft look. With a shrug, he dumped part of his sadness into the fog, turned and shuffled on into the Inn. The door clunked behind him and what wisps of sky came into the Inn-by-the-Bye soon melted away. The room was full of the smell of soup and rolls. Thyruid sniffed, twitching his nose at the fragrant panorama presented to him. This wasn't quite the sort of day he had planned, but it would do – it would *have* to do. For no one in their right mind would come out *today*, of all days. So the disappointed Innkeeper raised a smile and went to his table. Thinking briefly that too much was wrong today, he set his mind to enjoying what was yet right enough.

The middle of a corner table was filled with a tureen of soup and a basket of fresh hot rolls, wrapped in a cloth. A gentle and civilized steam rolled upward through the cracks and crevices of the tureen lid. Thyruid sat down unaccustomedly as Marthuida reached to serve their bowls. The notion slipped through his head that she was the one who was supposed to have the party and be served; he started to fuss, but she simply took the stage from him – so he sat back quietly, even timidly. The bowls served, the rolls broken, they ate a very good lunch. 'You certainly *are* an excellent cook!' he exclaimed with appreciation and a wipe of his face on the napkin. She smiled, mused, and wondered out loud: 'Now to attach the dishes …'. 'We'll be quiet today. Why don't I help you?' 'That sounds good; … I'll enjoy your company. Here: you bring the tureen.'

Between them, they quickly brought the dishes into the kitchen. Once they got them all stacked, with her cooking pans, Thyruid marveled that so many dishes would be needed for lunch for two people, even as fancy a lunch as Marthuida had prepared. 'Whew! These will take us a while to do!' 'Oh, I suppose they will. But what better is there to do … with that fog and all?' Thyruid remembered his plans, foiled by the weather, and he drooped a bit. 'Cheer up, Thyruid! Some good dishwater will warm your spirits!' 'Or at least my hands' he observed dryly, before succumbing to a twinkle in his eye.

Cleaning up took a long time. First of all, there were a lot of dirty dishes. Secondly, neither was in any hurry ... especially Marthuida. She began to talk about almost anything over and over again as they washed. He would speak quickly, and she would respond in a lazier drawl until Thyruid too slowed down and almost relaxed. The dishes went slowly, carefully, with a tortoise's speed.

Not long after the Innkeeper and his wife had retired to the kitchen, the front door had inched open slowly and quietly. Geoffrey and Clyde slipped into the room and hung up their raincoats – Clyde's slicker and a coat Geoffrey had found for himself. Tiptoeing about as silently as possible, they inspected the room and made some *very* careful arrangements. Not one table leg or chair scraped the floor, nor clunked into another piece of furniture. For their gentleness, they moved quickly, figuring the dishes would take only so long. Hearing Marthuida drawl slower and slower, bringing Thyruid's pace to a crawl, they smiled at one another.

That pair had barely finished when the door eased open again to admit the first of what proved to be a regular progression of people, all entering in silence. Mahara and Guerric came, bringing a heavy basket of food. Mary and Carymba came with a bundle of flowers which they set around on the rearranged tables. Vlad, Yev, Cons, Nike, Serg, Lev, Dum, and Alex came with food – and assisting Father John and Mother Hougarry and even Missus Duns. The Spinners – Chert and Effie, Gilbert and Martha – brought two groaning baskets. Benito and the Tinker, John, Gingre, James, Peder and his laborers – Charles, Gregory, Jerome, Cy, Jacques and Guido – Terzi and Tyler all came, laden with supper.

All was arranged, or so it seemed. But Geoffrey grew nervous and began to pace back and forth, worried. Clyde saw him and tried to settle him down, lest his thrashing serve to announce to Thyruid that something was up. Geoffrey tried to convey his concern over the missing guest. Clyde nodded and drew Geoffrey near, to whisper into his ear. Geoffrey nodded, but with a wave of mixed frustration and anxiety sweeping across his face.

In the kitchen, the dishes at last done, Thyruid confessed he had wanted a party for her today, an anniversary day of their time in the Inn-by-the-Bye. But even with the weather, I thought somebody would come.' Just then a rap came at the back door. With a puzzled look at Marthuida went and answered the door. There stood a wet old woman: 'Have you a glass of water?' 'Certainly ... and do come in from that awful weather ... here.' 'Thanks. The water seemed fitting today' she said as she threw her hood back to smile her presence. Thyruid grinned broadly: 'Missus Carney!'

The door squeaked behind him: Thyruid turned around and saw a house-full awaiting him. 'Go on' said Missus Carney: 'the party is for you.' She smiled, and winked, and drained her water glass.

1 September 1985

CCIV

Cool real rain fell lightly outside; Betsy watched the ground soak up the splatters of big drops after they had crashed into the soil. The dust was now clumping; as she watched, the wet clumps ran together slowly and as fresh bombardment from the skies brought them near to new neighbors. The clumps merged and owned the surface, finishing the transformation from thick and powdery dust to slick slime, yellow-streaked and glistening. Betsy stood in the doorway, watching, brooding. The air had been hot and heavy for days, lying upon the land like a giant blanket, a steamy blanket. Now the air hung light and crisp, a foretaste of nearing Winter, she feared. And yet that coolness which brought the lazy-falling rain to wash the air and earth brought as well a freshening of heart and body. She even rubbed her arms for warmth, then giggled at the realization that goose bumps felt good today.

Yves, hearing his sister giggle, grumbled: 'What's so funny out there?' he wanted to know. He could hear the drumming of the rain on the roof of the Great Dome. He listened to the regular patter, a drum roll of sorts, punctuated occasionally and randomly by larger splats where a leaf's gathering in the trees overhead grew too burdensome, and rolled off to crash more weightedly upon the roof. The sound generally meant a day inside, with Betsy, seeking something to do, being bored. That prospect hardly encouraged any giggling. All he heard in return was more giggling. He grumbled even more about sisters and all as he dragged himself off his bed, to his feet, and toward the door.

There stood Betsy, looking out the door at the rain, her arms folded in front of her. Yves stopped, his hands on his hips, his head tilted to the side in questioning disdain. He watched her rock up and down on the balls of her feet, bare on the floor. She looked so silly that he smiled, until she

13

giggled again. Curiosity won him: 'What is so funny?' he asked out loud, his voice narrow and strident, surprising even himself. 'Oh! Yves! I forgot about you!' That response left him somewhere between puzzled and hurt. He had never thought of himself being forgotten before; while *he* may have become preoccupied on rare occasion in the past, and have ignored Betsy, and even forgotten her (he half-smiled at the thought of forgotten little sisters), he himself had always presumed himself rather unforgettable. A semi-pout crept over his face. Betsy watched him: 'Not really forget you, Yves. I simply didn't think of you as I watched the rain and felt the cool. Have you seen the mud grow?'

Yves scowled, turning his pout into a frown: 'mud grow?' he thought, scrunching his face and spreading his nostrils in a gesture of distaste which Betsy did not notice because she had turned back to the outdoors. He wanted to think of his sister as being awfully stupid – largely because she was younger than he, and a girl, and a sister. Yet the question of mud growing taunted his mind and his pride. Which would win, pride or curiosity, he almost asked himself, and would have asked himself *if* he had had sense enough to realize the contest that was going on inside his head. He knew about mud: it was slippery and wet, became oozy when it got deep enough; mud clung to feet and clothes. Sometimes mud was fun; a grin flickered upon his face and vanished. He had never see mud *grow* before, however; it was always just there. Grow? does a mud monster rise yellow-brown and glumpy? slithery? stretching mud dripping paws upward with gaping slime? He shuddered at the visions in his head, and pondered going back to bed while the mud-monsters dried out.

But then, he thought of growing mud, and the rain drops gave fresh barrage upon the roof of the Great Dome. Rain, he knew, meant more mud. More mud meant more growing. The mud-monster wouldn't go away today! not with more rain coming to make more mud to grow bigger monsters. Yves' eyes grew wide; he could feel his pulse beat harder, faster. Betsy giggled again. This time Yves was sure is was nervousness and fright which brought the giggle. The mud-monster must be growing ominously now! He began to mutter, talking to himself under his breath so as not to frighten Betsy any more than she already was, poor girl! 'Now Yves, think. This is no time to become too rattled. Be brave! Think of poor Betsy; she is your sister, after all. Now, what to do; what to do.' Yves trailed off into anxious silence as the mud-monster grew bigger and uglier and fiercer in his mind's eye.

Suddenly Betsy opened the door and said 'Hi!' Yves froze, his eyes wider than he remembered them ever getting before. Betsy must be crazy, he thought. Her calm and pleasant 'Hi!' echoed frighteningly in his distorted hearing. He imagined the mud-monster flopping himself up the steps. He could hear the sloppy sound of mud on the steps. He tried to swallow, but could not; he did not need to swallow for he was suddenly dry of mouth. The tiny steps of splattering mud echoed large in his ears, the squishing ascent of a growing monster, the Mud-Monster. The door closed; he heard it rattle shut. He did not yet see the Mud-Monster with his eyes. He swallowed, but there was nothing to swallow, so he went through the motions. The dustiness clung at his throat. He watched for the monster to ooze at the screen door. He imagined it would squeeze itself – mud-like – through the screen and remold itself on this side. Betsy leaned over; he saw the yellow-brown slick mud gleaming through the door. In his panic he searched for breath, never thinking that he saw only the rain-slicked yellow clay path up the hillside. Betsy spoke: 'Don't worry about the mud. How could you not be muddy today? After all (and she giggled!) I've been watching the mud grow out of the dust all morning, I think.

Yves waited in horror for the Mud-Monster to ooze over him. He was resigned. Betsy looked at him, her head sideways because she was leaned over at the waist, her hands on her knees. He looked very funny; she laughed out loud. More than a giggle, she had to step forward and catch her balance in response. The muddy feet hurried aside, just in case Betsy would have more trouble. She stayed standing, however. But the sound of mud crowded Yves ears, almost enough to hide the ring of laughter on the startling, bright face, rung in curls which all belonged to Betsy.

Without standing erect, Betsy asked: 'Well, aren't you even going to say hello to our guest? What's the matter with you, Yves? You act as if you never saw Carymba before!' Glancing down to Carymba, up against the doorjamb, then back to Yves, she added: 'She isn't *that* wet. *I* had no trouble recognizing her, even as she slithered own the hill of the fresh mud.'

Yves began to realize the big shiny slithery yellow-brown glob was really the hillside he loved to slide down. He even began to wonder what

Betsy had meant. Weighing his pride and curiosity, he finally shrugged and said hello to Carymba. 'Come on in! We ought to be able to handle a little mud! Why, after a while, it even grows on you.' He blushed around the ears, but only slightly. Betsy wondered what Yves meant. Carymba smiled graciously and came into the center of the Big Dome. Yves glanced once more at the mud, shook his head and shrugged his Mud-Monster away.

8 September 1985

CCV

Low skies rumbled violently, shaking the huts of Apopar with the shock of nearby thunder. Sheets of rain riveted the walls and swept across the roofs of each little hut. Inside each hut quivered another family, hoping through the assaulting storm. One door creaked open as the storm rushed by; looking out with careful eyes, Missus Carney watched the not-quite-horizontal driving rain rush past the doorway. Brilliant flashes and deafening roars illumined and shook the huts she saw. The wind bowed the plants, the branches reaching far and shaking after unknown objects; perhaps they sought after the leaves which the wind so hastily stole away from them. The path to her door lay soft and oozy, pocked with puddles large and small, each puddle rippled by rain and wind. The safety of the hut, like all the huts, was questionable in the violence of the storm. Even so, the walls were friendly and dry; the mud was all on the *outside*.

As Missus Carney watched the sweeping sheets of rain wash by, she was suddenly surprised to find a drenched and mud-splattered body struggling toward her door. The lad came from some distance; she knew because she recognized him from an earlier meeting in need. Impulsively, she stepped out to help him; the wind drove the rain into her, causing her to stagger until she leaned her body stiffly into the wind. Then she reached for his hand to help him into her hut, out of the direct ravages of the storm. The lad came in shaking and quivering in fright, and chilled a bit by water and wind. Missus Carney brought out a towel and helped him dry himself. She found him some dry clothing and hung his wet rags up to dry. She heated some tea on her low, spitting fire and offered to him that he might warm himself. Taking the gifts offered, the lad nodded a thank you and squatted down silently in the corner of the hut, not too far from the fire.

Missus Carney looked softly at him. A gust of wind caused the hut to groan and shudder. The boy held his ears tightly as his eyes grew large to watch the flexing walls; every muscle was tense, ready to spring. They stayed tense even when the hut relaxed and the groan was past. Tight eyes looked to her, meeting her own gentle look. A smile crept across her face; he cocked his head to one side, puzzling over this woman and enjoying her fire, a refuge against the rain, at least for now. The thunder exploded against him before he dared relax; he cowered in his corner, frightened of the storm. Missus Carney looked away, out the door while lightning flashed, thunder crashed, the wind moaned and the rain drove relentlessly against everything. He watched her for a while as she stood in the doorway, her skirts swaying in the eddying blustery wind and her grey hair pouncing free and ragged in the wind's assault. All the while, he sipped his tea and savored the warmth of the hearth's low fire.

Suddenly the lad looked up again, toward the door, leaving behind the thought of the fire. For his eye had been attracted by her quick motion out the door, drawn into the storm even as the black clouds were being carved by bolts of fierce fire and his ears were ringing with the insistent cannonade of thunder. The wind-swept figure of Missus Carney leaned into the wind; he saw her mostly in the frequent, massive bolts of glare, outlining her and her snapping skirts. Enchanted by dread, he watched, anxious of being alone when the low groan returned in the frame of her simple hut, his only shelter. Gradually, he saw her return, helping in two, no, three more, drenched and frightened, chilled and shivering figures. These too she dried. These too she clothed afresh, hanging yet more dripping laundry to dry from the straining frame. More tea was readied, poured, given. A man, a woman, a young child squatted with the lad, looking anxiously at one another, at him, exchanging habitual suspicion.

Missus Carney knew suspicion could only wane over tea and warmth, in the sharing of a creaking, groaning but sound shelter. She smiled at the two camps – the lad: the man, woman and child. Her dress, wet with rain, now clung to her boney frame; and her hair, grey and frazzled, clung in dripping locks along her face; the drips ran down her face, following the channels left by age and wear. She shoved her hair back with gnarled hands, then shook free her clinging skirts and blew a drip off the end of her nose. The lad almost grinned; she noticed, and winked before returning to her sentinel duty at the door.

All the while, the weather raged in insolent assault upon the poor of Apopar. Missus Carney gazed blankly: watching, waiting, wondering. She heard a crash and looked outside. She could not see, so she stepped outside, leaning forward into the wind and squinting into the beating rain. Although her face was being stung by bombarding pellets of blind rain, she could see the hut nearby: it had collapsed under the strain. The woman living there was older than herself, a frail lady. Through the now shin-deed mud Missus Carney waded away, her skirts dragging in mud, her body drenched by relentless rain.

The lad and the man, his wife and child shared anxious and silent glances. They sat by the fire, warm and dry and afraid. They had seen Missus Carney disappear into the storm, and they shuddered as refugees from nature's brutality know how to shudder. The family huddled together; the lad crouched upon himself more closely; the beams moaned again under the wind. The child waved to the lad, inviting him over. He looked, uncertain. The man frowned; the lad drew back; the child waved him welcome. Finally, the man reached out his free arm to welcome the lad; he smiled; the lad smiled in return and took new refuge in the man's arm, across from the woman. The child grinned and held out a handful of tiny pebbles.

Missus Carney had found the hut and began pulling. Finally, an opening worked free, and within she found, bruised and confused, her neighbor. With frantic eyes, the neighbor looked at her drenched friend and quivered, not knowing what to do, nor what to say. She certainly could not move. The main beam had her pinned down, though not too tightly (she was fortunate, she said), but immovable nonetheless. Missus Carney grabbed the beam but could not move it. She tried again, gaining leverage and position – but it was too heavy for her. She tried again, but her muddied feet slid on the rocks. The pale eyes looked at her helplessly as the wind and rain ripped at her. The water ran down on the neighbor's frail, pale face. Missus Carney wept amid the rain-wash on her face. She shoved; nothing happened. She thought of her guests, but could not leave this friend for help. Sighing, she moved to pull. Nothing. She could not quit; she did not quit even as she felt the rain drive through her clothes and the chill eat into her body. She wavered, then looked at her helpless neighbor; she could not leave her hopeless, too.

A Guard's gruff voice sounded behind her, saying something about vandalism. Old Missus Carney felt angry. And then the Guard's hands, sticking out from the dreaded uniform, grabbed the end of the beam and lifted it, with a groan. Missus Carney quickly grasped her neighbor and pulled her free. She never paused but drew her neighbor to the shelter of her own house. When The Guard let go of the beam, it crashed with crunching certainly. Everybody shuddered.

Bringing the woman into her hut, her guests looked with pity. One rose – the woman – to help with wounds. A towel was grabbed. The lad helped, finding clothes for her. The child patted her face; the old woman wept. Dripping, Missus Carney tended her fire, her tea. The Guard slid in the door. No one noticed, except Missus Carney: she handed a towel and a cup of tea to him. She had saved him once, too.

15 September 1985

CCVI

Long grass blades sparkled brightly in the morning's first glare, the sun finally peeking over the Leaferites' Hill to blaze across the Fields. Catching the dew, the Sun once more set the Fields ablaze as if upon a treasure of diamonds. Into the blaze hobbled Carymba, having wound her way from the Fringe and around, down past the Spinners' Shop. She was really heading nowhere in particular, having finished her last chore very early and then deciding to take a tour of Hyperbia, checking how things were. She thought to herself that this was a fine morning – clear and bright, crisp with a promise of things to come in the Autumn of the year – and the sight-seeing tour would be interesting. Besides, she reminded herself, most of her best adventures came unexpectedly, when she had wandered into unplanned and unsuspected needs.

As she rounded the trail along the Fields, the early Sun turned brilliant the world in front of her. She squinted at the brightness even as she drank in the beauty of each droplet of watery dew. Walking along slowly, she smiled mistily, sharing herself with the prismed burst of each droplet, absorbing the loveliness and finding herself softening, even as she squinted. She thought of her shoulders and neck and even the little muscles of her face as she could feel them all relaxing. She thought of other she had watched relax that way, about how their faces softened and almost blurred, out of focus, gradually revealing a depth of person which changed the texture of the moment. She touched her face, just out of curiosity; the flesh was pliant and easy to the touch. Flexing her forehead in a quick pulse, she half-shrugged and moved onward.

Around the end of the trail she turned toward Mary's Flower Shop. The blaze of light was no longer glaring in her eyes; her squint relaxed, leaving her to amble in the memory of the morning's glory. In such a gentle spirit, Carymba came to Mary's porch. She had no thought of stopping. Indeed, she was not really aware of where she might be going, for she had slipped into a daydream-like state, blissfully unaware of details, the whole world blurred for her out of focus and receiving. So her pace was carrying her past Mary's porch when the door opened. Carymba did not respond, nor alter her walking. Mary stepped out as Carymba slowly moved past. She cleared her throat: nothing. 'Good Morning' she said; Carymba paused, gathering herself back toward the present. 'Ahh ... h: ... Good Morning.' 'Are you going somewhere today?' 'No ... not really: I was walking, nothing more.' 'You did seem ... uh ... preoccupied.' 'Not really ... no: I was simply enjoying in memory the prismed splendor of the Fields as the Sun came over the Leaferites' Hill.' 'Oh.' 'From this side you can't see it as easily. But over there, toward the Empty Area, the view is lovely.' 'I guess I never looked.' 'There is no reason you should.'

Mary watched Carymba as they talked. Like so many others, Mary had learned to observe things by Carymba's seeing. And now her newly-observant eye turned to her friend who seemed to be observing nothing. Mary looked into Carymba's eyes: they were bright and clear but indistinct. Mary frowned over those eyes; Carymba made no reaction. Mary wondered about those eyes, with their dreamy focus, or lack of focus. Her friend seemed to be barely aware of where she was; such seemed uncommon for Carymba. Indeed, Mary grew reflective in a tight and channeled way, pouring over the archives of her memory, seeking some scrap of memory of some time in which her friend Carymba had not been minutely aware and directly attentive to the myriad of details which regularly escaped Mary's own notice. She searched and searched, a dusty job in deep internal libraries; she found nothing to suggest Carymba had ever been known to be like this. She worried. 'Uh ... would you like some tea?' she asked, leaning slightly forward, her head cocked half-way to the side.

'Huh? ... Oh ... I'm sorry: some tea? That sounds delightful.' Carymba smiled, beaming her glance round about.

'Come on, then. I'll fix some' said Mary resolutely, nodding her head, spinning about and waving for Carymba to follow. She could only hope Carymba would, indeed, follow. Maybe some tea, something to eat, too, would help bring Carymba back to reality.

Mary walked into her house confidently. Then, the door did not close. At a corner, she peeped over her shoulder to see Carymba smiling dreamily at the open door, just beyond the doorstep. 'Come on in and have a seat' she offered hopefully; 'I'll have some tea ready in a couple minutes.' There was still no sound of a closing door; Mary only hoped Carymba had come in and not wandered away, uncertain of what was happening.

Barely minutes later, the tea steeping, she brought out her teapot and cups on a little tray. She thought that would make for a pleasant setting; besides, the process speeded her return downstairs to the Flower Shop proper and, she hoped, to Carymba stepping in. Mary noticed first that the door was open, and the doorway empty. She caught her breath suddenly and almost tipped her tray too much. She feared Carymba had just left absentmindedly until the shifting weight in her own hands brought her back to the immediate problem of the tea. 'The table: I'll use the table' she muttered to herself under her breath and went to set the tray down safely. Having the tray secure, she looked up on the way toward the door; she stopped when she saw Carymba in the window, smelling a flower. The light cast itself about Carymba's face, filtering through the strands of her strawberry blonde hair to create a sort of crown around her. Her softly rosy cheeks clung to her face with a fresh translucence. The blue eyes were still in the misty, dreamy soft-focus that so intrigued and disturbed Mary. Mary frowned, wadding her face like a crumpled paper. Then, recalling her relief that Carymba had not left, she half sighed, then asked: 'Would you like your tea now? I believe it is ready.'

'Oh! ... Certainly: I was admiring your flowers. It has been a while since I was last here, I guess, and I was reminding myself of their subtle fragrances. I believe the little orange ones are sharper in smell than the yellow.'

'I think so, too.' Then, frowning quickly, Mary added: 'What else were you noticing?'

'The Fields out there ... they are drying now. The Sun does that: creating beauty in the dew and then stealing the dew from us until tomorrow. Those who do not get up in the morning never see that lovely spread. They never feel that brilliant beauty enter into their eyes ... and more. Now: where is that tea?'

23

'Here' pointed Mary, more confused than relieved. Having poured the tea and taken a seat opposite her friend, Mary finally asked: 'Why are you acting so strangely this morning?' 'Strangely? Why, I hadn't thought anything strange.' 'I mean, you seem so dreamy, so unobservant.' 'There is more to see today than you suppose; I was seeing that, too.' 'Oh.' 'The tea is good.' 'Thanks.' The two smiled, Carymba with sympathy and Mary with resignation.

22 September 1985

CCVII

Crisply dawned the day in the valley of Uiston. Father John had risen early and dressed and tended his stove, both to fix some breakfast and to shove back the early chill. For that purpose he added a little to the fire, more than just breakfast required, in order to let the warmth work into his old joints. The fire going and breakfast cooking, he sat in his chair near the stove and rubbed his hands to help loosen them for another day. They would hold his cane and ease his step all day; when they are loose and pliable – or reasonably so, for he did recall his age and all – they did those hand-y chores more readily. Cool dampness always served to slow this process, he had found. And so with care and diligence, using the friendly warmth of his stove, Father John regularly and tenderly prepared a hand for today.

While yet the breakfast cooked and hands rubbed one another warm, there came a rap on Father John's door. He paused; the thought of who might call so early on a brisk Autumn morning flickered through his mind. 'Yes?' he squeaked, for he had not yet tried his voice this morning and he really needed to clear this throat. There being no answer, he cleared throat and then responded fully; 'Yes?' 'Father John?' 'I'm here. Come in.'

The door opened and in fumbled Yev. 'Good morning, Yev. I'm afraid I don't have enough breakfast for two, and mine seems about ready.' 'Go ahead. I can wait, come back later.' 'No, no: come on in. You can fix the coffee and get it on the stove. Fix enough for both of us. That's right. Thanks: these old hands are not always cooperative, especially this early in the day.' 'There: that should work. Um' he smiled. 'That stove feels good. I hadn't realized I was chilly already.' 'While I eat, why don't you tell me your story, Yev.'

'My story: yes, I guess there is a story which brought me to your door so early. I didn't come with making coffee in mind!' Father John smiled slightly around his breakfast. 'You know we came from Apopar'. Father John nodded: he knew. 'Well, we had been hearing strange things from over there. A message came that Missus Carney had been seen helping a Guard. The man was as good as dead and she nursed him to health. Most folk there would have said good riddance to see him buried, but Missus Carney, who had done so much to help the people in spite of the Guards, healed one. I couldn't understand that at all.' Yev gave up sitting near the stove – it was too warm for him – and he took to pacing back and forth across the room, inside Father John's little hut. The older man looked carefully, for Yev was almost taking up more room than there was. He could see a randomly flying hand crashing into a wall, or a stove pipe, or a window with less than fortunate results. Father John cleared his throat, but Yev did not notice, continuing instead his agitated walk back and forth across the room.

Father John ducked, none too nimbly, in time to avoid the flailing arms. 'Yev, Yev: be still. Your problem seems so slight. Why is a woman's kindness to be withheld from need?' 'You don't understand' Yev glowered; 'the Guards are the enemies of our people.' 'Speak on' returned the older man.

'Word came that she fed a Guard in the very hut which sheltered five others: my people, her people. Missus Carney was the one who sent us here, away from the Guards, away from the very sort of thing she is indulging now. The Guards there are the means the rulers have of keeping people in line, or under strict control. They are the tormentors of anyone who might grasp a scent of freedom. We always thought they were afraid of Missus Carney, but now there is a lot of confusion.'

'I take it, Yev, that that confusion in is Uiston.'

'*And* it is in Uiston, yes, Father John. The confusion starts in Apopar. No one can desert Missus Carney, because there is no alternative. But now we wonder if we can trust her.'

'Here in Uiston?'

'No. There in Apopar, or in the Borders.'

'And has anyone ever been failed by her?'

'Not that we know. When she helps a person, the person is helped.'

'When she helps, do the Guards stay away?'

'They were always able to be nasty. They nagged after her, if they could find her. She had a slippery way of walking through Apopar. No one seemed to know how she got anywhere. She sort of appears.'

'Is that good or bad?'

'Neither. I suppose we all learned to move as quietly and inconspicuously as possible, just to keep our noses clear of the Guards.'

'Settle yourself a bit, Yev. There is no need to get so upset. Say, isn't our coffee ready by now? It certainly should be.' Father John frowned slightly, and gazed onto the stove where the coffee pot steamed briskly.

'Oh ... yes: here, let me pour us some. Do you have an extra mug?' 'Yes. In the cupboard over there – you should find ... yes, that one is good.' 'There you go. Be careful: it is very hot.' 'Be careful yourself as well. ... Thank you for your help, and warning.' 'I should have taken my own warning, too. My tongue is burned now.' Yev made a face and rubbed his tongue inside his mouth as if to rub away the nagging feel. Father John sipped carefully at his mug: 'The coffee tastes good, Yev. Thank you. Now, while you sip, what really is the worry in Apopar?'

'Folk just don't understand how she – Missus Carney, that is – how she can be kind to a Guard, any Guard.'

'Excuse me, Father John, but your door was open.'

'Come in, Carymba. There may be some coffee left.'

'No thank you, Father John. I was passing by and heard Yev's complaints. What is the matter, might I ask?'

'Perhaps you can even answer; responded Yev, taking the lead from Father John. 'Missus Carney has been very suspicious lately.' 'Oh?' 'Yes. I have learned that she secretly nursed to health one of the Guards.' 'Yes. She did that. She found him in the night, moaning. She helped as she would anyone.' 'Oh. And then she fed a Guard in the same hut as five other people who had long known the Guard's heel. It is not right.' 'That is what I understand.' 'Was one of those an old woman whom Missus Carney had pulled from another hut, one which had collapsed in a storm?' 'Yes.' 'I suppose you also knew that the Guard she saved was the Guard she fed.' 'No.' 'And that he was the one who pulled the frame loose to free the woman.' 'No. That was not said either. But how do you know?' 'I found out by seeing Missus Carney.' 'Oh.'

'Carymba, how about some tea? Yev will fix it.' 'Sure, I'll be glad to fix it for you.' 'Alright, I will have some, to join you.'

'Thank you, Yev. Father John, I see you get even with stiff hands by rubbing them with firm, gentle warmth.' 'Nothing else works.'

29 September 1985

28

CCVIII

Mother Hougarry pushed herself, forcing herself to putter at the usual chores. She certainly did not feel like getting out of bed, so she dragged herself up, dressed herself a little bit fancier than usual, took a bit more time with her hair – all by the light of her lamp. The hour was not so early, but the grey skies dimmed the world, and even more her Hidden Cabin. Breakfast was next, she decided once she was up and dressed and prepared. She worked to fix the fire in her stove, and then her breakfast. Prepared, she sat down to eat by lamplight.

The grey drizzle which drummed upon her roof that morning kept calling her to the world beyond her cabin and to the visitors she had not had for a while. The grey entered her; and she felt grey from the inside out. She almost chuckled at the fleeting thought of grey blood in her veins; but she was too grey for chuckling just then. She was too grey to do much more than gaze through the breakfast she had prepared. For her mind blankly pondered the way through the tastefully arranged breakfast without, however, grasping what was there. She remained distracted, gazing at her cooling breakfast, but not really seeing it. Everything for her was lost in the grey which her lamp tried to push back with only modest success.

The fire in her stove crackled and popped as, for time to time, it would do. The sudden sound startled Mother Hougarry, causing her to jump slightly and to rouse herself momentarily from the abiding grey feeling. Having roused and thought again, she tottered on the edge of grey which was, in a way, marked by her flickering lamp. The comfortable slide back into her slouching dreamless vacancy in company with the overhung grey lured her with a settling appeal. On the other side, the lamp danced a golden glow, just for her, and her breakfast lay in a sort of self-offering for her – even if it was cooling rapidly. The struggle to get up and get going *anyway* waved a memorable banner in her mind's eye. Her hand, finally, reached for her fork, and took a bit of breakfast, raised it to her mouth; thence she ate it. Lukewarm, the taste was less appealing than she had hoped. She twitched her nose and blinked her eyes in a hard, rapid pattern, to help bring herself back from the brink of the grey.

Perhaps it was a snorting of sorts, but she wondered nonetheless when her lamplight flared up more brightly for her, lightening the way from her grey. Smiling at herself, Mother Hougarry forced her body to sit erect, to support her head aloft, to smile and to breathe deeply. The creeping odors of Autumn were beginning to make themselves known in the air. A few leaves had fallen, and more were turning gold and red-orange overhead. Their aging scents particularly flavored the area about her Hidden Cabin with a certain rich musk which tempered the now-cool, wet earth aroma from a Summer's fullness. Deciding the breakfast could only get colder, she pursued it hastily. In the end, she was satisfied, but her face betrayed the deteriorated taste she suffered on account of the greying of her life.

Breakfast done, the lure of sliding out of things again beckoned. Mother Hougarry pouted over the idea, and frowned; her frown even turned into a deep scowl. In no way did she like the idea, although the whole idea seemed as pleasurable – so relaxed, so in tune with the drippy day. She heard the lazy patter on her roof and thought of lazy days. She could get by doing nothing today, she thought to herself, pursing her lips in a gesture of thoughtfulness. The chair was comfortable. The dishes could wait. The grey looked soft and rather appealing, a cuddly fuzziness which promised to be warm and comfortable. She almost smiled, then shook her head with unaccustomed violence, flinging one of her hair pins out onto the floor with a pinging clatter. Muttering out loud to herself, she spit out the words: 'I did not drag myself out of bed for this. I'll do something today!'

Pushing on the arms of her chair with full might, she wrested herself erect. Proudly, she stood, looking with defiant glances at the grey shadows which parried with the flickering lamplight. Her chair squeaked on the floor as she pushed it further back from the table; the sound sent shivers up and down her body, leaving goose-flesh in their wake. Rubbing her arms and shuddering slightly, she laughed at herself and moved to tidy her cabin, even though she could expect no company on a day such as this one.

She snorted quickly: 'Who would be silly enough to come out on a grey, drizzly day like this? Not even the Sun has courage enough to poke into this day.' She repeated the sentiment just as she finished doing her dishes.

Hanging up her dish towel to dry, she started when footsteps sounded on her porch. She flushed quickly, then chuckled at herself. 'I must be hearing things' she whispered to herself. For, of course, the notion that anyone would be on her porch was made ridiculous by the enfolding grey and the steady drumming of the light rain upon her roof. She straightened her kitchen a bit more, closing her cupboard doors. And then the rap came upon her door. She tried to swallow, but everything caught in the middle of her throat. She coughed and held onto the edge of the counter-top. She felt confused and found herself frowning; she felt the furrows plow deeply into her forehead as she tried to imagine what tricks her ears must be playing on her. She had almost decided it was a trick when a deep voice came from beyond the door: 'Mother Hougarry? ... Are you alright?' Around her cough and non-swallowing throat, she gasped a squeaking 'Certainly'. She heard herself and, believing she had convinced no one at all, squeaked further 'Whatever *could* be the problem?' Her squeak did not convince her; how could it convince her startling visitor?

Flashing through her mind came the lure of the abiding grey, assisted by the rhythmic patter on her roof and a sudden desire to retreat from this uncertain anxiety into the sort of world she could control. In the grey-world, she would be in control. There would be no real intrusion, no door rapping, on unlikely days. She would not have to worry about that hair-pin that had fallen out. ... The hairpin! Her hand flew to her head. There the fingers found the straggled, loose, untamed locks which she had once consigned to that pin. Where was it now? Her eyes glanced frantically around the room. She moved irregularly toward the table in lurching motions, searching for the pin. Where? She felt a panic inside herself; her stomach and its breakfast-load developed a flutter. There it was! She stumbled after it, falling to her knees, grasping the pin and struggling to get it back into her hair.

The door opened. She gasped quietly, in sudden resignation. 'Are you alright?' The anxious concern in the voices was lost on her. She knelt behind the table, peeping over the top to see a bushy face under a bright yellow hat, over a bright yellow coat, gleaming wetly in the lamplight.

Just behind stared a long face under a drooping black hat, above a cut-away coat. 'Mother Hougarry?' 'Yes?' she said in a sudden calm, as the recognition of her visitors came upon her to shave aside her lure of grey and her make-believe, all at once. 'Are you alright?' 'Of course I am. May I fix you some tea?' 'Let us help you up first – and then, yes, some tea would taste very good.'

Mother Hougarry smiled. 'You know, I'm glad you came today, both of you.'

6 October 1985

CCIX

Morning stole crisply across the Fields, moving with customary suddenness to fill the corners of the place. The brightness of the day came stealthily, with the rich-colored preamble to the eventual wave of clear blue overhead preparing the way for the rising Sun. As that brightness emerged upon the Fields, it met a sultry brightness already there at the opened door of John's Foundry. For he had begun his day's work early, while the twinkling hosts of heaven gazed coolly down upon his fiery beginnings. The bright blue sky looked down on John's little Foundry and watched the heat radiate out his door in waves, pushing back the Autumn coolness. All the attending frost had been pushed away by the menacing glow which fluctuated between an angry orange and a vivid white.

Out of the Fringe slid a narrow figure, moving by habitual spurts along the path into the Fields. The grass hung high along the way, and he kept himself at the edge of the path, under the covering wave of grass from the Fields. His path brought him by the Forge, and near to the workman, John. At the Forge, the grass was withered and kept down, and brown, by the heat of the Forge. As a result, the cover along the edge of the path dropped away, leaving the wandering figure in the open. He paused at the edge of the heat-sponsored clearing; and he pondered. For he was much happier along the covered edges of paths, or even in the midst of clumped grass, where he could move discreetly and with a fair degree of slyness. This opening was not to his liking. He thought of retreating and taking a different route; a survey of memory proved unhelpful. He thought of going back and taking the other side of this path; looking across the way, he saw that such a move would gain him little, if anything, in protection. So he frowned, pulling his hand up to hold his face in a pondering mode.

The Sun lifted itself over the edge of the Leaferites' Hill, casting a direct brightness and fading the blue of the arching sky. Had the wanderer looked up, the sky would have looked as if it were receding, rising higher overhead as the blue faded near the Sun. Had he looked, he might have thought the sky was drawing up to see what he might do. Rather, his own forehead raised like the sky, and his eyebrows arched in personal indecision. Finally, the eyebrows sagged, even though the high sky did not. He had decided. Swallowing extra hard, he straightened himself, tried to adopt a very casual demeanor, and began to walk across the opening. Alas, for his composure, just as he was three strides free of his last shred of covering grass-wall, John, the Foundry-man, came out his door, wiping his heavy sweat from his face, coughing over the clean, clear, crisp air which startled his dusty, hot lungs. The wanderer tightened against his will; every muscle stood tensely and pointedly. Even so, he tried to ignore John.

And then John's voice called out loudly: 'Good morning!' John, of course, was only being friendly. He was shouting but had not yet realized that the roar of his Forge-fire was no longer right there, that he need not shout over it. The wanderer froze. He turned white, for his blood drained; he was used to silence and a slithery life among mostly frightened and scattered companions. His bloodless gaze looked back at John, browned by the bright heat of the furnace at his Forge, glistening from the warmth behind him, smiling confidently into the daylight. The wanderer coughed; he could not really remain silent and slinking away too long. The greeting which threatened him so rang *too* insistently for that. He squeaked out a thin, tight 'mornin''.

'Don't I know you from somewhere?' asked John, pondering.

'I don't think so' replied the wanderer, who hoped John didn't know him, although he did know who John was ... by face and name as well as by Foundry spot. He frowned as he said it, as though he were trying very hard to search the odd nooks and crannies of his memory.

John frowned in return, really searching his memory for this slight and slouching figure who looked as if he might really be *cowering* instead of slouching. John set his hand over his chin, one finger arched as an imitation moustache, his other arm folded across his stomach, holding his elbow. His eyes sank behind the furrows in his concentrating face.

The sunken eyes studied the man out of curiosity. Then he moved his moustache finger to the tip of his nose as if trying to assist the thinking along its way. His face half lit up: 'Jas ... per. Yes. You look a lot like Jasper, Effie's brother, the one who has been living out in the Fringe for a while now. Used to live in the Hills. You must be Jasper!' He broke out in a broad smile and laughed at himself for being so slow in remembering.

Jasper – for John's memory *was* finally accurate – winced slightly. He would have just as soon not have been seen. And seen, he would rather not have been greeted. Greeted, he would have preferred not to be recognized. But his choices had all been lost. 'Now what?' was all he could muster in his mind. He did not even have the will to wave and move on toward the Spinners' Shop, to find Effie and try to arrange a loan, just a little something to tide him over until the next time. Little did it matter that he had tried before, and failed. Little did it matter that there was little hope of success this time. There were no other options; besides, he was simply *bored* with the Fringe. He had gone there when there was nothing else to do. But there was nothing to do there, at all. Effie remained his only tie. But now, John stood there grinning at him, proud as punch that he had figured out who this was. Finally, Jasper simply nodded. 'Yes. My name *is* Jasper. And I am Effie's brother. And I used to live in the Hills, but have now moved to the Fringe.'

'I was sure I recognized you!' Breathing deeply, John sighed. 'This is certainly a beautiful morning' he said with a radiant face. 'And I'll tell you true: that crisp air smells a lot better than the old Foundry.'

Jasper raised his eyebrows in surprise. He had never thought of the crisp air as smelling good. It was just crisp, cool, not frigid and cold and wet ... but not steamy either. He decided quickly that living in the Fringe, without houses or foundries made a man have a different view of things.

Suddenly, as Jasper was confusing himself in the midst of the conversation upon him, another greeting came to him, sounding from the path he had intended to follow: 'Well, Jasper! I never expected to see you here this morning! How is everything going for you these days?' Jasper did not need to look: it was Carymba. He knew the voice too well. His body slumped a bit, and he could feel it; he wondered if John saw it, but a quick glance assured him that John had looked to Carymba as she spoke. He glanced at Carymba to speak a grunted 'Hello'. She had seen him slump; he knew she had. There was no escape at all. He even forgot why he had left the Fringe in the despair he felt. 'What am I to do now?' he asked himself, under his breath.

John eased the situation with the observation that he had grown thirsty, and that there was some water just inside the door. 'Would anyone like some?' Carymba answered: 'Yes, that sounds good. Thank you.' Jasper just stood there, looking for a chance to melt away, back into the forgetting Fringe. Carymba took his arm, however, with a wink: 'Come along; we'll make it a party on John's cool water!' Jasper blinked unknowingly, and came along less mechanically than he had expected.

13 October 1985

CCX

Midday came around and Missus Duns had soup prepared. She had decided on soup that morning when a frosty chill needled her, and everyone else in Hyperbia, too. The sod house had been damp and too cool for comfort, so she had stoked her stove and done some baking – more than she needed, leaving her an excess to store for later. Still cool, soup seemed so logical as a good way to change the climate in her home today. But that was before the sudden change, when the Sun came higher and the coolness vanished, and all the early dampness turned to steam and an Autumn seethe settled upon the place. Now, she was no longer cold and shivery; rather the sweat rolled down her face and her hair clung in wet splotches all around her face. The soup steamed her house further. 'I never thought July would return so soon!' she sputtered in aggravation.

Lunchtime came, and she was hot. She toddled out and opened her door; there was no breeze back in her little corner of the Hills. Curious, she wandered to the particular crook in the path toward her place from which she could see the Fields. The grass stood undisturbed. A great yellow-orange leaf broke free and floated downward in lazy swoops, obviously uninterrupted by any breeze at all. She watched again as one more lone leaf dropped free. It floated out, turning up on itself in the process. Then came the pause and a reversal, dipping lower but once more curling upward to pause and reverse again, slowly spiraling itself around and flashing the bright sunlight off the brilliant colors, and sighed at the breathless air which rose as steam from the suddenly-hot-again Fields. The Sun baked her head and the heat reflected in moist abundance from the soil underfoot.

There was no relief from the Indian Summer surprise, so she moved back to her sod house. She would try to encourage the fire to die out, and set the soup to cool. For now, the fine way she saw to warm herself on a chilly Autumn morning had vanished in the heat of an Indian Summer day. High noon was hotter than she liked … and just as she had begun to adjust to the cooler weather! She was hungry; so she ate the soup even though it was too hot for hot soup now. All that happened in her eating was that her hunger was eased, but she herself was getting more and more *un*comfortable. The steaminess seemed to come from inside her, as well as outside. She sat, and she sweat. She even began to cough and sneeze. She grumbled: 'my best plans fall apart … backfire … work against me. What a day … what as day!' Every word came out dispirited, and each word was more saddened than the one before. She sat in her chair and she slumped in displeasure. Slumping only made her hotter; she no longer cared, however. She was too miserable to care anymore.

High noon gave way to afternoon. The Sun blazed down upon her sod house. The air continued to hang silent and still. An occasional leaf surrendered to Autumn and floated to the ground flashing color and brilliance for anyone to see … but Missus Duns was not watching anymore. The remnant of her stove-fire smoldered stubbornly toward a slow death, but the heat kept pouring into her hot house. The extra soup, never really finished, kept hot and slowly steamed away, keeping her sod house humid and heavy, keeping her muggy and tired and miserable.

Come mid-afternoon on what was for some a lovely day, Carymba and Geoffrey came along the path beneath the Hills. Geoffrey had suggested the walk as the day warmed, for the enjoyment of the color. He had suggested it before the warming day got warmer than he had expected. And Carymba had agreed because she was restless and a walk would help, would ease her unruly anxiety to *go* somewhere. Some days, she knew, she was not at all restless; others she had to go – and her feet seemed to go where she needed to be. She had stopped trying to figure it all out long ago. So Carymba was ambling along, trusting her feet to take her along her limping way. And Geoffrey – ever proper, and a gentleman at that – came along with regular gait, somewhat warmer than he had anticipated being.

'Carymba, why don't we stop and visit Missus Duns? It seems like an awfully long time since I've seen her. I really ought to keep more in touch with her.'

'I don't see why she shouldn't – or couldn't.' Then, stealing a glance at her friend, she added: 'Besides, she might have some cold water … or even lemonade on a day like today.'

Geoffrey blushed just a bit to think that his interest was sparked by a dry, dry throat. But then he shrugged with an impish grin: 'That may be possible. Yes, indeed: that just may be possible. She usually has water … from her spring, you know.'

'Of course: I know she has that cold spring. It is refreshing in the Summer's heat and always clear in Winter's cold.'

'And today, most of all, it will be wet … most likely.'

'Most likely' she agreed with a nod and a wink. Together, they turned up the crooked path, cut back, climbed quickly, turned past the crook in the path where Missus Duns would go to look across the Fields, but did not themselves look back. They were indeed warm and quite muggy-feeling as they turned around that crook and ascended unto the opening at the end of which nestled Missus Duns' sod house.

The pair looked: Missus Duns' door was open and a thin, waning wisp of smoke was curling from her stove pipe. Otherwise, all was quiet. Geoffrey looked at Carymba, puzzled; Carymba looked at Geoffrey, also puzzled. They thought about the door, and looked at it again: indeed, the door hung open on the lazy day. They looked back at one another and read in each others' faces the puzzle of the scene. Each began to notice the questioning lines which had come to etch the other's face. Carymba first, then Geoffrey, experienced a twinge of humor, for that curiosity-streaked face looking at her (and him) was strained. As a result, she felt a twitching in her chin and the curious lines bent into suppressed laughter lines, accompanying a fickle giggle. Geoffrey struggled to remain o-so-proper in response, and failed. His stern face, creviced in curiosity, crinkled in kind humor with Carymba his friend. They giggled at one another. They laughed together. And, laughing, they wandered toward that open door.

The visitors made racket with their voices and their bubbling laughter. Even the muggy heat of the day could not swallow it *all* in persistent steam. The racket bombarded the sod house, inside and out; and within the sod, the slumping Missus Duns heard the first sound of liveliness which had penetrated her hollow. Even the leaves she had watched had fallen noiselessly, without even a rustle or a crinkle. Now, she lifted herself and her puffy eyes, looked blearily out to see the shadows form – a gentleman and a girl, in countered tails and in flowing skirts. She roused herself to think a bit. She smiled: 'Hello' she said, half asking. Her visitors caught their giggles, almost, and answered around the bursts: 'Hello Missus Duns.' The familiar voices echoed: 'Why you must be thirsty. *I am.* Let's share some water; *that* should be cool and fresh *even* today. A scone anyone?'

20 October 1985

CCXI

'Thyruid!' The cry pierced the room brusquely from the door of the Inn-by-the-Bye even as the now damp coldness rushed menacingly into the Inn, sweeping by the mud-clogged figure suddenly standing there. As for Thyruid, he was more concerned with the fire in the fireplace, started to help shove back the piercing, clinging dampness that now gushed upon him and threatened to overwhelm the still tiny fire than he was over somebody who was not closing that door very quickly. He was more concerned with the door than with the visitor whose intrusion came at such an inopportune time. The cold wind knifed into him; he shuddered. And yet a hot rage over that door being left open warmed him and blunted the knifing wind for him, but not, alas, for his struggling fire. 'Close That Door!' he bellowed, allowing the wall to reflect his outrage as he huddled himself over his whimpering fire, trying to preserve it in the face of that wind. 'Oh! … Sorry' came the surprised, apologetic voice just before the door came closed and timid little fire was allowed to settle into a nascent security.

Convinced finally that the flame had some hope of establishing itself, provided the door not crash open again too soon, Thyruid panted as he shoved himself up to sit along the hearth. He went to speak, but caught himself short as he made out the figure in the dim light of the foyer. Changing his demand into a more curious tone, Thyruid coughed lightly, than began: 'Why not come in some more?'

'I am a … little on the muddy side.'

'How muddy can you be?' Thyruid chuckled, waving his guest nearer. He watched the slow, stiff movements draw nearer to the step down into the dining room. Out of the shadow he moved. As the low lights about

41

the dining room illumined him, Thyruid's eyes grew large and his jaw dropped. The muddy figure stopped at the step and raised his hands to rest them on his hips. Thyruid swallowed noisily.

'About this muddy – that's all. I believe I could not get much muddier, even if I were fresh from the wallow!' The voice behind the mass of mud laughed. Thyruid choked politely, endeavoring to keep from gasping, for his visitor was heavily splotched with globs of yellow mud, gleaming in the light. His face and hair were pasted yellow-brown with crinkled gaps where nose and mouth and eyes broke through. The eyes in particular danced with devilment, sparkling in the low lights with extraordinary brilliance. The frame was light, beneath the mud. The voice … the voice was modestly familiar. Who could it be? was Thyruid's ponder. The voice interrupted him: 'Well, is it muddy enough?' Thyruid's head bobbed in rapid acknowledgment. 'Should I come in? or wait here?' Thyruid struggled to say something, without luck. 'Ha!' he laughed: 'I'll stay here! I could not imagine traipsing this mud into the dining room!'

'Uh … uh … you were calling me?'

'Oh yes; I was.'

'And what about … may I … uh … ask?'

'Sure: go ahead. Ask.'

'I just did.' Thyruid felt himself re-gathering after the initial surprise which had so disrupted his day. He felt somewhat indignant over the whole thing. Why should a man come into the Inn in such a mess. He was oozing slowly onto the floor before Thyruid's eyes. The Innkeeper saw more and more mess to clean up. So with a sharp, short tone, he continued: 'Well, what *did* you want.'

The visitor was startled. That should have been a question, he thought to himself; but it did not *sound* like a question. He had never heard the Innkeeper speak that way. The whole matter was incongruous. Even more were the tart words which came next: 'Cannot you tell me why you are dripping mud in my Inn!' The sparkle vanished from those eyes, replaced with a distant vacancy of disbelief. Now came the visitor's turn to be speechless. The words came again with rapidly repeating assault: 'Well? What do you have to say for yourself now?'

Nothing came to mind. So the visitor slowly turned and shuffled to the door, ready to leave. Behind him, leading from the edge of the step back to the door, lay a yellow-brown streak, gleaming where the light hit it, lying darkly suspicious in the shadows. He reached the door, taking the handle in his slippery hand when he paused. 'Oh yes, Thyruid … I was going to ask you to come and help.'

'Help at what?'

'The mess … down in the gully.'

'What mess? in what gully?'

'You don't know who I am, do you.'

'The mud *does* make a good mask.'

'You really don't know!' The amazement led to a chuckle, and the chuckle to a laugh. He tottered in his mud, and began to slip on the droppings from his feet until his balance leaned too much backward and his feet both snapped forward and he fell with a resounding splat, the mud scattering in clumplets all around him. He caught his breath at the jar; then he laughed even harder, holding his side.

Thyruid heard the splat as the abundant mud appeared to soften the fall. He could not see well, but he imagined the splatter, and the mess. He grimaced; then he hurried to help the visitor in his laughter. Very disturbed, quite concerned, the host of the Inn moved directly to his fallen guest until his feet began to misbehave in the muddy, wet drippings on the floor. His feet began to take their own directions. He pulled them into order until the difficulties of balance interfered and he felt that he was going every way at once … and finally down to the floor, his feet spread in front of him. Thyruid did not laugh. And now the continuing laughter of the other, the guest, sounded *un*musical in his ears. His ears burned. His neck grew warm. His seat was sore. And wet. The muddy floor was about him; he felt it with his hands and frowned greatly. 'Well! Who *are* you?' he blurted.

'Guerric, your handyman' he gasped out between bursts of laughter. He moaned in delight over his sore ribs – sore from laughing over a scene which Thyruid found far from funny.

'If you are Guerric, why are you so muddy?'

'This is mud from the gully!'

'So?'

'The Spinners were bringing some yard down to our house ... a lot of yarn for Mahara to knit. And, they slipped on the wet path and the yarn, and they themselves slid down. Mahara and I went to help. And we slid down ourselves. I am the least muddy, so I came for help.'

'Oh.'

And just then the door opened with five muddier figures in the doorway, the cold damp wind rushing about them. Thyruid looked up. 'Oh my! Some coffee may help for a start. ... And then some basins ... or should it be the other way around? Oh my!'

'Water first, I believe' came Mahara's steady voice, questioning the scene, the cold, the laughter she found at her feet.

27 October 1985

CCXII

Huddled onto himself for warmth, Alex sat in the still, crisp pre-dawn darkness, upon the edge of the porch of Father John's hut. Overhead, the black sky had been densely speckled with brilliant spangles, unimpaired once the moon set in the earliest hours. Underfoot, the ground was hard and cold, frozen with frost's paining hand. Alex had noticed the brisk stiffness of the white-plated grass as he came to the porch earlier, by habit and by starlight. As dawn approached, the chill nipped deeper into him; he curled his toes in response, creaking them inside his shoes. He shuddered and shivered coldly as he watched and waited. 'I must have come earlier than I thought' he muttered softly to himself, both to hear something and yet not to disturb Father John. The night swallowed his whispered mutter without a response – unless there might have been an extra twinkling of a cold high star for him.

Gradually, the stars began to fade. That was the first hint of change toward finally impending day. Alex noticed the fading stars; only the bolder ones remained, and they began to grow faint before the sky really lightened, greying and then growing light at the ridge of the hill toward the Sea while yet grey toward the Fields. Quickly then, Uiston's valley came to view and whitened blades of grass stood in rigid review for him. He almost smiled over their soldier-like attention, with whitened array. Overhead, the once black, then grey sky now vaulted in a thin blue. The air remained chilled and frosty; his breath crystallized before his face, then vanished in wisps of vapor into the still morning. Once more Alex wiggled his toes, then rubbed his arms. The morning was cooler, and slower than he had anticipated when he came during the night.

Finally, Alex heard the earliest shuffling sound behind him, inside the hut. He pursed his lips and nodded: that would mean Father John was beginning to get up. Now, thought Alex, the trick is to leave him time to be up and dressed and moving about become coming to his door. So he rubbed his arms some more, and sat, and listened. Thump: 'the feet must be on the floor now. I wonder how cold that is in there … with bare feet fresh from a warm bed? Oh well, we all get up some time. And we all put warm feet on a cold floor many times. … But Father John is not as nimble as he once must have been.' Thump: 'I wonder what that was?' Screech. 'A chair: it must be.' Alex nodded to himself as he imagined the chilled movements of Father John behind the closed door.

All was quiet inside the door for some time … longer than he had expected. Alex frowned and wondered about hurrying his step to the door. 'No. Not yet. I will wait a bit longer' he muttered, his frown becoming a scowl as the quiet continued. Images of all sorts of disaster flitted through his mind. At first he thought the chair had slid when Father John flopped down to get his bare feet off the cold floor. That image faded into Father John falling into the chair by accident, causing it to screech across the floor. That too faded into Father John being hurt and hanging desperately onto the chair, and thence to deepening desperation. Alex's eyes grew big in the middle of his scowl. He began to sweat and to breathe more heavily, in spite of the cold. He was half frozen in concern over his worsening conception of the state of old Father John; the other half simply did not know what to do. He began to bounce back and forth from one side to the other, uncertain and unable to bring his growing agitation to the point of doing something.

The quiet inside lingered for a long, long time. Alex had become more and more certain that something terrible had happened. His agitation had grown and grown until he nearly fell over from tossing himself back and forth. Then, he sat still, bolt upright and attentive. He listened to the quiet as the Sun began to peek over the edge of the valley and gleam against the white soldiers on the other side of the valley. His eyes went to the glittering frost as it melted quickly into runny dew, and the attention-proud grass blades wilted once again. He too wilted. His apprehension gave way to sorrow. His posture slouched and his face drooped. His spirit was wrung from his heart and his eyes fell into dull reverie. Something dreadful must have happened; and he did nothing.

Alex sat there in a sort of stupor, disengaged now from all the sounds which began to stir around him. As he drooped and sadly watched the rising Sun melt away the frost in steady increase, he did not hear the steadier thump, a double thump inside. He did not hear the sigh and the grunt which followed. Nor did he hear the muttering, the tapping of the cane, the plodding steps in triple precision. He did not even hear the door creak over behind him, nor the voice grate his way. He was lost in imagined sorrows until the cane had come across the dirt porch with Father John, and the old man's boney hand had come to lie upon his shoulder, wrenching poor Alex back to reality ... by way of imagined ghosts and mirages and untold other distortions. 'Alex! What brings you out so early on a chilly morning?'

'Why, ... Father John ... you ... you ... you're alright?!'

'Of course. Of course. Now catch your breath, Alex. I did not mean to frighten you, but you were daydreaming, it seemed.'

'I ... I ... I'm fine. Really. I had come to chat with you and just waited until I heard you. I guess I heard you get up ... the chair screeched, and I fell to imagining things ... for I didn't hear anything again until your hand hung onto my shoulder.'

'Well, Alex, I'm sorry to frighten you. Some mornings go slow for an old man. I don't move as quickly as I once did. Now ... do you suppose I could trade you a bite of breakfast for some help with the stove? This frost came quickly overnight. And I didn't get my stove set. The thing is cold now, and needs to be started.'

'Sure. What's for breakfast?'

'We'll have to look into that, won't we?'

'Yep. ... Here, I'll get some wood and the stove will be ready shortly.'

'Thanks, Alex.' Father John let the younger man move first and get out of his way before he began to turn himself toward fixing breakfast for the two of them. By the time he was through the door, closing it behind himself, Alex was on his knees, attending to the needs of the fickle stove. Father John moved slowly, carefully across the room, around the stove in a wide arc (just to make sure of the distance Alex might require). He approached his kitchen area just as Alex sat back on his heels.

'There!' exclaimed Alex, causing Father John to start. 'That should be going well in just a couple more minutes.' Looking up at Father John, Alex pushed himself erect, shuffling his shoulders back broadly, as if to get a kink out of his back. 'Let me help you' he offered.

'My hands are already clean, Alex. Let me putter through it. Meanwhile, you tell me why you came over.'

'Well, … uh … I guess I wasn't … uhm … feeling too with it. And I wanted to talk. Well, I have forgotten that; I'm hungry now! And that stove is warming the place. .. Can I wash my hands? …'.

3 November 1985

CCXIII

Having finished his polishing chores for the morning, Thyruid looked at his gleaming brass trim with a certain definite satisfaction. The glow warmed the room to his eyes, a feeling he enjoyed with an enjoyment which sent him to polish every morning. His eyes glanced at the curtained window and quickly looked away. He had peeked outside once: that was enough. Now the fireplace needed tending; Thyruid paused over the fire's needs on the way to cleaning up for breakfast. The flame danced once more in brilliant array, charming the mind which had been so disturbed by the window views. Thyruid smiled again as the dancing brightness warmed his eyes and his body at the same time; he liked that feeling.

As he replaced his polish pot and wiped clean his hands, Marthuida swung through the doors from the kitchen, carrying their breakfast in her hands. Setting the steaming dishes on the counter, she swung herself onto a stool. Thyruid similarly dragged himself onto his stool and leaned toward breakfast, allowing the fragrant steam from the fresh-baked biscuits and the piping hot coffee to mist in his face and tease his nose. He swallowed quickly as his mouth began to water in eager anticipation. For her part, Marthuida glanced his way and smiled softly over his obvious enjoyment in anticipation. 'My eyes have been warmed, and my body; now my nose is warmed as well.' Marthuida simply nodded in response. She appreciated his appreciation.

The windows rattled softly and the flame in the fireplace cowered. Thyruid grew sullen and Marthuida shivered. 'It sounds cold out there' she commented as casually as she could arrange. 'Yes. It does' responded Thyruid in measured, dull tones. His eyes were dull, too, as his mind flashed over the drizzly weather, wringing moisture out of heaving, low slung, slate-grey skies. With mechanical precision, he broke open his biscuit, releasing trapped steam; he layered the butter on top and watched it turn into a golden ooze, saturating the crumbling biscuit with a gleaming lode of soft gold. Sullenly did he crown the gold with globs of translucent red jelly, to watch that also melt and slither into the waiting biscuit-face. The biscuit became a carrier now, leaving in his fingers the crowning load for breakfast satisfaction. His teeth sank into it, as the aromas wafted upward, tantalizing his nose and leading him forward. He sniffed a bit deeper and basked in the moment: Marthuida's breakfast was a delight for the day. He sniffed again and the warmth in his nose became warmth in taste as well. 'Inside this Inn, my sensory enjoyment lies in multiple warmth' he commented in drawled softness.

Again the windows rattled in the wind, and a regular drumming rhythm took up its cadence upon the panes. The waning fall was fussing, and the bleak black skies were gripping the land in the mood of anger. The Inn herself shuddered timidly under the gusty oppression of the morning's tiff. Thyruid looked about the walls and considered pensively the memory of the building of this Inn so many winters before. He nodded to himself in confidence, for he had set those walls and the beams which framed the Inn. Angry weather would yet pass over the Inn, and they would all remain safe inside. Content, he lifted his mug of coffee and drew a long draught: 'Ahhhh …' was all he could say.

Clyde's characteristic clomp sounded from the stairs. The echoing sound gave ample announcement of his imminent arrival. Marthuida patted Thyruid's arm as it lay upon the counter, and winked her sparkled eyes before spinning around to prepare Clyde's customary mug of coffee. She knew he never complained if it came slow, but that he too appreciated the prompt arrival of the coffee to open the day. So, by the time Clyde's heavy face, bloated with leftover sleep, bounced with the weight of his beard as he flopped into the chair before the hearth, Marthuida was already approaching with the mug, full and hot. Clyde glanced her way with bleary eyes, open technically but not yet sufficiently under control truly to focus. He half smiled, a noble effort before breakfast, or at least coffee had infused his gullet. 'Good morning, Clyde. I heard you coming and thought you might like some coffee.' Gazing her way, he nodded and half grunted, the initial excuse for express gratitude.

Marthuida left the mug on the table. Clyde looked toward it and blinked heavily a few times, enough to draw up his own awareness of the curling steam. He decided to let it sit a moment while he watched the dancing fire, his private entertainment on the way toward morning and wakefulness. The enchanting dance was beginning to entrance him, but he shook his head and frowned; turning to the table, he groped for his coffee; finding the mug, he pawed it to himself, lifting it and sipping long. Lips, tongue, gums, gullet arose in indignation: the hot, hot liquid singed his mouth. Disgusted with himself, he puckered his face in disdain, then shrugged, blew the steam away and sipped so lightly from the mug that he barely gained a taste. Gradually, life came into focus and he too noted the glow of polished brass, heard the drumming rain and shuddering of framing timbers in the Inn-by-the-Bye. The Inn moaned; Clyde sat up more directly now.

Listening to the muted reports telegraphed through the curtained window, Clyde felt very comfortable and warm. Aside from the tastelessness in his scorched mouth, he smelled and saw a sensory warmth which invited his settled ease. His coffee was cooling now and he was almost fully awake. Looking about the dining room, he saw Thyruid puttering over something. 'This sounds like a nasty day out there.' 'It sure does.' 'I think I will stay right here today. Only a fool would go out there now.' Thyruid merely nodded his agreement. 'I don't mind snow. And Winter is merely inconvenient, but this rain just drives through a fellow.' 'I plan to stay right here. I looked out that window ... that one ... no, the next one ... when I was polishing earlier. Rather, I peeked outside, and then closed the curtain quickly. Then it got worse sounding; I don't even want to look outside now.' 'May I?' 'Go ahead. I'll go in the kitchen for a bit.'

Clyde laughed over that decision and pulled himself upright. Pausing, he drained his mug before the coffee got too cool. Clunking the mug to the table carelessly, he turned to go toward the window. He pulled back the heavy curtain and looked. His face grew heavy in the face of the low leering slate sky, rushing along, swirling around the Hills, the Crossed Hills, the Leaferites' Hill, and all the barren, waving trees. Rain rushed almost level to the ground; then swung and slapped the window, turning away with a haughty wave only to spit again toward Clyde's bearded face. He let the curtain fall again, hiding the Inn's inner court from the insolence of the hurrying weather. He nodded: 'Only a fool would be out there now. In here is warmth and beauty: only in here.

The door broke open and a rush of wind investigated the corners of the Inn's inner courts. The fire flared and flickered. Clyde spun around to see a dripping figure shoving at the door against the taunting storm, but with little final success. He hastened to help seal out the ravaging day. The floor was quickly slick with water-splatter. He almost fell, but managed to overcome the rage and close the door: click. Once in victory, his new companion uttered: 'Thanks.' He looked at Carymba, drenched, her hair in cold strings, clinging to her face, her dress and cloak plastered against her tiny frame. 'Let's get some tea; Marthuida must have some dry clothes.' 'Thanks ... but, no: you see, this rain has damaged Mother Hougarry's Hidden Cabin. And I hoped to find some help.'

'Let me get my slicker. I'll be right there.'

10 November 1985

CCXIV

Chill knifed through whoever and whatever might stir from home that morning. Little stirred, leaving the eager chill prepared and ready to carve into the flesh and joints of the very few who arose insufficiently wary. It was an early chill, and laden with too much dampness. No one was ready yet for Winter's freeze; that lay a ways away as yet. The chill was not yet frozen: only almost. To certain fingers, that rawness ate more thoroughly than the crisper cold of deeper Winter. From over the Fringe thin trails of smoke arose from isolated huddled fires where speechless folk shivered and sought a brittle warmth in body now. Out of the scruff at the base of the Fringe climbed a bundled figure, taking strong steps, the arms pumping briskly in support.

As he walked up onto the Fields and then along the path, billow of breath blew out in chugs which puffed the air like steam exhaust from his inner engine. The heavy damp air, cold and raw, would take no more moisture from his breath and so condensed the whole in foggy expanse. Were one to look at him, they would see a rough red face enhanced by an uncharacteristic twinkle in the eyes. The pace, once leveled onto the Fields, settled into an energetic swagger along the path at the base of the Hills. His stride had a single-minded bent to it; he moved forward eagerly. Thus he came by the large rock which juts out alongside the Way Down.

'Hello Walter! You look fresh and eager this morning.' The voice came to his ears; Walter stopped abruptly. He snapped his head from side to side: no one was there to be seen. He spun around on his heel aggressively, placing his anxiety into action: again, no one was there to be seen. He leaned forward, cocked for action, just in case it was necessary. But nothing was necessary, it seemed. 'I'm up above … on the rock.' He looked up sharply, snapping his head in eagerness to be ready for any danger. Balance tottered slightly, which bothered him most of all because that might leave him less that fully prepared. Puffing yet more billows of vapor, he gazed up to see the tell-tale grin and strawberry blonde hair, the sharp blue eyes on a rosy face. 'Carymba! What are you doing up there? You could scare a fellow half to death!' he scolded harshly.

Peeping down, she saw him there. His feet were spread apart for sturdiness. His fists were folded upon his hips, his elbows spread wide to the sides. His head was cocked back to see; the angle was sharp, forcing his jaw to hang down, his mouth agape. The intensity of fear flashed from his eyes. Obviously, he wanted very much to be ready for most anything. Just as obviously, he was ready for nothing, least of all a gimpy girl like herself. With great effort of self-control, she managed not to giggle over his specter down below. For poor Walter was at an unexpected disadvantage. Swallowing very hard, she croaked an answer, barely audible: 'Sorry, Walter: I was only watching the day go by … or drizzle down … and saw you coming from the Fringe with such zest. .. Saying hello was simply the honest thing to do.'

Carymba's tones of natural innocence shoved back on Walter's proud apprehension. He had always assumed his own importance, and so he read flattery in her speech. Rising in his mind came the image of himself as a young warrior, or an athlete at least, rushing confidently into a daring, dangerous contest. Every step was taken as the foe trembled. He rushed toward victory: he was sure. Every sense was prepared, aware, attuned for lightning response to any threat … and yet he was boldly committed to the challenge. Walter smiled at his view of himself and thought of how Carymba must be proud of him now.

For her own part, Carymba watched poor Walter and truly considered giggling. She had a notion what he might be thinking behind that satisfied grin, and a sound giggle would be appropriate, she thought … but unkind. Instead, she smiled over her own image of a hurrying toddler, rushing along in great earnest, arms pumping, breath puffy like a runaway steam engine, anxious, eager, full of show and bluster, ready to be thrown into a flutter by a gentle greeting. She leaned back on her heels so that Walter could not see her face crack open in a wide, impish grin.

Having gathered herself once more, Carymba leaned forward, ending up in a crawling position. She looked pleasantly down on Walter who was basking in his pride. 'Now, Walter, tell me …' 'Huh?' .. 'Tell me what brought you here with such zest'. Walter nearly burst open, he was beaming so proudly; Carymba's eyes watered as she held back her laughter over his silliness. 'It must have been something very important' she added with just a bit too much sweetness mixed in for most situations … but Walter missed it entirely.

'Of course it was important' he began. Then, pausing, he frowned; concerned, he turned the frown into a serious look of reflection; stalling, he gathered himself up and tried unsuccessfully to overcome the fact that he had forgotten where he was going. Or why. In the midst of his confusion, he reported: 'in fact, it is so important that it is top secret' (he smiled, proud of himself for that one!) 'and I really must hurry on'. 'Oh.' 'Good-bye. … Perhaps I can explain it some other time'. 'Oh.'

She watched him hurry onward, toward the 'Y', swinging his arms and puffing great clouds of steam into the chilly air. He walked with mechanical eagerness, but without the assuredness of before, when he was charging forth from the Fringe, leaving those thin smoke trails pointing upwards from the silent fires. With a softer smile, she sat back onto the rock, pulling her knees up, wrapped in skirts and also in shawl, to watch the day some more.

The dampness thickened and the still air felt cooler; the chill sharpened and plotted to carve into anyone available. That meant, in particular, Carymba. She did not want to leave just yet, but that chill was bothersome. She squirmed a bit upon her rock. Her hip felt stiffer than usual, and her seat was sore from the hard, cold rock. Shrugging some, she gathered her shawl – the Winter one now – more closely about herself. She shuffled some more and watched as the Fields began to fade from sight as fog collected to gradually enclose everything. She shivered, and waited.

At a time that might have been noon, she heard a step coming from the 'Y'. She listened carefully and heard a soft humming coming too. She smiled as the ambling tune came nearer, and nearer, slowly and steadily through the fog. The steps ended nearby. A soft slapping sound followed right beneath her. 'Ah yes: this is a rock, the second rock; this must be the place. No one can find anything today. If I had only known it would be this chilly, I would never have moved from my mound'. 'Hello Geoffrey' came the interrupting voice. 'Hello Carymba. Did you realize? …' Yes, Geoffrey, I realize now how cold and damp it is. Let me come down to you'. 'Careful!' 'The back way … not on your head'. 'Good.'

'There: I made it. I believe lunch is at Missus Duns'. Are you ready?' 'Certainly. … Say, did you see Walter coming by here?' 'Yes, I did. He seemed confused, but hurried.' 'He came by the Inn, wondering what you were doing out in this weather'. 'He is always so worried about *something*'. 'True enough'. 'Does he ever worry about anything worthwhile?' 'I don't know'. 'I don't think so. he is so busy with himself. … Oh here: this is the way up there/' 'Are you sure?' 'Yes. Come along … there's the twist, see?' 'I follow, but I do not *see*'.

17 November 1985

CCXV

Drizzled darkness nestled closely around the timid huts. A cold mud squished under foot, forcing the feeling feet to slither and gather unseen goo. The accumulating mud clung in layered squalor about the feet, causing each step to be a bit heavier than the one before. Coming at the end of the day, each step was weary already; the mud merely made them wearier. Missus Carney sighed as she wiped the moisture from her face. Day had begun in darkness and fog for her. And day's grey light had given bleary witness to the slow labors of care. Now the day was long over and she was returning home, to her own hut for a bite to eat, some tea, some sleep.

She pulled up each foot out of the muddy path; accompanying the labored life there returned a soft schlump sound as wet-mud suction broke free again, and again. The cold drizzle soaked her body. Her clothes had long since become wet, clinging to her flesh and holding the fresh cold wet of late soft rain all about her. She felt the cold trickles down her skin. Her legs felt chapped from rubbing against her plastered skirts. Her muscles in her thighs ached, threatening to rebel as each suction grip grew slimier, stickier. Her hips grew stiff in tiredness and gnawing chill. Her arms hung limply. Her shoulders slumped. Her head bobbed erratically with the pace. The vision of warmth and dry clothes, of hot tea and even a cold biscuit or two danced in her mind's eye, tantalizing her, overcoming the anger in her muscles for another step, and then another, and another through the oppressing night.

After a while in her lonely walk, as she mechanically threw her body to lug a foot forward, then repeated the act in mirror image to fight the other mud-encased foot forward, she began to hear a doubled schlump from behind her. She almost smiled at the thought of an echo in the heavy night. But her face was drawn now, worn and weary, dripping the rain from jowls and nose. Everything on her bones seemed to drag, being stretched against too-tired muscled by dribbling water and the drag of downwardness. The echo sound was the first distraction she had found, to lift her heart from the drudgery of dragging her soaked self home to her own hut.

Schlump – schulmp ... schlump – schlump ... schlump – schlump ...: the echoing pair continued in the black of a wet and lightless night. Habits of familiar places led her along; there was no other sure way this night. The sound was losing its novelty for her and attention was waning from the present in favor of the fulfillment of her journey, a stop yet ahead, when the last clomp and schlump of the night would be past. Even as she found herself easing into general forgetfulness, the soft and misty mind of the very weary, she had begun to almost notice that the second schlump, the echo, grew louder, more energetic-sounding. She would have frowned in concentration, but she was beyond that stage. She was too tired to focus her mind on the event, or any event. She floated about, no more than brushing along the solid ideas or visions which would normally dance in her head. So she plodded slowly, heavily onward. Her bones ached now, too. For the cold had tightened her tissues and seeped into her joints. Everything in her was tight and angry over the force of her wet muck.

The second schlump came louder yet, approaching her from behind, coming nearer to her although she could not be seen. Her customary dark clothes clung black to her slight body. Her dark shawl lay plastered over her stringy grey hair. Her pale, washed-out face stared forward, but even that was hidden in the blackness which encased the night. She turned the corner; the echo followed closely now. She almost wondered who it might be when the steps came up alongside her. 'Missus Carney?' came the whispered tone. She looked: all was black, although she could hear the matching schlump beside her step for step. She sighed; then breathing again, she muttered 'yes' by force of will. 'Good: I thought it must be you, so steadily marching so late on a night like this. We are nearly home, to my home, that is'. ... 'Oh ...' she muttered.

As step ached after step for her, Missus Carney thought of stopping. And then she feared. She had worked all day with those whose lives had come too close to the Guard, or perhaps to the Guard's other side, the ruffian side which raged over trials fruitlessly. She saw the poor girl weeping bitterly and recalled the roughness of her story. Her empty stomach knotted on her, and hurt. Fear and grief and rage and sorrow and bone-aching tiredness combined in her. She knew all the reasons to hurry onward from the ones who live that life. Rebellion was feared, she knew, and tight controls were being laid upon the people, keeping fear alive, a force of uncertainty and anguish as the unseen extra Guard to keep the people fully under control. She looked toward the sightless accompanying schlump, and asked: 'Who are you?'

The words hung hollowly in the rain-pierced air. The night swallowed them swiftly. The answer was unheard. She almost said 'oh' once more, in a knowing way. But then the word returned: 'a friend'. 'Not a Guard out like this?' 'A friend'. 'Then why be out this late? Curfew passed some time back.' 'It passed for you, too.' 'True enough, I suppose.'

She fell silent, remembering the many homes she had entered late at night or under the reign of fear. She had come inside and given care, even when she had been unknown, a younger woman sneaking a trace of good into this land. She almost chuckled at remembering her midnight visit to young Thyruid and Marthuida so long ago, ordering them to leave and create the Inn-by-the-Bye. They were terrified of her knock, and afraid of her presence. She had always been slight and not very powerful in look. Yet they feared her then, and obeyed for good. Now she was being met in need by 'a friend', he says. Saying much is dangerous now, in the listening silence of the night. No commerce covered those voiced sayings, even the whispered ones.

'Here' he spoke as softly as he could, and stopped. The aching rebellion in her bones and the stubborn reluctance in her step made her pause. The 'schlump' broke stride. She sighed and wept, the tears joining the wash of rain, which was freshening now, coming harder and colder. She shivered through and through. How far home, she thought to herself: her hips screamed at her in cold ache a terse 'too far'. She looked as she heard a door open. Soft light from a low hearth fire revealed dry warmth. An old woman looked out at her with deep-sunk eyes and pasty cheeks. She gave a mellowed look, of uncertain depth. At the door dripped a young man, cloaked and bearded. 'No Guard here' she thought. She turned to follow but her feet would not rise again. Her knees quivered. Her legs melted. She slumped into the mud.

Strong hands gripped her; she was helpless to refuse. She was led uncertainly, carried almost, and definitely into the hut. The door shut behind her at his kick. Now the rain was heard on the roof, not on her shawl. He set her near the hearth. The old woman reached her hand and touched it silently. Missus Carney saw the gnarled hands giving cragged touch to her. Softness flowed. She looked and smiled: 'Missus Carney?' 'Yes.' 'Let me help you now. Here ... some dry clothes: those must be cold.' 'Hurry, please!' 'Sure Ma'am', and he turned aside to give her private room to exchange muddy cold for gentle warmth.

'Some tea?' she asked, once the chore was done. 'Yes: thank you.'

24 November 1985

CCXVI

The window which looked over his garden rattled with the mist-laden wind; Osburn shuddered, even inside the window, with the heat of the stove warming him well. The wind was of a penetrating sort; early had he learned that wind, and the cold it bore into the bones. Memories of campaigning days lay frozen in his mind, and contributed to the deep shudder he now emitted. He had learned early that glory came in discomfort and strain, even though he had struggled long to get beyond that point. And he had before he was kept up here, to tend his garden in retirement. He snorted to himself; no one was there to hear him, or to respond. He snorted again; the window rattled in a new gust, the pane new-splattered with mist-drops; he shuddered once again, without thinking at all.

The wind which lashed the window before his face had already swept across the garden which he had tilled in softer days of Summer. Stubble quivered in the wind. The shorn remnants of last Summer's produce stuck stoutly from the clumped mud. The mud itself, black and lumpy yet, grew a gleam, a pasty film which seemed to deepen and soften the mud. And yet the clumps clung to the roots of the barren stubble, testament to the season gone and a shivering preparation for the Winter barrage yet to come. To Osburn's eyes, there lay the aftermath of his labors of the Summer, retirement labors he had decided to call them, even though he had never wished retirement on himself. He had planted and tended and harvested. The produce was all safely stored for himself; he would not go hungry this year, no matter how that wind howled and threw its frigid dampness upon his window. 'Better the window than the body' he said, patting his modest paunch, and turning away. The wind rattled the glass more harshly, but he did not look back. Rather he left the raging cold to sneer at empty glass and cast its chilled droppings away from his weary face.

Slow steps brought the older-now Osburn to the far side of his house, to gaze out another window out over the Plain and, in particular, the City on the Plain. He sighed to himself, as he usually did when looking out this window. He had built that window to watch his own city, then saw the power slither through his fingers, like silver turned quicksilver in the twinkling of an eye. Today the view was hampered by the wind which rushed over his house and off the Cliff, tumbling down and away in vicious swirls. The mist displayed the fury of the wind, splattering back upon the pane. He shuddered again. Beyond the splatter, he could yet see the swirling mist eddying wildly off the edge of the rock race. Through the mist, he could make out the trail down the Cliff and, further, the outlines of the City on the Plain. Pondering what he could almost see this day, he figured that the harvest was well stored there, too. He had always been concerned with food, and had made certain that his storage facilities were more than adequate; only now they were no longer his own, but the City's. Osburn rubbed his balding head and frowned into a scowl. He had done a lot down there; they should have appreciated him more. Instead, they took his power and retired him to his nest on the Cliff.

Out of the corner of his eye he noticed movement coming up the trail, up the Cliff. He smiled: the traveler could be going nowhere other than this house, to see no one other than Osburn. The figure moved slowly, slipping a bit on the mist-slickened stone. Osburn's lip curled by ancient habit as he imagined the traveler's knee touching: it would once have been a gesture of respect – but now, he knew, the traveler had merely slipped. From a snarl, his face drooped into a frown, and then into a scowl. He closed his eyes and blanked the image from his mind, as being his lingering pain.

Curiosity roused in him, however, and he opened his eyes again. The figure had come closer, moving carefully, staying close to the Cliff-side of the trail. A bag hung over his shoulder – or Osburn assumed it was a man who came up today. He chuckled at the thought of anyone coming up that trail on a raw day like this one, least of all a woman. From experience, only a man would be foolish enough to take the stone face of the Cliff when it was all wet. But then, who could he imagine might come up? All his old cronies had deserted him ever since it became obvious he could do them no more favors. All he had now was his garden, and that brought few friends among those who clung to power. He furrowed his forehead in a form of concentrated thought. Nothing was making sense to him. There would be no reason for anyone to come up, even if the weather were good. Now Osburn stirred his mind as he peered out his window to watch the huddled figure inch his way up the face of the Cliff, carrying that bag which increasingly looked awkward and hard to handle. 'Who could that be?' Osburn spoke out loud, surprising himself with the sudden break in the quiet of the house. 'And what might be his errand?'

Osburn could figure no alternative to waiting. Oh, he did think of going out to meet the traveler; but just then the wind gusted and dashed a burst of mist, almost rain against his window, and the shivers succeeded in eliminating such a plot from his mind. The window in front of him began to fog over. At first he thought the fog was outside, but finally he realized he was standing too near the glass and his breath was condensing there. Laughing at himself, he stepped back and wiped the pane clear once more. The path curved out of sight as it neared clear the top over beyond the house. As the visitor came to the blind spot, Osburn found his face pressed gains the glass to watch as long as possible. Vision cut off by rock, he suddenly realized his face was getting cold, and wet, from that window; so he pulled away to rub his face for dryness and for warmth.

Standing and pouting to himself, Osburn tried to figure out what to do next. His habit as a man of power was to make guests come to him, on his space, under his control. Then he could be kind or cruel as occasion or whim suggested. As a man of pretended power, he would act that way. But now he was curious about his visitor who risked that path in this cold and wet weather. Such an effort seemed foolhardy to him. And yet there must be some urgency to the person, to make the effort today, of all days. He decided to sit in his big chair and let the guest find him. So he sat down and arranged himself for guests, just the way he used to do. Soon, the visitor would knock at the door, and then … . Osburn turned red in his aggravation. He had forgotten that he no longer had a doorman. The last left as he ended up with more pretend than power. Hurriedly, he rose, and then rearranged himself to greet his visitor.

There came no knock at the door. He frowned some more. The visitor should be there by now. He wondered if he had slipped and fallen, perhaps been hurt. He shrugged and half-scowled. Now, he decided: he would wait. A long pause left no sound. He walked near the door to listen more carefully. The wind rattled the door harshly; he shivered, then wondered if it were the visitor instead. Curiosity won; he opened the door. Kneeling there was an old woman; he stepped back in surprise. She looked up at him.

'Oh, Osburn!' she started. 'You won't remember me. Once, years ago, you helped my mother. Now I can help. So I brought a bag of bakery goods – my family, we are bakers – for you. To say thank for once, years ago.' Leaving her bag, she turned away and left. Finally, Osburn called after her: 'Wait!' She waved: 'No: I must go. Do enjoy your cakes.' And he was alone once more with a bag of fresh cakes.

Weeping, he went inside with the bag. He went to the window to watch the old woman inch back down the trail along the Cliff face.

27 November 1985

CCXVII

Waves crashed upon the beach, washing part way over the Sea Road along the beach with cold-driven water, a hard spray stinging its way farther yet, into the hill-slopes to the south of the Valley Road – all this when the sun first peeked over the watery horizon. Huddled at the edge of the Valley Road, protected by the last of the trees, sat Carymba. She watched the sun rise upon behind the wind, as if that orange glob were pushing the wet cold wind against the beach, chasing it all away from its distant face. She laughed at herself for such a notion, but the angry Seas did rage *away* from that sun and toward her … and the Sea Road she planned to travel.

Carymba had come to huddle in that corner earlier, for she had thought to follow her way this day with a brisk and early start. In the black night, she could feel the stinging wind and hear the crashing of waves, both distant and near. So she paused and waited for the light, to see the harsh washing of the Sea before they engulfed her in their brusque indifference to whoever may stray into their way. Now she could see, almost; she needed just to ease herself from her huddled condition and wrap herself within her shawl and draw her warmth inside. And then she could step out from the shelter of her barren tree and dare her walk to the Sea Road, and on. So she did.

The wet wind flung the droplets torn from the breaking waves at her with dart-like force. Her hair twisted and spun in the wind; she drew her shawl more closely about her shoulders as she dipped her head into the wind and pushed forward down the Valley Road as the terrain dropped toward the Sea Road, and beyond to the beach and strong Sea. The darting droplets beat erratically upon her head, slowly wetting her hair into plastered clumps of darkened strawberry blonde. Trickles began a forced route, windblown down her cheeks or over the back of her bowed head.

Turning along the upland edge of the Sea Road, beyond the wash of most of the waves which burst upon the sand, Carymba began her battled way. Her skirts flapped to her side; her other, Sea-ward, side clung plastered to her body, gathering and clustering in folds which got in the way, making her gimpy gait more irregular and strained than ordinary. She scowled at her uncooperative skirts, and kept going. Her walk developed a necessary lean into the steady, hurried wind. Her left leg bent to take the lean; her right leg stretched, again accentuating the syncopation of her stride. The shawl held warm about her arms and body; and yet the darting wind was felt intruding now into her. Worse was the knifing cold mocking her and stabbing the accented left leg, compromising that hip and stiffening the leg. Gritting her teeth, setting her jaw, she plunged onward along the Sea Road, down the beach, relentlessly.

Relentlessly, too, whipped the wind upon her, holding her to her unnatural lean in order to raise her step upon the Sea Road without being blown up the beach-slope, into softer sand, where steps would come far more difficultly. She did not want to fight the softness, too; so she kept the lean, step after step. As the Sun rose higher in the blue-grey sky the wind felt harsher. As she stepped along the windswept Sea Road, the waves washed nearer and nearer her path until she had to walk through the water streaks. Her feet got wet and cold. The wind blew more; the waves washed more; her feet and her hem soaked water and hung heavily in the cold wind.

Finally, Carymba finished her walk along the beach. The Sea Road passed into a scrubby section of land, cutting the harshness of the wind and the fierceness of the dart-like droplets. Carymba slowly eased her lean, straightening slightly onto a rebellious leg. Surprising cramps startled her, hobbling her doubly in a further protest of nastiness. Idly, her thoughts turned to Mother Hougarry's warm Hidden Cabin from which she had left in the middle of the night, while her old friend who raised her slept. The Cabin was dry; she had been comfortable, except for the sense inside that she had to go, to come out and down the Sea Road, for something. Now, here she was, past the beach, approaching the wind-waved woods toward the Great River, and she was still uncertain why she was here. Sometimes, the delay in her certainty would frustrate Carymba, particularly when she was wet and miserable, like now.

Nevertheless, she trod onward, for there was nothing else to do. Having arrived here, there was no desire to lean into that wind the other way on the trek back: not now, anyway. The lurking cover, even laid bare for approaching winter, cut the wind down to size for her. She shook her skirts; reluctantly they flopped free again and dangled as they ought to do, making her walk far easier to take. She slowly rubbed and stretched her left leg as she hobbled along, trying to ease it for herself. Nothing was working well; even through the wind was cut, she was already pretty wet and cold. She almost wanted to mutter and sputter over the whole thing when a youngster popped up ahead of her with eyes big and brown.

Gathering herself, she put her discomfort aside. 'Hello' she said. The eyes got larger, a feat Carymba had not considered possible. Then she shivered in spite of herself. A glace of self-perturbance must have swept across her face, because the youngster opened her mouth and spoke: 'It's OK, Lady. I know where someone can help you. Come on.' She waved her arm and began to trot off. Carymba sighed and began her hobble again in the general direction the child had gone. She frowned at the split in the path until she saw the little form return for her. 'This way, lady. This way.' She waved eagerly. Carymba nodded and smiled to herself because she had not often been called "lady" by anyone. With half a chuckle, she moved onward down the narrow, little-used branch of a path.

Everything came to an end. There was no door. There was no further path. She puzzled. A giggle in the brush directed her gaze into a crack in the briars: two eyes beamed at her brightly. 'Well, is that where you called me?' 'Yep! … here' and she rolled back the briar-roll from a low entrance into a tunnel. Curious and suspecting she was where she ought to be, Carymba followed. She had to duck down to go through the tunnel. The farther she went the darker and the warmer it became. She loosened her shawl, but not too much. Suddenly the tunnel turned and she followed it and the sounds of the child ahead of her. At last, they entered a space lit by a low fire and with several people round about. 'Look what I found!' chanted the enthused youngster with the big bright eyes.

Other eyes looked warily at Carymba, their unknown visitor. She felt the eyes examining her, and she suspected they suspected her. Who, in their right mind, would be out in this storm? Besides, she must look a fright. She ran her fingers through her straggled hair; everything was a wet tangle. She pulled it more than once, wincing each time until the whole began to fall into place. She laughed at herself and the child took her hand. 'She came from the other way. I watched her. … Honest.'

'She is right. I lived in the Crossed Hills, mostly. And I came along the Sea Road this morning, even if it is a terrible day. Did you come from across the Great River?' The nods answered silently. 'You'll like it better over here. … May I sit down?'

An old woman near the fire watched for a minute or two, then slid over. 'Here: join me. And Tonya! bring her some root tea.' The child scrambled for some. 'Here. … Now tell me why you are here.' 'Well, I knew I needed to come out, and my path led me this way until … Tonya, is it? … Tonya led me here. I guess I'm here to greet you. Hello!'

1 December 1985

CCXVIII

Uiston's cup-like valley huddled in the shadow of the Crossed Hills and the Leaferites' Hill. Toward the Sea there stood a high-rolling land. And out beyond, toward the Great River, rose another band of hills. Uiston nestled in between. And so, when the stormy winds blew hard in Hyperbia, they tended to rush over little Uiston, leaving a relative calm. But there were times when that wind curled underneath itself and tumbled mercilessly around and around the valley. This was one of those latter days. The moan of wind which often is heard from the peaks of the sundry hills had come closer now, to rattle hard the hut of Father John of Uiston. The moaning wind slid over the Leaferites' Hill on the way to the mouth of the Great River, and beyond. The wind took a bent-direction detour around Uiston, poking icy intrusions all about the valley.

Inside his hut, Father John lay curled and cuddled beneath his blankets in his rather cold, small home. Winter had always come hard on him, and more recent winters even more than those of youth. In the dark of night, he lay awake to the tunes of the long mournful moans of the storm. He told himself it had to be the wind, for no living thing could howl that long without gasping for breath. Even then, one moan dies out only to be quickly succeeded by another, giving a lowly pulsating rhythm to accompany the creaking boards of his hut. Father John lay and listened. The creaks and moans were accompanied by the low crackling in his stove, staving off the bitter cold from his little home. Many a storm had he weathered in his time. He knew the sound of them, almost by heart. In the memory of years gone by, he pulled himself out of bed to check his fire, and try to insure its continuing warmth throughout the night.

He took his cane and shivered slightly. Using the edge of his rocking chair, he leaned over to the face of the stove and carefully adjusted the fire, judging by practiced eye how best to keep it arranged for the long cold night. He nodded agreement on his work and pulled himself up to shuffle his way to the bed once more, and crawl between the cooling sheets. A shiver raced across his chilled flesh as he snuggled in once more to warm the bed and thence himself.

After a while the moaning faded and natural drowsiness closed his eyes; Father John slept an uneasy sleep under ears retraining to hear the wanton list of storms. He did not really know that the wind moaned just as hard, just as mournfully, just as bitterly, but over the thickening deposit of Winter's snow. Slumber hid that much from him, and the more insulated warmth inside the hut did ease his aged body and permit him leisure to sleep the more. The fire did double duty, as it always did: heating the room and keeping clear the chimney vent. Thus Father John warmed and sank into sleep. He even smiled in the warm comfort of the bed while he slept.

On the edges of Uiston the eight young friends of Father John huddled in their place against the driving cold. The snow was not piling in their faces, but blowing away to expose the raw and freezing turf. The remnants of last Summer's grasses lay brittle and mostly broken under the heel of the storm. The streak lay barren before it gave way to deepening snow in front of the hill-inset lodge they had scraped out and built for themselves. Their comfort was secured by the hill. They had even found a way to use some huge old roots to hold up their space. Passageways suggested themselves and sprawling room within the hill in which their eight-fold privacy might be found. The project had intrigued them once, in warmer days, and now proved useful and warm. They looked, however, out the window and over their porch to see the Winter's rage, as best they could in the swallowing, snow-swirled darkness of the middle-night.

'It is cold out there, Vlad. You can feel the bitterness at the window.'

'True enough, Yev. It is enough to make a body glad for a fire, and those inner rooms away from the rage. I've found mine to stay quite comfortable so far.'

So far, I have too. I don't know how far frost will nip. That might be a problem.'

'True: we will have to wait and see. Dum might be luckiest of all; he has the deepest room, farthest from the light, farthest from the hearth but most protected, nonetheless.'

'How deep is that snow, I wonder.'

'I have no idea, Cons. We really can't see very much from here. The little the light shows is barren and grey. But beyond that ... well, all that snow in the air must be going somewhere!'

'Yes. I was thinking that, too. If it is thick in the valley, that might be a problem for Father John.'

'I hadn't thought of him! Yes: it could be a problem.'

'Yev, Cons: do you think we should go and look?'

'That sounds good to me, Vlad. Shall we ask the others?'

'It would make a good adventure tonight. Besides, what's the use in staying warm when there is potential excitement in the air?'

'Being cold is no fun, fella. We go out to check on Father John: that is all. I know of few things which would draw me out there tonight.'

'Father John is one of them.'

'Right.'

Over the groans of complaint that the night's wind moaned harshly and threatened them with cold, just as it did in Apopar in Winters of past dread, Vlad argued their trip. And Cons added his weight to their going. Slowly, they agreed, one by one: Nike and Dum and Serg and Lev and Alex. Slowly, with an occasional grumble, they pulled themselves together and dressed themselves as if to romp in the snow instead of trudge through the snow, the heavy Winter hard upon them now.

The eight clustered at the door. They paused to look back at the warmth of their hearth, the secluded promise of the branching tunnel to their sleeping quarters. A multiplied sigh rippled through them as they collectively looked to the door, the last barrier between them and the swirling, biting wind, driving snow as if determined to penetrate any audacious body who would wander out in foolishness. The door creaked open; the wind-driven cold hastened to poke inquiringly into their home; the fire trembled, then bravely flared. With hesitant resolution, the eight stepped out upon the frozen ground, closing the door behind them. At the now-sheltered hearth, the fire settled itself into a gentle and warming blaze.

The ground crunched, the grass crinkled like broken glass under their feet until, that is, they began to hit the deepening drift which lined by far the most of Uiston's valley floor. They knew the direction to Father John's hut, but soon found their way somewhat lost. Only by looking back to the dim glow in their home's window could they judge direction. But where, O where were they now?! The snow gripped them. Each step sank to groin height; each movement required a heaving step. They moved, wandered, kept check of home's warm glow until they sniffed the underlying presence of Father John's hut. The faithful stove marked the place. Together, they dug against the drift which this time sought to insulate too well the tidy hut of Father John. Down, down they dug, following near the smoke-hole in the snow: a roof at last, and then a porch, a hollow there before the door. Cons did not knock, but walked right in, into the warm and cozy, stuffy place. Father John smiled in his sleep. Cons woke him with a start: 'Father John, the snow is so deep: let us carry you to our place for now … until the storm melts free of here. It will be safe.' 'Are you sure?' 'Yes: come.'

8 December 1985

CCXIX

Crisp air nipped at the windows, drawing a mist upon the panes. Beaded there, with occasional running drips sweeping down the glass, the translucent blue of the high Winter sky was caught in an untold number of prisms on the way into the room, past the pulled-back curtains. Curious, Mary took a cloth and wiped away the moisture on the glass, leaving a broad smear of filmy water, more directly set toward her seeing. Tufts of fading green poked through the light white crest of yesterday's snow. Bare bleak branches stood in stately pose, unbent by any breeze. A high white blue sky arched overhead, aloof from doings down below. As yet the high Sun had not finished emerging from behind the Crossed Hills, to poke a cool yellow glare into the corners of the Fields. Mary nodded and smiled to herself: the day began pretty. She dropped the curtain back in place and turned to change into daytime clothes and choose some breakfast. Then, once fed and presentable, she could go to her shop downstairs with confidence.

Breakfast done, she dressed. Through the whole process, she hummed favorite little melodies, simply because that look out the window seemed *so* promising, so beautiful. Even with the crisp look, the brightness warmed her from the inside out, eliciting her song as she progressed through her early morning chores. Her dress was on, as were her fluffy slippers. The hair was next in line for consideration. A glance in the mirror indicated she had some work to do there! for it flopped and pointed in almost every direction, gathered into random clumps, branching in indiscriminate directions. Her hands searched for her brush, left somewhere other than where it belonged. She muttered under her breath some words concerned with the pleasures of having a roommate she could blame for such inconveniences, if only she had one. For now, the music departed in the pondering over the hairbrush.

She wandered around, looking for it, away from the mirror. She looked up and did not see herself, a fact which softened her eager frustration.

While she was looking for her hairbrush, Mary discovered a number of out-of-place items. A few pieces of laundry had fallen in out-of-the-way places. She decided to retrieve them. Also, there were some tools left around; she gathered them and decided to take them down to her work room in the back of the shop – where they belonged. So, she trudged downstairs to do that chore. In her work room, there were pots and all sorts of stuff just cluttered around. Clucking to herself, Mary set about reorganizing her room, so she could find her things when she wanted them. There were some potted plants there, tiny little buds gleaming with promise, but with the roots all cramped too tight. She just knew nothing would happen with those plants if they were not repotted, with root-room. 'I really should have done this yesterday' she sputtered as she began to loosen the assembly, and break it open into smaller clumps, each of which would go into a pot like the one she just emptied. Her fingers poked into the black crumbly soil. Her fingernails quickly collected the flaking earth as she used them to scrape and mold gently the root structure before replanting. She watched her work carefully and began to smile just a bit. The tunes returned to her and she hummed away at her work. One project gave way to another. She took the finished ones out to her showroom so as to have a bit of room in her work room.

After some time, she reached for a different tool; it was not there. She looked around, puzzled. She looked up and she looked down. Perturbed, she looked in the place it was supposed to be: there it was, one of the early victims of her morning zeal. 'That will show me!' she said right out loud as she turned with intrigue to the planting work once again.

Usually, she would have put on her apron for work in here. But she had not intended to putter there this morning, at least not yet. She began while she was in the process of forgetting what she wanted to find in the first place, and why. As a result, she had dripped dirt all over her dress. When her nose itched, she had rubbed it, leaving a large smudge of potting soil on her nose and across her cheek. In all of that she had continued to pot plants, and repot them with generous glee.

Outside her window, the cold snow gleamed in bright sunshine. There as a sunbeam bursting through one window right into her room, warming her marvelously. She smiled all the brighter; she hummed more strongly. She almost sang out loud. Had the quiet continued, she probably would have sung shortly. But the quiet did not continue. Instead there came a rap at her door. 'Oh my! That might be a customer' she said as she stacked her work on the table and wandered to the show room and on to her front door.

Opening the door, she greeted Geoffrey. 'Why didn't you just come on in? I thought you must be a customer, or something.' 'Or something?' 'Come on in, Geoffrey. You know what I mean! I was potting plants … come on back here while I finish.' Geoffrey watched her go, plodding along in her big fluffy slippers; he grinned and shook his head, for he had already noticed the strayed and smudged dirt, and the hair for which she had forgotten she sought her brush. Nevertheless, he marched along behind her, taking off his hat and gleaming in his always-right demeanor. 'Well, Geoffrey, what is it you want today?' 'I thought once of buying some flowers; but now I guess I'll just visit. Do you mind if I use your stool?' 'Of course not. I use it more for visitors, gossipy and otherwise, than I do for myself. I had thought I would use it more while I worked in here, but I found it simply got in my way more than it was worth.' 'Thanks. … My, you look busy today.' 'I just got started and kept finding something more that needed to be done. You can see, I have not been bored.' 'Certainly not: but, Mary, I do need some flowers.' 'Well, I certainly have some.' 'I need to buy some, Mary.' 'I am in business to sell flowers, Geoffrey. You knew that.' 'Yes: I came here because I knew you sold flowers and I wanted to buy some. I do enjoy chatting, but I wanted to collect some flowers for Marthuida. We are having a surprise party for her.' 'Oh, that sounds very nice.' 'Do you *ever* take a break from potting plants to sell some?' 'Certainly: all I need is a customer.' 'Mary, you have customer. 'I do! Who?' '*I* am your customer.' 'Oh! I'm sorry. Nothing was registering in my head, I guess.' 'I know. Now, …'. 'Come along, we'll see what we have.'

As they began to look at the possibilities for Geoffrey's purchase, a new customer came to the door. Mary let Effie in. 'Effie, how good to see you.' 'Uh … thank you … uh … Mary. I was wondering if you had some flowers, for a party. I mean, you are open, aren't you?' 'What an odd question! The Shop is open every day, as long as I am around. And when I am not open, I stick that sign … Oh! I forgot to take it down this morning.

There: now you can see that I am open.' Mary smiled broadly, wrinkling the smudges of soil on her face; she cocked her head differently, causing her random hairdo to flop to the side. Geoffrey swallowed hard. Effie looked somewhere between embarrassed and confused and horrified. 'Well, I had expected to look for some …'; her voice trailed off as she looked at Mary's fluffy feet. "is something the matter, Effie?' 'Oh, no. No. I'm fine. … Um, yes: I expected to find some flowers for Marthuida. We are having a Party.' That's what Geoffrey just said. Strange: I had not heard of it before.' Yes: I thought everyone was invited.' 'Perhaps you forgot.' 'Nonsense!' 'You do forget some things, you know.' 'Such as?' 'Such as aprons and dirty hands, and fluffy slippers, and hairbrushes. Little things.'

Mary's eyes grew big as many things came to mind. She looked out at the Sun-dazzled Fields. 'Oh yes: THAT party. Well, let's get busy.' …

15 December 1985

CCXX

Clear black sky sprung high overhead, supporting a spangled spread of stars flickering above. Barren trees and waist deep snow stood witness from the ground as Carymba slowly plowed her way down the Crossed Hills toward the Valley Road. The snow had come down cold and in brittle fluff until the clouds vanished after sunset. Thus there was no crust at all, and the gimpy waif was left to plow her way along, slowly, down the path. Mother Hougarry's old standard words rung in her memory as she left her wake in the snow: 'Why now? Stay here until things clear.' She always said that; Carymba always smiled and said good-bye for now. Mother Hougarry always sighed and said 'Do come back again'. She would. But now the need of the night drew her onward until she found the covered root-steps to the Valley Road.

She shoved the snow and probed for footing; then, finding a step, she leaned forward once, twice, then flopped the last part of the way face-first in the puffing snow. She pushed herself up until she could get her feet underneath her body and stand. There, in the hollow, the fluffy white reached her armpits. It made no sense to brush away the fluff from her falling upon her face, for there was the snow, nearly to her chin, in one big pile of fluff all over the Valley Road. She looked at it all. 'I'm tired already' she muttered under her breath, 'and this snow makes going a lot more difficult. Nevertheless, I go.' Setting herself, she began to plow, pushing the snow. Soon the snow bunched up on her in front, so she began to swoop her arms up together from the waist and then out as she neared the crest of the snow. 'There', she stated right out loud, 'that works better, even if the arms get tired. This deeper stuff ought to let up once I get to the 'Y' ... I *hope*.'

Gradually, Carymba forced her way into the snow. A drift rose to her nose; the puffing of her laboring breath blew away the uppermost snow, her arms surging to clear even more. The words of Mother Hougarry, so familiar she hardly heard them, echoed in her ears now, tauntingly, in a way Mother Hougarry never said them. Weary shoulders turned the remembered plea into a projected laugh. She shoved the snow, throwing up a fresh billow, taking another step. The air breathed cold and swept into her lungs, chilling all the way: she coughed at it all, and sputtered. Another sweep, another puff, another step: one pattern after another plowed her way down along the Valley Road. The snow would drop to her waist, then rise to her nose, but her feet remained in deep snow, and her canyon-cut collapsed behind her, leaving a loosened track under coldly looking stars.

The late rising moon was brightening the night and hiding the more timid stars by the time she had pushed her labored steps all the way to the 'Y'. There, as she had supposed, the deeper snows faded away and she could pantingly move through only waist-deep cover. She shivered now in the cold and pounded her body to puff away the clinging snow. Her labor now was eased, and cold was the cost for her. Again, Mother Hougarry's voice taunted with a whining tone of safety and warmth, security on a crust-less night like this. She shook her head to chase away the twisted memories of unheeded pleas to stay. She scattered them and then relaxed, stepping forward with a freer mind, down the Field's path, past Mary's Flower Shop, down to the corner.

Everything lay silent and dark under the bright light of the now over-arching moon. The houses were huddled as dim spots in the gleaming countryside. Carymba had no difficulty at all in finding her way. The moon took care of lighting her path in the snow. Mary's house lay in silence. The Spinners' Shop squatted in peace. At the place she knew the path to turn, and the graveled drain to dip down toward the Gully, she turned to descend once more.

The ground dropped away underfoot, and the snow went with it, more or less. At times, the extra snow packed high over her head, and she burst through it with mild anxiety for having lost all sight of the way until she poked her head through on the other side, where she found a drop in level more pointed than the drop in footing. Down she went; she slid and then she gathered her feet, moving onward until she met the path. She recognized the path because it offered a brief and regular plateau across the general drop to the Gully. For safety's sake, she stayed close to the upper slope, away from the edge.

Up the path she plowed, breaking the smooth reflecting face of the snow on the way to Mahara and Guerric's door. Once there, she rapped upon the door, and waited. She rapped again, and waited.

Inside, Mahara heard the rap upon her door. She sat up in bed, and frowned. She lay back down until the second rap and then she decided to rise and investigate. Pausing, she looked at Guerric, a slumbering lump who never rises well from sleep. Shaking her head, she stood out on the floor; the cold nipped her feet; she curled her toes and grabbed for her robe – something, anything to cover herself again from the chilled room. Her toes complained; she poked around, looking for her slippers. A third rap came, steady and patient except in Mahara's bothered ears. Finally, the slippers were found in their careless places. She fumbled her feet until they slipped on in to find some warmth. Still, it was not as good as her already cooling bed, under the covers – a fact she knew too well. Shivering, she tiptoed toward the door, for she was curious and yet concerned about who might come in the middle of the night. The filtered moonlight made it easy for her to step across the room. She paused and frowned; sometimes a cooperative Guerric, who would wake up in the night, would be helpful. Shrugging her shoulders, Mahara went on carefully: there was no other choice.

Another rap came. Mahara tightened in reaction. Frowning at herself, she consciously relaxed and eased near the door. She put her eye next to the edge of the curtain and held her breath so as not to steam the window more. A slight snow-splotched figure stood there, shivering. She spoke: 'Hello'. A muffled, chattering voice responded: 'Hello. Mahara?' 'Yes'. 'This is Carymba. Can I see you?' 'Not till I open the door.'

Opening the door, Mahara shivered at the cold. 'Come in quickly. Let me close the door again against the cold. … There' she sighed. 'Now, what brings you out now, of all times?' 'It *is* a nasty night, except that the stars were out, and now the moon gleams'. 'Yes: it is lovely, but cold, … and, looking at you, deep in snow. Was it over your head?' 'Only on the slide down from the Fields'. 'Brrr'. 'Yes: it is cold.' 'Maybe we can stir up some heat in that stove; it does not smell completely out yet.' 'I would not mind that at all'. 'Can you bring me some fuel from other there?' 'Sure. Oh, my: those fingers are stiffer than I expected! ... Here, I can hold some in my arms easier.' 'Thanks. It is chilly in here'.

The two of them shivered over the stove for a bit, teasing the fire back to life, gathering a small flame, which then became brighter and warmer. They added some fuel, and the flames danced and the stove warmed. The air began to warm again, and they warmed with it. Hands stretched out to the face of the stove and the rawness of one pair, the pale chill of the other shone in the light. 'That feels good on my hands.' 'My feet are warming, too. That floor was awfully cold when you got me out of bed'. I imagine it was'. 'You never said why you came ... now of all times'. 'That stove is warm now'. 'Yes'. 'Where does it vent?' On the roof, of course'. They both looked up as they heard a shuffling sound, one they knew as ice shifting on the roof of the hut. Mahara shuddered. 'I'm glad you came, whatever the reason. Ice is our worst winter problem. My uncle's house was crushed by ice build-up that was left unrelieved. ... Let's have some tea'. 'That sounds good to me, too'.

22 December 1985

CCXXI

A deep darkness had fallen over Hyperbia, lending a bottomless sinking to the damp chill of the day which was gone. Thyruid looked about his Inn, wearily. The chairs were sloppily shoved about, a reminder of the folk who had been in and out of that dining room in unusual flurry ever since mid-morning, before Geoffrey had made his usually belated entrance. Now, however, the Inn lay quiet, deserted. Marthuida was in the kitchen. He needed to straighten the dining room, and so he began that chore, slowly. With a great yawn, Thyruid stretched himself and flexed his shoulders around frontwards, then twisted first the left then to the right. He bent over forward, to each side in turn, and back, looking to the shadowed ceiling overhead. He crinkled as he went and yawned a few more times in ready succession. The day had been long and weary. He had greeted and served more than he could count. His face was even tired from smiling. His eyes hung heavily; he had to blink repeatedly to bring them into approximate focus.

Thyruid bumped the chairs and the tables erratically as he wound his way around the dining room, sleepily arranging the place in some proper order. Along the front, he paused to put out his lamps, then moved along the way to turn down, and out, each one in turn. Finally, he reached the fireplace, where the fires burned low, crackling toward glowing embers. Stifling another yawn, he blinked hard and smiled softly in response to the fire. The Inn looked sleepy. His guests had left or gone upstairs to bed. The only sounds remaining were the hissing cackle of the fire and a gentle clatter from the kitchen. The world, at least Thyruid's world, was at peace.

Marthuida poked her head out of the kitchen. 'Thyruid, I have some warm cider left. How about we share some before we settle in for the night?' 'That sounds warm and soothing. A good end to a full and busy day: I am amazingly tired!' 'Give me a minute'. 'You have it'.

Another lamp was put out, leaving but one, near their paneled door (matching closely the paneled wall opposite the fireplace). That one lamp he lowered to a soft glow as a restful companion to the fire-place on the other side. Looking at the counter and the stools there, he slowly shook his head and moved over to the table by the hearth. 'Clyde won't mind if I borrow this now; he ought to be snoring by now'. Sitting down, he yawned again. Warmth radiated from the fireplace; he leaned back in his chair, turned half way to watch the fire, as tired-looking as he felt. The chair nestled him into itself, soaking up his weight and inviting him to relax even more. He decided to indulge himself and set his feet upon the hearth. They hadn't felt much in their late-day shuffling. Now, raised, they began to quietly throb in a blissful pain, the sort of anguish which a tired body knows when it allows that tiredness to ooze, acknowledged and accepted as that into which surrender is aptly due. Thyruid closed his eyes and sighed. They burned just a bit; the smoke, perhaps, he thought to himself, although the cause was merely tiredness compounded by the settling-in. 'I wonder how Marthuida is doing. She ought to be here momentarily. Hmmm: I wonder if she needs some help'.

Thyruid had not moved when Marthuida came out to end his extended musing. 'Oh, I was just beginning to wonder if you needed help' he drawled. 'No. I simply needed a moment or two to get my fire under control, and have the cider hot, and spiced. I thought you might enjoy it that way'. 'The odor is tangy on my nose' he observed. 'I suspect I will enjoy the whole cup'. 'You do look comfortable there. All you need is your slippers. ... 'Sure, but not now. Here: sit with me and let's take a bit to watch the fire die down for the night'.

Marthuida set the cider mugs down, pushing one steaming cup to Thyruid and setting the other down for herself. 'Ahhh ...' she sighed as she melted into the waiting chair. She leaned back, letting her arms plate the arm-rests. 'I had not realized how long today had been. Was there any break between the time Geoffrey arrived for his late breakfast and the time Geoffrey ended his snack and went to bed, leaving us here to finish out the day?' 'No. But the steady rush began even before Geoffrey came down. Some days we have no one; today more than compensated for that!' 'I love to cook. This day made an exception. Too much is more than enough!' 'It certainly is. Now, is this cider cooled enough to drink?' 'Try some: carefully'.

Thyruid blew the steam away, then sipped at the cider: 'Whew! That is hot! But very good. I'll sniff the aroma for a bit more before I try again'. Marthuida chuckled. 'The only problem I am going to have is that I will have to move my arms again if I am going to have any cider to drink'. 'A just observation, I must say'. 'Oh, you old sage: your wisdom is almost as great as your yawn'. 'Pardon me. I've been doing that for some time. Then I have to blink repeatedly to find some focus in my eyes again. I must be getting old'. 'Don't say that: I'm as old as you. Let's just say days like today were easier some years ago than they are now'. 'I believe that is a fair statement. ... Ummm: you ought to have some cider. The warm spicy taste tingles the throat;. 'I will. Just give a minute ... or five'. 'You'll let it get cold'. 'So what? My arms don't want to move just yet; they are in that delightful stage of aching pleasurably in their relaxation'. 'My feet are that way. At least I can sip my cider at the same time'. 'Lucky for you'. 'Yes, it is'.

The flickering wisps of low blue flame fluttered on, then off. A hiss came from the coals, leaving a burst of gasses which popped into flame, casting a yellow flare upward. The light flashed against their tired faces, then died away into a wavering orange, increasingly coated with a chunky white ash layer. The warmth was nearly visible now, the slight glow showing the rippled waves of heat which softened Thyruid's aching feet. 'There is a pleasantness to the ending of days' Thyruid commented. 'Yes, there is' returned Marthuida. 'Now *my* cider is nearly done. One more sip and ... ah'. 'I'll need to hurry up and join you. Then I'll wash these quickly ...'. 'Oh, just leave them. Morning will come soon enough'. 'Too soon: and yet I never just leave things. The kitchen does have certain needs. I notice, by the way, that you straightened the chairs'. 'That was nothing; I did it *before* I sat down!' 'You were just lucky'. 'That says the truth'.

Thus savoring their ending day, as the coals crackled less often, less vigorously, they began to move. Thyruid dropped his feet to the floor and leaned himself forward. Marthuida pulled and pushed herself up. 'Ha: I got up first. Maybe you *are* older than I am'. 'Poof!' And he too stood up with pretended energy. 'Careful you don't fall on over, Thyruid! Those coals are still hot in there'. 'You be careful yourself, Marthuida. You seem a little tippy'.

While they were thus urging each other onward toward bed, the door opened. That was a most unusual happening this time of night. Thyruid spoke first: 'I must not have latched it'. But no sooner did he speak than Carymba hobbled into the Inn: 'Sorry I am so late. I was detained, and now so dearly need some help'. 'What is the problem?' responded Thyruid, just before another yawn overtook him. 'The snow has started again. The flakes are as big as my head as they float down. They cover the ground quickly, although it is warm enough to have a soft snow, clinging and wet and tight. Some folk find travel hard now. I came across one lady, from the gypsie area out by the Great River. She says she has been here before, that she is Mahara's aunt. She intended to reach their home tonight, but she came more slowly than she expected. And this snow has worn her out. She is slower now than ever. Anyway, she is hungry and cold and tired. Can you help?' As she asked, a soggy, shivering old woman in heavy long clothes appeared in the doorway, full of sadness.

Marthuida felt the chill and tiredness all through her own body. She sorely wanted to say no. So did Thyruid, until he held up his empty mug. Then, he said: 'We are tired, too. So we know how it feels. Come in and warm yourselves the lazy, tired fire. There is still some warmth. I'll add some fuel. Perhaps we can find a little left over food. Do come in: we will make ready. Come along. ... There'.

29 December 1985

CCXXII

Morning had arrived. She could tell by the dull greyness which had emerged from the dismal black of the huddled night. The fire she had left in the pit the night before, when weariness of bone and flesh dragged her into a thorough sleep, lay cold: time had indeed passed – too much time. Without the fire to hold back Winter's gnawing cold, the ravages of icy touches had begun to poke their way nearer and nearer to the hearth, the stones which lined her fire pit. Shivering, she inched out of her covers, one long bony arm ending in stiff, gnarled fingers reached to shove together a potential fire while preserving whatever body heat she could. The preservation proved minimal; she shivered more thoroughly and crawled out to adjust what needed to be done. Her knees poked the hard-packed floor; the cold hurt. Her toes and feet and ankles poked free, bare and chilled-white in the icy room. She watched her breath cloud in mist, then vanish, puff by puff. 'There', she sputtered: 'that is ready. Now for some fire. Then we can worry about warming these old joints again, for another day in mud and daub and snow. I think snow is our worst enemy – worse far than mere mud'.

'Missus Carney!' The voice pierced the hut from the crack in the door. The old woman started, jumping up to her feet with nearly forgotten nimbleness. She stood there: the voice repeated its shrill call. Suddenly she realized she was standing barefoot, her feet spread in readiness, her arms bent upward, her hands flexed into fists. Her neck was rigid, every muscle taut. Her nightgown hung half tattered to mid-forearm and mid-calf. She imagined her hair was its usual fright, the usual aftermath of a long night's sleep. Her heart was pounding; the sound echoed in her ears. She was panting, puffing out billows of steam. 'Missus Carney?' came the piercing sound again, more pleading now than before. She laughed at herself, a low chuckle. Her hands dropped to her side; she dangled them loosely. She was cold. 'Just a minute' she called in crackling tones as she grabbed a blanket to wrap around her wiry frame.

With her makeshift cope cuddled about her, her shins and toes shining free below, she shook her hair into approximate order and moved to her door. Cracking it but a little, she saw her neighbor boy there, with big dark eyes peeping into her dim room. 'I didn't see any smoke this morning. And it is awfully cold. I was worried about you'. Missus Carney smiled at her little friend: 'You look a little cold!' 'Oh, not me, Missus Carney. I was afraid you would be cold'. 'Why not come in? That door is not of much value closed, but it holds out more cold closed than it does open'. 'That makes sense! Sure. Your hut is always warm, even when it is cold'. 'Here, share my blanket a bit; we can sit together and blow smoke with our breath'. 'Yea! You always have good ideas'. 'I try. Now, what are you doing out on so cold a morning as this?' 'I guess I was looking for warmth. Our fire went out, too'. 'Ah, I see'. 'But then I saw your smokeless house, too. And I was worried about you'. 'As you can see, my fire has gone out. I noticed that when I quit sleeping'. 'Don't you mean woke up?' 'I suppose I could say it that way. Except that I feel more like I just quit sleeping than like I actually woke up'. Her neighbor boy leaned away from her, looking back with a strange and puzzled look: 'Are you really alright?' "Yes: Honest'. 'OK'. And, reassured, he snuggled close to be warm, or warmer at least.

Missus Carney continued talking: 'Anyway, when I found a cold fire, I began to arrange my fire-pit to bear a new fire, to warm me up this morning and fix some breakfast'. 'Food: *that* is interesting to me, too'. 'I thought it might be. But I haven't found a way, yet, to light my fire, to make the warmth'. 'So you need fire. My Daddy does, too'. 'That means we can't borrow some from your house'. 'No'. 'Well, don't be too sad. There must be someone around here with fire'. 'Nope'. 'Nope?' 'I looked all around and saw no smoke. That was before I came here. I was worried about you. But I was also figuring you might have some idea of how we could get warm'. 'Well, we have our blanket here. Otherwise, someone having fire would be pretty handy on a morning like this'. 'Yea'.

Missus Carney wiggled her toes. They were cold. 'I think they need to be inside my blankets. They need some warmth!' 'You don't know about fire, do you?' 'No. I am not sure just what we need to do now'. 'In that case,

I had better go'. The young lad crawled from the blanket, being careful to give it back to her quickly, to save the heat as best she could. 'Where are you going to go?' 'I don't know yet. But you stay here and stay warm'. With that, he left, closing the door quickly behind himself, leaving Missus Carney to watch her breath in her icy hut.

Figuring that clothes might help her keep warm, Missus Carney began to gather them into her blankets – but first she added a second layer about her bony self. Within the folds, she twisted and bent as best she could, gradually arranging herself into her garments. She was generous with layers on her feet and body. Her hands and her nose presented problems with layers; she kept a blanket handy to add one more layer on hands and, in shielding part, on nose. The combination did serve well to preserve her own warmth; but the chill poked about her anyway.

The silence outside began to distract her. She wondered about that silence. Normally, she heard noises outside by now. The mud had long encouraged the rough, sloppy sounds of squishing feet on daily commerce, even on the minor scales common to Apopar. Curious, she shuffled to her door, fully dressed now, and more than just that, all underneath her triple blanket load. She pulled open her door but a crack. Outside, she saw no mud. Rather she saw a driven snow, pounding upon the huts, hurrying along in soft, swishy motion. She closed the door again, and shuddered. She was cold. And she had nothing handy to offer her neighbors. She peeked outside again, squinting against the rude hard snow crystals cutting at her face with seeming disdain. There were no fires visible. Shaking her head, she closed her door again.

Barely was the door closed when a rap came on the door. 'I must have missed seeing someone' she said as she re-opened the door a crack. 'Missus Carney: we have no fire. Can we come in?' Certainly, but I have no fire either'. 'Nobody does. We decided to come here'. Another knock led to another entrance. Her little hut now held eight. Another knock came: her attendance swelled to twelve. The many huddled together, sharing the blankets they had brought among three and four, trying to be warm together. One man asked: 'Have you seen my son?' 'He came here early, seeking fire. Then he left. I don't know where he went'. 'He must have sought warmth somewhere. But where?'

In better times, Missus Carney knew – even in better times for the never-very-good Apopar – a debate would have followed over the child and his doings. Now, however, everyone sat numb, huddled for a tiny bit of warmth. Missus Carney frowned and huddled herself in her blankets, wiggling her toes, rubbing them together for heat, thinking over the neighbor lad. She had not realized the weather earlier, or she would have done something different: but what? She stewed in herself, frowning and looking older than her years.

The door thundered. Everybody huddled onto the other side of the room, instinctively. All the eyes looked at the door with a wide hollowness. Each breath puffed out a billow of fog – first here, then there, then again nearby, in a nearly random array, from cold reddened noses. The door thundered again. They were too numb to fear any more. Missus Carney was already on her way to the door. She stood herself erect and bore her own dignity against the cold. She opened the door a crack. A Guard stood there, richly bundled for warmth. Guessing, she nodded. 'Won't you come in?' There was a gasp behind her. She watched carefully as he entered; a small huddled figure followed closely behind. 'I understand no one kept a fire going last night. That was foolish. Nevertheless, for the lad's sake, I brought some fire. Here'. He knelt to the prepared fire-pit and set it ablaze.

The Guard stood and warmed his hands. 'We Guards have a right to be warm, no matter who else may benefit'. The neighbor's lad grinned, and winked at Missus Carney. She winked back, quickly, slyly.

5 January 1986

CCXXIII

Mary stood on her tiptoes, barefoot, to look out her bedroom on the second story of her Flower Shop home. The upper quarter of the window was still free from the outside snow, and she had decided this morning to take advantage of that peek-a-boo space in order to determine what kind of weather she intended to avoid today. She remained there, stretched as tall as she could muster without a stool, studying the sight. Over the top of the pure white snow fluttered small, hard-looking flakes of snow under an indeterminate grey sky. Content that she could find happiness out of that snow, she let the curtains fall back into place and rocked herself back onto her heels. Her feet hit the floor, and she rocked quickly onto her toes, although with less exaggeration than before. 'Brrr' she shuddered to herself, now newly aware of the cold floor.

Having scurried into her fluffy slippers first, she grabbed a housecoat and wrapped it around herself snugly. Warming inside, she turned to early chores, straightening her room, and then moved toward breakfast. While the tea steeped, she began her day. Around the sippings at her tea, she dressed, a little warmly for today. Then it was time to go down and visit her plants. She frowned as she thought of how they dreaded these long dark Winter days. She could keep them warm enough, and watered. But the light was dim, and all from lamps; the snows – deep by wee folk standards – huddled her inside a dim house.

Determined not to permit the deep snows to depress her, Mary adjusted the heating stove and lit the lamps. She gathered some water and began the needed chore of watering her plants … all of them. The task, as always, took up most of the morning. As she turned to examine each plant in turn, she began to hum to herself, little tunes both familiar and concocted on the spot, in a quite pleasant, absent minded manner. She found that the lamps lit the room enough. Her leaves turned toward them – toward one or another of them – with appreciation. There was enough warmth for her to be comfortable, and for her plants to be happy.

Mary lingered over her plants because there was little else to do. She knew full well that few visited flower shops when the snow neared her roof. She knew many of the wee folk half-way hibernated in the Winter. That last fact limited her potential market! Her strategy had become that of building a repertoire of flowers for the drab days of early Spring. A certain resignation to such patterns had long ago crept into her style of doing business. She loved the plants, and let her business go as it would. She found such ways fit in the world of her Hyperbia best of all.

Because she was so clustered on herself by the snow, and so absorbed in her plants, Mary was rather startled to hear a knock at her front door. In wondering surprise, she started toward the door, then paused. She set down her watering can and listened, frowning. She folded one arm across her waist, holding the opposite elbow as she raised her fingers to her chin. Shaking her head, she sputtered to herself: 'Why am I even thinking this. No one can get to my door; there is too much snow out there. I must have been imagining it all'.

And another knock came at the door, more insistent than the first. Or at least the knock seemed to Mary to be more insistent than the first. She had barely noticed the first one, but now was quite attentive to the door. Puzzled, she stepped pensively to the door, careful and tentative in her movement. She was next to the door, wondering what to do next, when the knock came a third time, right in front of her nose. She jumped and caught her breath in its fleeting moment. Gasping slightly, her eyes wide, her mouth ajar, her heart racing, she gulped. 'Ye ... ye ... yes?' she choked out.

'Mary? Are you there?' The voice sounded soft and timid and far away on the other side of the door. She could not mistake the location: the voice was on the other side of the door, not upstairs, not at some high window, not in some distant place.

Mary swallowed hard and choked over the words again: 'Yes. I am ... here. Who are you?

'Mary?' The voice sounded needful, so weak and distant in the snows. Mary breathed hard, taking a few deep breathes and thinking to herself how silly she was being. Thus she reached to the handle. 'Mary?' came the voice again, nearly pleading for an answer. She took the handle and turned: the door was locked. Mary felt herself blush; her cheeks were suddenly warm; her ears tingled. She moistened her lips and swallowed hard. She straightened her hair for delay purposes, then unlocked the door, and opened it.

Standing before her was a snow-covered figure, all flushed and weary from trenching a way to the door. Mary looked at her, and then at the narrow slice extending back from her door, sloping in rough, snowy steps to the surface high above. The grey sky peeked down on her, sending cold air at her. Mary shivered. 'Come in. Come in. That cold must be hard on you!'

Mary gave way to her visitor, then closed the door behind her. 'Come over by the stove to warm, and melt. May I help you brush off your extra snow? … There: that should be better now. … Let me get you a chair. Certainly, I must do that much'.

Having chosen a chair, Mary set it next to the stove. Almost automatically, she lifted her tea kettle and, having judged that it was full enough, set it atop of the stove to heat. 'I might as well get double use of that fire' she commented with a grin. A sturdy, low shelf lent itself nearby; Mary half-leaned, half-sat upon it as she sat opposite her warming, resting, surprising guest. 'Why not open your cloak? You'll find it more comfortable that way'. 'Oh. Yes. I can do that'. And she slipped off her shawl and threw her hood back off her head.

Mary looked with surprise: 'Effie! I hadn't recognized you in all those clothes, and all that snow! You must be tired! How did you get here?'

'I came out my window. There is a good crust on the snow and walking wasn't too bad. I had to go slowly, and there were some weak spots in the crust, where I fell a few times, but you don't live very far from my loft at the Spinners' Shop'.

'I realize that. Oh! ... That teapot is hot! Now I'll need an extra cup and some tea. Would you like some?'

'That sounds very pleasant to me'.

'There: sorry to be so long. I didn't want to fly down those steps nose first!' As she fixed the tea, Mary continued: 'What brought you out today, Effie? That was a lot of snow to remove just to get to the door. You should have banged on a window upstairs; they are nearer the surface'.

'In the Hills, we always went to the front door. Besides, those huts up there didn't have second stories. But I came because I needed to get out. A body gets snow bound after so long. And even with the others, I felt I needed a change. So I came here. ... Your flowers are so cheerful. Mary, how do you keep them so nicely?'

'They aren't so hard, Effie. They have to be my companions on a day like today. They keep me busy. And they demand little but some water, warmth and light. In return, they give me a great deal in quiet beauty'.

Effie's eyes sparkled in the light. She sipped her tea. 'This tastes very good to me. Thank you'. 'That is no problem. I'm glad to have you come by. Would you like some more tea? or perhaps to save that and look around at my flowers first?'

'Let's look at the flowers, first. May I leave my cloak here?' 'Certainly. Here: let me show you what I have …'.

12 January 1986

CCXXIV

Yev found himself awake in the dark of his room. Normally, dark meant night. And, normally, Yev was unaccustomed to lying wide awake in the middle of the night. So he stretched himself out, looking into the dark over which, he knew, reigned the ceiling of his corner of the root-framed home he shared with his seven friends. Only in the middle of the night was the ceiling hidden in deep darkness. So he closed his eyes; they were most uncooperative, and flew open again. He rolled to one side and curled up under his warm covers, and shut his eyes. As long as he squeezed them, they stayed shut. But one he tried to relax his way toward sleep, they bounced open once again. Yev thought to himself: 'I wasn't dreaming. That did not wake me up'. He thought over other things which might wake him; one by one, he checked them off in his mind as not applicable today. He turned the other way; his eyes flew open to view a gentle and unthreatening darkness. He asked himself if he were afraid. But his pulse was normal; his breathing was normal; there was absolutely *nothing* unusual about him … except that his eyes were open, his mind was rumbling, and he really wanted to get up, even if it were black and bleak outside.

Yev, disgusted with himself for he knew it must be the hour for sleeping, gave up, and got up. Strangely, at least to his own mind, he felt more natural, more comfortable standing than he ever did in the middle of the night. The natural impulse in him, as he felt it now, was to rise and dress and get ready for the day which ought to have begun, were he to believe his bones and his stomach. The stomach grumbled and turned his thoughts to food. Yev scoffed at himself, and patted his rumbling mid-section. He felt like it must be mid-morning, except for the unusual dark. Either his eyes or his body was deceiving him. With no resolve to return to bed, Yev pulled on some clothes and fumbled toward his door.

The hallway lay just as dark, darker than usual even. Yev scowled at himself, then groped along the hallway, slowly feeling and sniffing his way step by step. He found no surprises in the darkness of the home, a fact which nearly surprised him. The hall gave way to the front living room, which also lay snuggled in unaccustomed darkness. Yev found the stove, which was nearly cold; he looked inside and saw no spark. He bumped the stove, and no coal glowed his way. He found a poker and stirred the bed of the stove where coals ought to be. He met all the resistance of loose powder. But there was no glow, no spark. He felt the air over the should-be-coals; it was cool. Wondering if this really is the stove, Yev withdrew his hand and groped around some more. It certainly felt like the stove, even if the thing was as cool as all around him. Yev scowled again, and shivered vigorously. He knew the stove should keep some spark all night long. This looked like night, and he heard none of his friends up and about; so what is going on? He puzzled to himself, his hands on his hips.

Deciding he should investigate further, Yev felt the darkness with his hands, shuffling his feet slowly so as to avoid stumbling. He moved around the chairs; everything seemed to be in order, a fact which pleased him. Indeed, Yev almost smiled, for that was the first piece which had seemed right since he woke up and could not go back to sleep. He fumbled his way across an open spot, to a window. The curtain hung exactly where he expected it. He pulled the curtain aside, and saw nothing. He touched the window; the glass was cold and wet with condensate. He wiped his now-cold, wet hand on his trousers and let the curtain fall back into place.

Another window was over a bit. So he shuffled himself to the spot that window ought to be. The window was right there in the dark silence. He pulled back the curtain and saw darkness. He reached to the windowpane. The glass was cold and wet. He wiped his hand, again, on his trousers, and let the curtain fall, a barrier between darkness and darkness, between silence and silence.

Yev knew where the door stood. If the windows were exactly where he expected to find them, then the door *had* to be in place, too. He went there without hesitation, following blindly the route he routinely took. The door was there. That felt good, for it served to reinforce his touching with reality, even though he moved like a blind man. The thought struck him. He blinked hard, and still saw nothing. He rubbed his eyes, and saw nothing. He squeezed real tight and made himself see the unseen images in his eyes. That was normal, and halfway served to satisfy him. Boldly now, he took the door and pulled it open. He saw darkness. He reached forth his hands, palms forward, to find that darkness. He took one step and his hand slapped the face of darkness. It was cold and wet, like the window, except that it gave way to the force of his step. 'Snow!' exclaimed in a half-shout.

Leaving the snow-blocked door wide open, Yev hastily retreated, his unseeing eyes wide open in the dark room. He stumbled in his new-found carelessness as he maneuvered himself around chairs less successfully than usual. The inconvenience frustrated him so that, flustered, he reached the door of a room. He tapped. A low moan responded. 'Vlad!' he called. 'Uhmmph' came the very muffled response. 'Vlad!!' he repeated. 'OK. OK. Give me a minute. ... What is this? the middle of the night?' 'I don't think so. But we *are* all snowed under'. ;So?' 'So!?! Don't you think we ought to do something?' 'Like what?' 'Like find our way free!' 'Free for what?' 'For whatever we need to do'. 'Aren't you a little wide awake for the middle of the night, Yev?' 'I think we will find it is not the middle of the night. The stove is stone cold'. 'Stone cold?' 'Yes. And it isn't stone cold at breakfast time'. 'Let me get dressed. I'll look at things with you. Just wait for me. Find a seat, and wait for me'. Vlad yawned as he half-heard the stumbling steps of his excited friend bounce toward their living room area.

By the time Vlad had moved his slumber-laden self to the living area, half-dressed and still stretching in the pitch-black darkness, Yev had roused the other six and all were bumbling their way toward the dark room. Everybody grumbled, certain that Yev was dreaming or deluded, or at least very, very confused. They came only to humor him, to overcome this little game, and to get themselves back to bed. Straggling into the room, they groped for chairs. Serg asked why it was so cold. Yev responded that the fire was out. Cons, who found the open door, complained that the open door caused all the cold. Most mumbled and grumbled some more – at the cold, at the open door, at Yev.

Vlad moved through the room, seeing nothing and rubbing his arms for warmth. 'Dum, can you do something with the stove? Yev tells me it is cold, and I believe it!' 'Sure, if I can find it'. 'Thanks'.

Everyone sat around waiting while Dum clanged about. 'There is the stove. It is cold. The ashes are even cold. That makes things harder, particularly in the middle of the night like this. A little light would help'. 'Maybe I can find a lamp to light. ... There's one. And now a light'. Everyone blinked at the sudden brightness. 'Thanks, Alex' said Dum as he set out to get a fire going in the stove. Yev, with the light to help, reopened the door. 'See, Vlad: snow. All the snow you could want, and then some'. Nike answered 'Yes! If it is that deep here, what is Father John doing?' Everyone stopped, except Dum. Then, as Dim fussed over the fire, the others disappeared, to reappear in warm clothing to begin the chore of finding a way out.

Dum finally got his fire going. Then he sat back on his heels. 'That ought to warm us soon' he said in satisfaction. He looked around: the lamp flickered on a table; otherwise, he was alone. 'Where did they all go? Back to bed?' Dum shrugged. 'I'll be warm anyway' he said as he sat on a chair to watch the stove warming everything for him.

19 January 1986

CCXXV

Yves turned back from the door and looked toward Betsy as she sat against the wall near the door to her room. The look outside was hardly encouraging as the sky hung low in a dull slate grey and the branches quivered in a rushing wind. The edges of the brook which ran under the great Dome were iced, although the gurgling rapids bounced freely. The window felt cold, too. Turning back, he looked at his sister, painted with the standard pout of boredom. And he shrugged. 'I wonder about days like today'. 'Huh?' responded Betsy after an awkward pause. 'I said I wonder about days like today'. 'Why?' 'Because it is so grey and damp and raw. Even looking out the door is depressing'. 'So why look when you can sit here and be bored? … like me!' 'Yech! Boredom looks ugly!' 'Thanks a lot'. 'Not you, Betsy; but you *bored*'. 'I am bored. We ought to do something'. 'What?' 'Be bored, I guess'.

Yves slid down the wall next to the door to his room, just across from Betsy. He too was getting bored, and was settling into his ways. He grew grumpy and disgruntled. He grew *really* bored. Betsy looked at him and saw his face grow slack. He slumped and seemed to turn a dull grey – not as dark as the sky but nearly as unpromising. 'Yves, I believe you now'. '… Uhmm …about what?' 'About boredom being ugly'. 'You're right: I *am* bored. There is nothing to do'. 'Tell me, Yves, do you ever wonder what it would be like if we had never come here?' 'Sure. Particularly when I get bored. Like now. You can get boring, Betsy'. 'Don't feel too lonely. You can be awfully boring yourself'. 'Compliments needn't run strongly between us'. 'Who is complimenting who?' 'At least you are boring'. 'I suppose that is more than I can say sometimes'. 'About you, Yves'. 'Thanks a lot. But you are right. I do wonder about our old home sometimes …'.

The two sank into silence, a silence beyond or below their boredom. They looked at each other blankly, without recognition, without emotion. They were lost in memories they could no longer recollect for themselves, the memories which might have been, might have given them someone with whom to do something on a grey bleak blah day, like today.

Such sitting consumed the morning, unawares. They sat until their stomachs began to rumble on them, and thus to rouse them from their struggles to imagine what might have been had they not found themselves here in Hyperbia, surrounded by all the kindly wee folk, but with no one like themselves. Yves noticed his stomach first, as it began to turn flip-flops inside. 'It must be lunch time, almost' he said without any feeling whatsoever. Betsy raised her eyes to him blankly: 'My stomach says so, too. I suppose we will have to go get some lunch'. 'Marthuida will be expecting us soon'. 'It will be cold out there'. 'We can bring our lunch home and eat it here. We can be warm enough, even on a day like today'. 'You are right, for once'. 'What do you mean, 'for once'?' 'Settle down, Yves. I can't let you think you are better than you are, you know'. 'Alright. But you ought to admit I am as good as I am'. 'Fair enough. You are right, this time'. An impish grin crept across her occasionally serious face. She watched Yves as he grumbled, then stole a wink toward her.

Laughing now, the two dragged themselves up and rounded up their coats and hats – all of a patchwork sort, for their helpers who sewed the coats for them were all wee folk who labored hard for them, for the adopted children of all Hyperbia. Bundled against the cold, they both went out and shivered. The air nipped at them. Playfully, Betsy nipped back – and they both giggled. The worn path was a streak of brown, frozen hard and gouged by heels from when it lay softer in the uncertain days of Winter, where hard frost is parted occasionally by slight thaw, a teasing before Spring arrives to claim the world for goo. The frozen gouges gave foot-hold today and eased their scamper up the hill.

Having rounded the curve and brought themselves behind the Inn-by-the-Bye, the pair dropped to their knees beside the special big door Thyruid had installed so they could get fed on (for them) reasonable sized dishes. They never knocked; they never needed to knock; the thud of their knees tumbled the Inn sufficiently to effect the announcement of their having come to eat. Shortly, Marthuida poked her head out her little door and smiled. 'You'll have to wait a bit; I'm not quite ready. You will want to take your lunch home to eat, won't you?' 'I think so. The cold is damp today'. 'Just a few minutes" I got behind this morning'. 'We'll wait' they replied, in chorus.

As they would sometimes do, the two sat down, back-to-back and watched the world go by, each telling the other what was happening on the side they saw. Looking down the hill, into the gully which swept under the Great Dome, Yves admitted: 'I see a few drips almost falling from the high twigs. They would fall if it were warm enough'. 'Sounds exciting'. 'It isn't. How are things you way?' 'The Leaferite Hill is standing there, like always. And … oh … wait, here comes Mahara from the Plain'. 'Oh? What is she doing out on a day like this?' 'Walking'. 'Everybody hates a wise remark!' 'Well, she *is* walking. She's walking slowly; she swishy skirts are barely moving – not like they usually are. But it *is* Mahara; only Mahara wears those bright, bright colors'. 'Is she by herself?' 'Yes. I see no one, not ever Guerric. That is odd, now that you mention it; they usually travel together'. 'I wonder where she has been'. 'If we wait a few minutes, we can ask her'.

Their lunch had not emerged from Marthuida's kitchen before Mahara ambled up. 'Hi Mahara' said Betsy, softly because Mahara looked so sad. Mahara looked up, her face drawn and mellow, her olive complexion drab, her dark eyes lacking in fire. 'Hello' she said, more softly than had Betsy. Betsy wanted to cheer her: 'Your dress is so pretty, especially on a drab day like this'. She smiled warmly, in her best little girl fashion. Mahara nodded to your young, large friend. 'Thank you. I think it not so bright as your smile, however'. 'Oh' said Betsy, and blushed: 'where have you been this morning?' 'I was visiting; and now I am going home'.

Betsy cocked her head to the side in interest. 'I was thinking about home this morning, wondering what it is like there. Neither Yves nor I remember any more. We don't even remember forgetting. Geoffrey can't say that'. Mahara half smiled, and sighed. 'I suppose you could say I thought I was visiting home'. Betsy frowned, then said: 'You look tired, Mahara. Sit on my knee and tell me what you mean. … Here: I'll help you up. There!' 'Thank you. Sitting does feel good, if only for a couple minutes. I really must get home'. 'Yes. But do tell me what you mean, first'. 'Alright: I will. I had been lonesome – homesick some would call it. And I went back to visit. I saw my dear aunt, the one who came here to see me.

I saw the people I had known. We had a good time, a good visit. I was glad to be there. Then I realized that I enjoyed the place and was warmly welcomed, that everything was set out as home had been – except that that wasn't home anymore. Home now is on the little ridge overlooking the Gully, in the cabin you can see from your front door, if you look the right way. I thought I was home; now I need to *go* home. I guess home is where I do *my* work.

As Mahara slid down from Betsy's knee, Marthuida opened the door. 'Here Yves, Betsy: sorry to be so long. Take them on home before you get any colder'. Then, seeing Mahara: 'Oh, Mahara, do come in; Guerric, I heard, just came for lunch. He'll be glad to see you'. Mahara nodded and, blushing slightly under her olive tones, she followed Marthuida through the kitchen … as a surprise.

26 January 1986

CCXXVI

Betsy yawed and stretched. Her stomach growled. 'It must be morning' she moaned to herself as she stretched and yawned again. She sat up in bed, the covers falling to her lap; she gazed in a blank stare across the dim room. After long enough, she mustered herself and crawled out of bed. Her feet did hold her, and the tottering was slight. She grinned at herself in smug satisfaction until her stomach grumbled again. They she rounded up her clothes and changed to be ready for the day.

Dressed and as perky as she could muster herself to be, Betsy strode into the central hallway of the Great Dome. Yves was still snoring. Her own stomach rumbled in reply. Curious, she went to the door and looked out. Snow was everywhere. Snow crept up the trees and lay thickly upon the landscape, with only the dark opening for the rapids in the book marring a clean bright surface. With all the snow, there was no sign of activity, no hint of motion. She saw nothing but snow and trees. Sighing, and nodding to herself, she retreated from the door.

Having meandered to Yves' door, she banged on it. Yves snorted and gasped. She heard him heave himself in bed, then moan. 'Yves!' she called. 'Uhhhh …; he grunted. 'Yves, there is snow outside'. 'So? It is Winter. It is supposed to snow'. 'There is lots of snow out there'. 'Sounds like good sleeping weather'. There is too much snow out there'. 'Are you going to let me sleep or do I have to come shut you up?' 'I'm going for breakfast. Aren't you hungry?' And with that she walked away, to her room, where she gathered her Winter playwear, pulled it all onto herself, hat and scarf and mittens and all.

Yves, for his part, lay there, his rest disturbed. He scowled and frowned. His eyes had fought to open in the midst of the exchange with Betsy. Now they were reluctant to close again. He muttered under his breath: 'Sisters can be *such* a trial'. He did not want to get up, and yet his mind kept meandering insistently. He tossed himself once; then again; then again with a violence born of the anger of waking against his laziest wishes. Finally, hearing the front door open, and close, and all footstep sounds vanish simultaneously, he wrenched himself from his pillow and heaved his body out of bed. Erect, more or less, he stretched and yawned and wavered a bit in the cool room. Curiosity was driving him, and a new awareness of a grumbly stomach. His clothes covered him. Over them came the Winter wear. Finally, he emerged to the empty echoes of the central room. 'Betsy?' he called. There was no answer. He went to the door and looked out the window to see her footsteps plunged into the snow, which (he thought to himself) must be nearly waist deep on her. He hurried out the door after her, slamming the door behind himself and triggering a dumping of snow from the Dome's roof … onto his own head.

Picking himself up out of the snow, Yves began to shuffle after Betsy's tracks. The snow was deeper than he had expected as he labored after her, plowing through the fluff. He lunged, step after step, up the hill. Panting, he paused there to collect his breath. 'I thought you might come soon. Even bed could not give you good enough of a reason to miss breakfast'. Yves had not expected to hear Betsy's voice there, then. He was startled and he jumped. Betsy grinned. 'Of course, we may need to dig out the Inn-by-the-Bye in order to find some breakfast'.

Betsy waved her arm in the direction of the Inn, or where the Inn supposedly stood. Knowing where to look, Yves recognized the hump of snow. 'Our friends might be in trouble today'. 'I suppose. We could romp some and open them up'. Yves' eyes lit up with a sparkle. Then he lunged after Betsy, to grab her and throw her into the snow. He failed to surprise her, though, and she too leaped away from his grip, only to fall into the white fluff, puffing forth a billow of white. Yves also feel face-first, carving a slot in the thick white blanket. Separately, the two laughed and giggled and tossed themselves through the snow, leaving canyons and craters as the result of their frolic.

Inside the Inn-by-the-Bye, Geoffrey was up: even Geoffrey. The hour was very early by his standards, but the others had roused him from under his comfortable mound of blankets to take counsel together. Together with

Clyde, Thyruid and Marthuida, Geoffrey sat in the dimly lit dining room. He shivered: 'that snow is so inconvenient! I get cold'. 'And so do we'. Poor Marthuida can't cook until we get the chimneys free. There seems to be much-too-much snow out there'. And so had they talked for some time. No one could conceive a way to free the Inn of the over-abundance of snow. Clyde admitted he had dug out a channel before. But then the snow was not this deep. And he had been younger then. Geoffrey scoffed at that, but knew himself to be no match for the snow. He could only suggest that there are certain advantages to living on hilltops. 'There are also good reasons for staying under the wealth and warmth of many covers' he added with a whimsical glance toward the underside of his corner room overhead.

At about the moment of despair, the Inn began to quake and quiver, as if it had been bombed, or an earthquake had ensued. The chairs rattled upon the floor, and the tables danced. Clyde sat down upon the cold hearth. Geoffrey groped for the same security. Thyruid and Marthuida held onto the counter. All of them trembled, along with the Inn, having visions of disaster: avalanches from the Leaferites' Hill or general collapse of the Inn, burying them all in the haughty onslaught of the overbearing snow. Geoffrey looked at his room. 'Bed and that delightful mound of blankets would be *so* delightful' he confessed with a tremor in his voice. The Inn shook again, and again, with agitated vigor. Lampshades became cocked; dishes fell to the floor; pans rattled and clanked in the kitchen. The foursome looked at each other to see a set of pale and ashen faces reflecting the uncertainty in their own minds.

The tremors ceased. Clyde sat up coolly. His nose twitched on him and he could not stop it. He felt his chest pound. His breathing was short and quick. He felt warm all over. 'I ought to get my shawm' he sputtered. 'In fact, I will'. With that declaration he went upstairs to retrieve the shrill and plaintive instrument. He walked into his room as bravely as he knew how. Just as he reached for the shawm, a rasping sweep flashed past his window. 'Impossible' he thought to himself. Then it came again. He heard a rasping, scraping sound across the side of the Inn. His jaw quivered; he tried to set it but he could not. Under his beard he felt his flesh creep. He thought of all sorts of things to do. The most prudent, he decided was to go downstairs, taking his shawm with him.

The stairs quivered under him on the way down. And his knees wobbled, too. He held onto the railing firmly, and over-firmly, until he managed to stay upright and move down into the dining room again. There, the scraping sound persisted. He heard all around. Glancing at the others, he knew he was not alone in hearing. Geoffrey buried his head in his knees. Clyde wanted to do the same. Thyruid and Marthuida held each other, unable to move. Clyde thought to play, but he had no breath control.

The Inn shook again. A banging came at the kitchen doors. 'Make us some breakfast! We're hungry! We'll be back after opening some more houses!' Breathless shouts came, the voices of Yves and Betsy, followed by a thundering rush and a peal of giggles. Clyde sat down. Thyruid swallowed hard in the quiet. Marthuida wiped her hands on her apron. 'Well, now we can get to work, I suppose' she said.

2 February 1986

CCXXVII

As her footsteps carried her back and forth again and again across the trodden floor of her sod house, the notion flickered through Missus Duns' tired brain that she may be wearing her floor out. She almost looked to see if she were wearing a trench, but stopped short of that with a snorted laugh at herself, short and crude. 'That old floor is packed as hard as can be'. Her pace took her to one window to let her peek out. And then she returned to the other window to do the same. And finally she checked her active stove before beginning the cycle once again.

At each window, she watched the drizzle fall into the waning snow. There had been a lot of snow piled all through her little corner in the Hills. And now it was all turning to water, and the once frozen turf became an intermittent slick of mud, maybe ankle deep on her now, all full of water, oozing. She knew the water seeped into her sodden walls, her roof. She stirred her fire, more necessary now than ever to hold her dry home for another season. Again, she moved in anxious fear, keeping watch over the wallowing of mud, over the crackling of the fire in her heating stove.

Missus Duns had lost her momentum in time for measuring the limit of her annual watch – or so it was, at least, for thaw and rain together came to threaten her house of sod. She moved and moved, wiping her hands upon her apron, then dropping the apron to wring her hands together in fretful antic. The routine seemed very natural, having taken up hours of her time. Then, suddenly, she stopped. She glanced about. 'Which way was I going that time?' she asked herself out loud. She blinked, and realized how tired she was. Her routine grew heavy now. The stove crackled boldly. Her legs ached. The mud wallowed outside: she knew. Her eyes were heavy. The air was warm and dry, keeping the walls as well as she could do. Her shoulders slumped. Her hand reached to the back of the chair nearby. 'I can sit, for a minute. I'm sure that will be alright. I am so tired'. And so she did sit down.

The dripping sounds outside were muted in her hearing, slumber bound. Her eyes grew heavier, and closed. She blinked open, to close again. Warmth snuggled around her. Her shoulders eased. Her legs, relieved of standing, grew nearly numb. She felt the comforts of sleep easing upon her while the fire crackled again, reassuringly. The chair received her weight buoyantly. She slept. And all the while the dripping made oozing outside and the fire shoved back the cold damp, heating her walls and vaulted roof against the mud of a wet Winter's thaw.

Looking for the crevice which gives entrance to the niche in which her sod house nestled were the wet and muddy pair: Geoffrey and Carymba. Between them and Missus Duns' door spread a gooey sea of mud, puddled in places with cold water, the fresh melting of snow. Geoffrey looked with dismay while light drizzle dripped off the rim of his hat. 'I don't know why I ever agreed to this'. 'I thought it was because you liked Missus Duns'. 'I do. But we could come at a decent hour. You didn't have to get Clyde to clomp in and rouse me. I was so warm. And this is too early in the day for me. I ought to be asleep, under my delightful mound of blankets'. 'Well, Geoffrey: you *could* have said *no*'. 'I know. That is what I have been thinking ever since we came out into this mud-producing weather. I really do *not* like mud, Carymba'. 'I know that. Unfortunately today proved to be muddy'. 'Precisely'. 'I suppose we will need to use a technique of movement very much like the one we have been using all morning'. 'Oh?!' 'Yes. I propose that we walk'. 'Wouldn't wade or wallow be a better verb?' 'Perhaps ... by the way, it looks as though her stove is going. I expect she keeps it warm and dry in there, particularly now'.

Geoffrey thought over the prospect of warmth and dryness. The idea was almost as pleasant as sleeping in his high-piled bed. And the warmth was closer, even with the wet mud which looked so cold and squishy and lay between him and the door to the warmth. 'Carymba, since you have dragged me this far, I suppose it only makes sense to go onward. But my spats will be hard to clean from that yellow-brown paste. I have cleaned them before, and the task is most unpleasant'. 'Poor fellow!' 'Your sympathy hardly seems very supportive'. 'Should it be? Come along!' 'Alright, alright: wait for me. ... Yuck'. 'Careful, Geoffrey: the mud is slippery. You wouldn't want to fall, too'. 'Whoa! Come back feet! Oops. … Oh! … Darn it!' Then came the splat: face first, the hat even falling off into the mud, brim up to catch the drizzle. 'Are you alright?'

Geoffrey shoved himself up, his fingers and hands sinking into the mud, mud which oozed over everything. He pulled his knees under him. Then, reaching to his hat, he retrieved it for his head. Only a little drizzle had collected and now trickled down his mud-caked face. Carymba offered him a hand, but he waved her away. 'This is all your fault' he sputtered, spitting out mud with his words. With care, he eased himself upon his feet and stood erect, his ankles poking out of the oozing mud. Carymba wisely eased away, dragging her skirts in the mud. The two stepped high, toward the door, pulling the one foot out of the sucking mud until it loudly surrendered the foot to step forward. Then the trailing foot repeated the labored way, step-by-step-by-heavy-step until, new wearied, they meet the door of Missus Duns' sod house.

Carymba knocked, and waited. Inside Missus Duns snoozed soundly; the knock was lost in the irregular drips of water round about. Carymba knocked again, more loudly than before; still, Missus Duns slept on. Puzzled, Carymba frowned. 'Might she have been nursing that stove all night and only now have gone to rest?' asked Geoffrey. 'Perhaps. Should we leave?' 'No'. 'Should we enter?' 'Let us knock again; here' I'll take my turn'. He rapped more loudly. Missus Duns snorted in her sleep. Geoffrey nodded: 'Hear her?' 'Yes. Knock again'. He did, with hasty harsh raps which hurt his unaccustomed knuckles. Misses Duns snorted again: 'What?!' she called. 'You have company' responded Carymba. 'On a day like this?' 'Yes. It is cold out here'. 'I imagine it must be'. She fussed to get up, then sat down again. 'Oh, I'm lazy! Just come in, Carymba. Just come in'.

'Hello, Carymba' greeted Missus Duns. 'I must have fallen asleep. I get so worried about mud this time of year. I must keep my fire going! … Geoffrey: is that you?' 'Yes. I am here'. 'What happened?' 'My feet slipped on me'. 'Oh, dear: let me …'. 'No, no. I will be fine. I will leave my shoes and spats and even socks here. Then I can seek some warm water to wash away some of this unsightly excess. Some days, being a gentleman's gentleman, but without a gentleman, is difficult. This is one of those days'. Missus Duns looked with bleary eyes; she blinked only to have them turn bleary again, with tears from laughter she was too polite to let out. 'Do clean up. The stove will warm some water promptly, particularly if you stoke it some'. 'The water?' 'No: the stove; stoke the stove to heat the water'. Carymba just laughed out loud. 'Let me get some tea ready'. 'That sounds good. Some help will help today. … Poor Geoffrey' sighed Missus Duns.

9 February 1986

CCXXVIII

Mother Hougarry poured another cup of tea for herself, offering one to her guest, Carymba. 'Thank you' she responded; 'that will set off a perfectly delightful lunch'. The two of them sipped and chatted over pleasantries and memories shared while the stove's fire crackled out a warmth to keep the Hidden Cabin and the pair protected from the Winter cold. Outside, the wind moaned in trees overhead, a none-too-subtle counter melody to the stove's cheery insistence. 'On a day like this, Hidden Cabin is truly a haven, a refuge, an island of warmth in a land grown cold' Carymba observed. Mother Hougarry smiled knowingly: 'I find that often true, but in particular on days like this one, and with the gift of warm company'.

In the midst of gentle chatter, Mother Hougarry began to plot a supper for two and to think of arrangements for freshening a place for Carymba to sleep. Certainly her old bed is still in place on chance – in hope – she would take it up again for ready, consistent use. Too long, she felt, Carymba had followed her whims and gone off impossibly – late, in bitter weather, in storm and rage. Involuntarily, she shook her head over thoughts. Carymba, noticing, smiled: 'I see your thought turns to less likely topics than your tongue'. 'What?' 'You speak agreeably of old friendship and our days together – precious days – and yet you shake your head as over the most disagreeable of happenings'. Mother Hougarry sighed: 'Well, I suppose you find me out again. Discovering comes too easily for you!'

Carymba waited until it became clear that Mother Hougarry did not intend to divulge her secret thoughts, even though she knew they both had a good idea what was going unsaid. Instead, Mother Hougarry pursed her lips tightly and frowned, half-scowled, before relaxing her face quickly into a renewed warm glance. Carymba smiled, knowingly; and as if in return, Mother Hougarry moistened her lips pensively, then began: 'This fire makes the room cozy'. 'It certainly does do that'. 'And, of course, the company does too'. Carymba nodded deeply, largely to disguise the nearly-involuntary smirk which stole across her face; she looked up again, slowly, when once it had passed. 'Your being here, Carymba, makes this Hidden Cabin warm again'. 'You like my coming, don't you?' 'Yes'. 'And you really *dis*like my going'. 'Yes. I do that, too'. 'That is too bad, for my leaving does arise, in spite of my willingness to sit'. 'You have to leave" asked Mother Hougarry in sudden gloom. 'I fear I do'. 'But the wind moans so oppressingly. You will be cold!' 'I know. Your fire, your company, even my old cot over which you nursed – they tempt me'. 'Then stay!' 'That would feel good, except for one fact: I cannot'.

Carymba rose, setting her empty cup aside. She warmed her hands once more over the stove as the crackling resounded inside. Giving a sigh and shrug, she turned with swirling skirts to seek her winter shawl. On the peg where she left it hung she found it. The cold walls left it chilled; as she threw it about herself and flipped the hood upon her head, she shivered. 'The coat is always cold until I warm it'. 'Not so here: we – my stove and I – are warm to welcome you'. 'I know. And I'll remember. Thank you for so much'. 'You can stay'. Carymba heard the anxious tone and glanced at the warm stove as overhead the wind moaned long and low, rattling the windows of the Hidden Cabin. 'No. I cannot stay, no matter how pleasant that would be'.

Carymba slid out the door, avoiding opening it too far so as to minimize the rush of cold wind into the warmth of Hidden Cabin. Her last glimpse was of Mother Hougarry sadly waving a good-bye. The door latched; she pulled hard to make sure it had. And then she turned into the gale which was needling her with tiny crystals of snow, frozen hard in tight pellets to crash into the random targets, including now the lone traveler, Carymba.

Taking a path of ease, she turned up hill, her hooded back to the biting wind, and eased her way to Uiston. 'I need to leave, I know: but I see no need as yet to plow into the face of the storm' she muttered to herself while she felt the warming shawl-cloak pressed against her back from her knees to the top of her head. Beneath, the skirts lay plastered to her legs, all the way to her ankles. In front, she clasped the cape to keep it all from fluttering free and cold in the hasty breeze. Her steps clomped over frozen, clumpy ground, each clump holding a face of white, streaked along the edge with icy brown, soil on which the snow had failed as yet to collect.

Into Uiston she descended, the wind now churning in haphazard eddies about the cup-like valley. The wind, still cold, spun round to slap her in the face and bend around, seeking a way – or so it seemed – a way beneath the sheltering cloak. Moans gave way to sharper whistles as the wind could not decide just what to do. She looked into the swirling wind to see the hut of Father John, collecting a little snow only to see it puff away when fickle winds changed angle of assault. Dancing and vanishing almost as quickly as it appeared came the smoke from the stove of Father John. His window gave a cheery glint, sparking the thought of warmth inside. Carymba wandered near the cabin, so welcoming in the midst of the wind-rattled Uiston floor. She knocked; he answered slowly, leaning on his cane. 'Oh! Do come in, Carymba. That wind is nasty out there'.

Once inside, she loosened her shawl-cloak and hung it on a peg beside the door. She moved to a stool near the stove and near Father John who had already flopped again into his rocking chair. They sat and visited for some time, a pleasant place by the crackling warmth within the shelter from the roaring wind. At last, she added: 'The hour grows late. Did you have a supper planned?' 'I thought a sandwich, perhaps'. 'May I fix you some soup, or something warm, on a night as cold as this?' 'I am a little low on provisions right now, but that sounds good. And help on cooking would be convenient for these old bones. You'll join me, won't you?' 'I needn't if you are low on goods'. 'I'm not that low! Besides, soup tastes better when I can match slurps with another'. 'That sounds fine. Shall I?' 'Go ahead: it is all over there'. While she prepared a simple meal, the two shared warmth of conversation, a further insulation against the cold.

Supper done, slurp for slurp, they talked and shared a bit of time. Carymba washed the dishes and straightened things for him, hobbling more agilely than he could do in days of age. All done, she meandered her way to the stool. Father John sat there in ease and comfort, appreciative of the help. He smiled at her in his own, old-fashioned way. The stove was warm. The wind rose to rattle the hut again. The soup felt good in her stomach. The snow crystals drummed suddenly against the windows. She looked; her cloak wavered in the wind which leaked by the door. The stool was there; she bumped it with her knee and thought of sitting down again in warmth and comfort. 'You are welcome to stay, Carymba. The place is warm enough, I suppose'. 'It is lovely, Father John. But I really must be going. The boys – they will get you some supplies, won't then?' 'Sure'.

Taking her cloak in hand, she pulled it around herself again, and shivered, for it was cold. She looked longingly at the stove, half-smiled with a wincing nod; 'Good night, Father John'. 'Good night … and thanks'. The door closed behind her and the spinning wind twisted her around in the cold. She shivered again, grasping the wayward cloak – and took her resolute step onward, toward the narrow way to The Plain, huddling her steps against the dark cold.

16 February 1986

CCXXIX

Ice gripped Apopar, stopping everything until relief should come in sun or warmth to melt the awful stuff. The Guard stayed home, a relief in itself. But the ordinary, necessary, subtle commerce of folk stopped, too. People could not trade goods. They could not buy food. They could not go visit. Ice covered over all the simple needs with a chilled pall. Whatever lay beyond the doors of huts was fundamentally unavailable.

An old woman grasped her door, and shoved. She shook it with anxious earnestness, and shoved again. The heavy coating covering her door would not yield. She wept, and in her weeping pounded upon the door with flailing fists. Her hut echoed with the beatings on the door until she sank and sobbed. The echoes muted to those of anguished sobs. For she had counted on firewood stored outside, and the grocery for food. Cold, she huddled to herself in a spare blanket. Her eyes gazed blankly, widely into the dim room. Her sobs gave way to dazed blankness.

A young man stood at his door and shoved. It would not give. He lowered a shoulder and bounded on the door with his whole weight, driving with his legs. The door quivered, and held firm. He turned the latch; it was loose. Holding the latch to be sure it remained open, he flung his body against the door violently. The whole hut shook. Some twigs broke free on the ceiling-roof. But the door held firm. He listened to the gripping noises outside, the patter of drizzle upon the ground, a hard rattle as if it were uncertain when to freeze. The sound caused shivers, and he thought of settling in for the day and hoping for warmth or sun to soften the seal upon Apopar. He stroked his chin thoughtfully, for there was a nagging attraction to being lazy today. He sat down to muse over unopenable doors.

Missus Carney arose in silence. She pulled her clothes over her boney frame and gazed at the day from dark-sunk eyes within a pallored face, lean and long. Sitting, she pulled on her winter stockings and slid her feet into the boots she saved for Winter's wars. She pulled together food, and ate mechanically. Having taken care of morning necessities, she packed her bag for the cares of today, the needs which waited her visiting hand. She stretched herself and bundled against the cold; the old cloak was oiled, repelling almost all water. She selected that one, pulling the dark hood over her head so that her eyes peered long and haunting, but from deep under the hood. Ready, she reached for her door. The handle was stiff; she set down her bag. She yanked and the door gave for her; she yanked because she had the only door in Apopar which opened inward; the outward opening door preserves room in the tiny huts. Her overhanging shingle held the ice away, but did not preserve her from a thickened wall of rippled ice. She took her poker and rammed it into the hard curtain, spraying chips of splintered ice. She rammed it again and yet again as gradually the curtain parted, then broke free and crumbed at the step. Kicking now, she scattered the ice away, clearing a path on the slippery way.

Taking up her bag and using the poker as a sort of cane, the betrayingly frail-looking figure of Missus Carney moved tentatively from her hut. She closed the door and gingerly moved alone across the puddled ice. 'I'm glad I learned to move on ice long ago' she muttered to herself as she made slow progress, being particularly gentle in controlling her balance when her feet slid together on the wet ice.

A lone dark figure in the dripping landscape, she came first to the young man's solid door. She looked and saw the tiny stress cracks at the edge of the door, too small to do any more than betray his effort to break free. Balancing carefully, she jabbed with the poker, breaking ice and sliding backwards. She moved into place again, poked again, scattering chips again, sliding back again. Over and over again, she repeated the process until the larger chunks broke free and clattered to the ground.

Inside, the young man sat and listened. He waited for her to call for him to wedge open the door, for he did not want to fling the door into her. He knew it must be Missus Carney; there was no one else who would be there then. The voice called: 'come on out'. He rose and leaned against the door. It gave a little. He backed up and threw his shoulder against the door. It gave, and splattered chunks of ice across the way. Standing free in his door, he looked out. 'Well, get yourself ready. We have work to do.' The Guard is in. We are free, as free as ice will let us be, free to do our work and care for one another'. 'I'm coming'. 'Bring an ice-breaker'. 'Yes, ma'am'.

Together they toddled gently to the next door. They combined to smash the ice and free the door, opening it upon the huddled, frightened, cold figure of the old woman. He got some wood, breaking it free from the icy grip of the morning. With little stuff he found, he fired her stove. All the while, Missus Carney eased the hopeless, huddled woman to her chair, leaving the blanket in place. The old woman looked at the hooded figure, feeling the boney grip of Missus Carney's old, gnarled hands. She peeped with concern into the overhanging hood, for inside the look was that of chalky paste, ending in the dark and sunken glance of eyes. 'You're ill!' 'Shh. Here, I brought some tea. It will help you. I'm not ill: merely tired. There is much to do today'. The fire begun, the water was set to heat for tea. Missus Carney deftly did the chores, sending the young man on to free some tradesmen, bring some food. 'Broth will do for a start. She is hungry'. A gentle, tender glance stole from her eye, under the cover of her hood. The old woman said 'Lay back your hood. You're inside now'. 'Alright' came the response and her hands laid back the hood by either ear. The cheeks betrayed some color now, as work unfolded for her. The old woman sighed, relaxed: 'I'm glad', she said.

The tea prepared, Missus Carney served her hostess. 'Do have some, too' she pleaded. 'Oh, I think not'. 'But I insist. Do sit with me. Just for a moment, sit with me and share with a cup of tea. You free me here on a day when ice' bonds release our hearts. Now sip with me'. Missus Carney nodded, then fetched herself a cup of tea and sat herself upon a stool, balancing her cup the while. 'There: I can be half a hostess now'. 'I sometimes forget how important that is. Thank you for reminding me! The tea is better shared'. 'Tell me how you keep going, striving in days like this'. 'These are days of freedom, as you said. A body moves in freedom, grasping to do and reach to share in the spread of an icy day. Strange, but the cold comes to warm us'.

The young man burst in, his arms loaded with goods. 'Where shall I put them?' 'Set them over there, on my little shelf, or by it, if you will'. 'I'll try'. 'Let me help you with the groceries, and all, lest you have more trouble than need be'. 'Thanks. Ahh. Those get heavy'. 'That is a dozen trips for me, young man'. 'The ice is bad; you needn't journey'. 'O but I must. Today is the best of days for journeys. Don't you see?' I suppose I do. Later then, you can go, after you have arranged these'. 'OK'.

Missus Carney rose from the stool. 'Shall we go? We have some more houses to visit. You take care. I'll see you again'. The old woman nodded as the two stepped carefully out her door, closing it behind themselves. The young man asked her: 'What drives you so?' 'Oh, I simply follow a promise, a promise and a dream. Now, let's go. There are lots of tight houses and people to see. ... Thank you for your help'. 'Sure'.

23 February 1986

CCXXX

Tumbling over in bed, once and again, Clyde found himself finally awake enough to remember the *last* tumble, the last grasping after uncooperative covers. Half of him did not want to waken. Half of him wanted to sigh and proceed with the day he assumed to be at hand. He tumbled over in bed once more, once too many times, sending the loosened covers off, into a heap upon the floor. He lay there, dissatisfied with events as they had happened. He grumbled at the chill in his room which now cooled him too. He debated pulling the covers in a sort of lump over himself and staying in bed, but the difficulty of decision and the anticipated difficulty of accomplishment discouraged the project. The chill encouraged him to rise and get dressed. The last, at last, he did.

Roused and dressed, Clyde stirred himself for warmth. Stocking-footed, he moved himself to the window. The frost painted curls and sprays of flashing crystals which sparkled in the light. 'When the Sun gets over the Leaferites' Hill, that window will be glorious. Unfortunately, I won't want to stay here and wait for it. But I do want to see out. I know what to do'. And he began to rub a splotch on the window, causing it to run clear and runny, then to melt free and leave a small little patch through which he could peek. His one eye looked through the very small patch to see the frost-painted landscape. 'A lovely day, but it looks cold. I'll take a second pair of socks ... and my shawm, for after breakfast'.

Having completed his readiness, and putting his shawm in his pocket, Clyde took his coat and hat and went downstairs. On the stairs, the smell of fresh coffee and breakfast cooking greeted his nostrils. He twitched his nose in appreciation for the odors in the air. He swallowed quickly, as his mouth watered in anticipatory response. Hanging his coat on the coat rack in the foyer, Clyde stepped briskly off the step, down into the dining room.

With ready appetite, he strode to the chair at the table by the fireplace. He sat down to await his meal, knowing that Thyruid had heard his step on the stairs. As he waited, he watched the flames dance and flare, casting a comforting warmth upon the hearth, and him. Within his bushy beard, he smiled. The whiskers spread a bit, bristling slightly. But the surest sign of smile lay in his eyes and the lines upon his weathered face. The flames danced for him. His eyes danced back, both in reflected and in original dance. He leaned back in the chair, letting his eyes grow misty, watching the warming fire dance to its muse, and his. The tunes rolled in his mind. He sighed and mumbled: 'I could accompany your dance on my shawm. That would be fun for me ... but not, perchance, for sleeping Geoffrey'.

Thyruid emerged through the swinging door, carrying a mug of steaming coffee and a plate, a wrapped biscuit basket, a pot of butter and another of jelly. The tray came to Clyde's table. Thyruid had it all laid out before Clyde realized he was there. In fact, Thyruid cleared his throat and almost spoke before Clyde turned and greeted him: 'Good morning, Thyruid. The breakfast looks beautiful. It is a morning of beauty. I imagine that is why my covers fell off: my muse was calling me to indulge in today. I looked at my window, a perfect spray of painted frost. I made myself a peephole to see outside: a wonder world in stillness and frost. I came here and watched the fire: a dancing dervish play for me in lovely turns. And now, breakfast laid forth in beauty – of steam and jelly and butter – as yet I imagine Marthuida's biscuits'. Thyruid looked at him strangely. 'Are you alright this morning?' 'Yes. I must be in a mood. Dance music for my shawm was just roving through my mind. This is just one of those days'. 'Well, do enjoy your breakfast; offered Thyruid as he slowly backed away.

Alone again, Clyde adjusted his chair to face the table, even though he couldn't watch the fire dance so well then. He opened the wrapping on the basket of biscuits, and watched the steam curl up into the air. He twitched his nose to sniff the aroma. Reaching in, he grasped one biscuit, then folded back the towel, to hold in the steam and the warmth as best he could. With eager anticipation, Clyde cradled the biscuit in his large and strong fingers. Gently, he broke it open and watched the trapped, moist heat burst free. Setting it upon his plate, he quickly capped each half in butter, which melted in with a golden rush. The jelly melted in next. He watched it with pleasure; he sniffed it with pleasure; but not so much pleasure that he forgot to eat. The biscuit crumbled in his mouth, bite by bite. He repeated with the second, and then with the third, until he was fully satisfied.

Taking his coffee mug, Clyde turned to the fire, squeaking his chair in the process. 'Now *that* is disagreeable music' he sputtered to himself. With his spare hand, he brushed free a few stray crumbs from his beard. Then, leaning back, he watched the dancing fire and sipped at his mug of coffee, cooled just enough to avoid burning the tongue which had so recently savored Marthuida's biscuits. He slurped at his coffee and put his feet on the hearth; there, the warm fire baked them, basking them in the radiant glow.

Thyruid came out. 'How was breakfast?' he asked directly, having decided to ignore the strange comments Clyde had offered before breakfast. 'Lovely' was Clyde's reply, curt and surprisingly direct. Thyruid was startled and stood upright with sudden surprise. 'What does that mean?' he asked with a defensive note. Clyde sat there, involved in the dancing fire and finishing his coffee. Finally, he set the mug down. 'Thank you'. At that, Clyde clomped his feet on the floor: Thyruid jumped in response. Clyde stood up quickly; Thyruid took a half step back from the far side of the table. Clyde smiled, and pushed in his chair. Nodding, he strode back across the room, stepping up and grabbing his coat, pulling it on, and his hat as well, all on the way to the door. He left. Thyruid shook his head: 'He's preoccupied about something' he said as he cleared the table, and looked in the fire for those dancing dervishes. 'Nothing there'.

Clyde, outside in the breathless brisk air, sniffed at the cold and smiled. The nose tingled in the frost. The sun was almost high enough to flash its chilled brightness upon the frost-covered branches. Underfoot, the snow, light as it was, and fine, crunched at each step. It crunched and squeaked under his weight. His hands were stuffed in his pockets ... until he began to dance, the same dance he had watched in the fire. His fingers, stuffed in his pockets, itched. He pulled them out, bringing the shawm with them. Thence he brought the instrument to his lips and began to play those dervish dances he saw and heard in the fire. His fingers danced on the shrill pipe as the reeds buzzed and the tone fluttered free across the Fields. His feet began to dance and in lively step he moved about the Fields, down the paths, charming the frost as it blazed in brilliant glory, an offering of beauty in the Sun's eager rays.

Mary rushed out to dance with him. Then came the Spinners – Martha and Gilbert, Effie and Chert – hurriedly gathered in winter coats, dancing in the morning beauty, upon the squeaking snow. Then John and Peder, and the Tinker, and more came out and danced and danced. By whim, Clyde returned with his band to the Inn-by-the-Bye, and entered, leading them to the dining room where they danced and danced the more. Thyruid and Marthuida, safely behind the counter, watched with eager glee, tapping toes and fingers. Thyruid looked: there was the fire, dancing for him. He smiled and laughed. Clyde sat himself int his chair, playing still the furious dances of the fire, until he paused too long for breath and all stood still, and quiet.

Carymba walked in: 'Play on, Clyde, a softer tune for frost now melted in the rush of glory in the early Sun. The beauty of the day needs take a steady turn. Lead on, Clyde'. He returned his shawm between his lips and raised a plaintive tune, a grace for this day's new beauty.

2 March 1986

CCXXXI

An early grey softened the pre-dawn black and muted the many stars overhead. Along the eastern rim of the sky, a brighter grey, with streaks of brilliance began to press itself into the space of sight. At his hour there stole across the Commons a lone figure. He stepped surely and directly around the Inn-by-the-Bye and onward, past the door and along the muddy paths. He could have been seen stepping carefully in the dimly lit way, for the ground was soft and muddy under a very thin crust of overnight frost. He was not one looking to be bogged down in mud. He was straining onward quickly, though with the appearance that his pace was hampered by the sticky softness underfoot.

The Commons, always soggy when snows have melted, added a clinging mud to feet on mission. When he arrived at the rim of the Commons, amid the wet and plastered grasses of last Fall, the figure paused to shake his feet, then scrape them on a stone to lighten their slippery, glistening, mucky load as now the sky revealed an arching blue, high and bright overhead. Lightened once again, he stepped toward the stone-laid path along the ledge unto the cabin in which Guerric and Mahara lived. Walking with care, he took his ease arriving in safety at the doorway. The quiet cabin huddled before him in dim silence; he listened carefully before he reached to rap upon the door.

Inside, the rapping echoed loudly. Mahara sat up in bed, startled and curious. She looked at the neighboring lump – Guerric in his undisturbed slumber – and wished once more that he would move a bit easier in the morning. She sighed, then jumped again as the knocking exploded into the room once more: morning had never been, would never be his strength! Hence, she would have to go find out what the matter might be. Pulling on a robe and stuffing her feet into some slippers, she responded to yet another rapping: 'Just a minute. I am coming'. The knocking paused, awaiting her arrival.

Shaking her hair into some sort of order, Mahara pulled back the curtain to see Malak standing there, his hands stuffed into his pockets, his head down, his shoulders hunched against the borderline frost and the penetrating damp. Opening the door, she spoke: 'Yes, Malak?' He looked up with darting eyes, drew his packet from his pocket and gave it to her. She took the envelope and opened it as Malak turned in silence and began his trudge back. 'Do you need a return message?' she asked while he was still near. He shook his head and kept plodding on his way, never turning his head. Shivering, she closed her door against the damp chill. 'His job is simply delivery, I suppose. His feet looked muddy. And mud meant heavy, slippery steps'. With a shrug, she turned from the door and emptied the envelope to read the contents. She paused half way across the room, wrinkled her forehead and shrugged in exasperation. 'That aunt of mine!' she exclaimed as she dropped the message on the table and began to dress.

'First I need to make some breakfast. Guerric will be hungry … when he finally wakes up. The best alarm clock for him resides in his nose!' With that, and a tacit admission that she too was hungry, she turned to normal preparations. In fact, she became involved in her normal work and in her hunger so that she forgot about Malak, her aunt, and the message which had pulled her out of bed in the first place. Before long, the stove was hot and the coffee was coming toward a steam, the biscuits were baking and she had some dried fruits warming. The whole hut billowed with fresh aromas. She swallowed a couple extra times and rubbed her stomach in anticipation. Looking toward Guerric, she saw him begin to stir. She smiled and her eyes danced mischievously. Then she shook her head and decided to behave. She set the table and savored the fragrant offerings she was preparing for herself … and Guerric, if he ever decided to get up. He rolled over and moaned; she listened to hear him swallow the new-flowing juices. Yes: there it came. 'Good morning, Guerric', she called. 'I'm getting hungry; get up'.

After multiple calls and much cajoling, aided by the finishing breakfast which she spread on their table, Guerric struggled up. He stretched and yawned, then rubbed his stubble-face in both hands until he had garnered some degree of wakefulness. He sat down and watched the coffee pour, gurgling, into his cup. Half a smile was all he managed until he had sipped a bit to shock his system into wakefulness. Mahara piled an over-ample breakfast before him and sat down herself, on the opposite side of the table, in order to enjoy the breakfast which had so well and thoroughly teased her onward. Looking at it all now, it seemed somewhat more than it had as she had indulged herself in its making. 'This is a large breakfast' she observed, gulping. 'I'm glad you noticed that, too. I wondered if we planned to hike, with the leftovers for sustenance along the way'.

At Guerric's comment, Mahara bounced in her seat, placing her hands over her mouth: 'Oh!' 'What's the problem?' 'I forgot!' 'Forgot what?' 'The rap on the door you didn't hear'. 'I didn't hear: that is correct. What did you forget? A hike for us?' 'In a way, yes: a hike. We may need to do that, in spite of the dreadful mud out there'. She waved her hand toward the door. 'Might I ask why?' 'Yes. Malak brought a message. I set it her on the table. Now, where did it go?' 'Is that it, on the floor, over there in the corner?' 'Perhaps. Let me see. ... Ah, yes. Here it is'. 'And what does it say?' 'To Mahara ... that's me ...' 'I know'. 'To Mahara: you should know your aunt left for your hut last week and no one has seen her since. Is she there?' 'Your aunt came?' 'That is what it says. But she never came *here*, not recently, anyway'. 'So, you think we ought to go looking for her'. 'What else would we do?' 'We wait for her to come here'. 'Yes. But it hardly takes a week to get here'. 'How do we look?' 'With our eyes'. 'Wise: and where do we look?' She took a deep breath and held it, pensively: 'I'm not sure' she finally emitted.

The two nibbled on breakfast and pondered what to do. 'We will have to look for her. But which way did she go?' Mahara shrugged in response and took another bit of her biscuit and fruit. 'I know what you mean. She just may be *lost*'. 'I hate to think of my aunt as ... as, lost. The word is so hollow'. 'I know. But is there another word to use for such an occasion?' 'No. ... I cannot think of one. Not one'. They fell into silence until breakfast stopped being eaten, and they noticed that they had stopped. 'I'll pack some food for us. We will need to go'. 'Yes.'

The two arranged themselves and the cabin and soon were out the door. They slid along the path, then reached the Commons and mud became more of a problem, for the Sun had banished the frost and softened the fragile crust Malak had found. Their feet dragged. And they dragged all day as they wearily made their search from the Inn to the Great Dome to the City on the Plain, back into the hills from which Guerric had come. They sat on the plaza there. No one had seen Mahara's aunt. They wandered into Uiston and back, on toward the places Mahara knew in her childhood. They came at last to her aunt's wagon-home, a place detached from the meandering community because she had decided to do that. Mahara, on a whim, knocked before she entered. She heard her aunt call to come in; she entered, weighted down in clay-mud and the weariness of along-spent day. Her aunt smiled: 'Mahara, so good to see you again. But you look so *lost!*'

9 March 1986

CCXXXII

Puddles no longer dotted the paths. Now the paths dotted the puddles, and left there a slick and muddy, meandering track along which feet may remain modestly dry. The crests of the not-yet-puddled strips were already deepening in mud. Soft and oozy were the ways and many wee folk were wary of these paths, or became content to splash their way knee deep in cold water and clinging yellow mud. They shivered in the wet of the late winter thaw; they shivered at the expected price of going somewhere, anywhere this time of year. Rather, the *very few* who dared their journey shivered. This was a time for a tinker to make his lonely rounds undisturbed.

The wind gusted boldly from off the Empty Area, back beyond the lost gully. The wind burst warmly on the thawing sod. The now-bare grass lay plastered brownish-yellow with timid, lingering splotches of dull green. The ground was soft now, as frost was shoved into a narrower band beneath the gooey surface. The frost beneath held the water in the mud, and held it cold. Combined, the warmth and melted sod over sealing frost made the puddles reign over every trekking foot.

Among the rarity of feet came the syncopated pair of Carymba. Her skirts already hung limp and heavy, soaked with water, splotched with mud halfway to her knees. The puddles welcomed her. Even as she tried to hold the gooey ridge, she slid and slopped along, as she had since leaving Hidden Cabin after breakfast this morning. The Sun had risen, giving ample light through overcast skies to see the mud and puddled goo through which she trod. The way she took from Hidden Cabin to the Valley Road was drained by slope so that the exposed roots which made her steps at the last, served also as a cataract of falls. The Valley Road lay puddled and spongy underfoot; each step left a tiny puddle in the imprint as last year's now decaying leaves held water in the sod. After having turned onto the Fields, following the path along the edge of The Hills, her steps left the spongy soil and entered the mottled clay way.

Thus she had come toward the Fringe. She had passed by all the slithering paths, the Way Down and the twisted path to Missus Duns' sod house. She hadn't thought of Missus Duns; the path sparked a thought. She glanced up and could see the smoke from Missus Duns' chimney: the stove is working to keep the house dry, she thought to herself with a little smile. Onward she went to where the path disappeared into the marshy clumps of the Fringe. There, the mud predominated even more, and all the wearied paths were puddled over. Each step now must splash, warning any listener of approaching visitors. She paused and looked at the way before her, frowning into a scowl before shrugging her shoulders and plodding onward, into the flooded marshland of the Fringe.

Wandering her way through the Fringe, along what might be pathways in more pleasant times, Carymba watched and looked. She remembered some of the routes, although they now lay in lost and hidden camouflage, under the overlay of stagnant waters, the now elevated level of marsh. Her feet got colder and she felt the water wick up her skirts, causing them to cling to her legs in cold insistence. She shivered and muttered to herself: 'All I need to do now is get lost in here! I wish I could find Jasper quickly'.

Splashing steps scurried away from her. She was startled, for she had not been aware of company in the area. 'I wonder who that was?' she commented, and turned to follow the sound of the splatterings. Soggy step gave way to a wetter one, over and over again as she trudged through the marshes. Her feet squished at every step as the water which had entered her shoes sloshed around, squirting between her toes in little icy jets. She began to wonder why she had joined the few who even tried to go out until the mud had subsided or the crocuses bloomed. She gave herself a disgusted look – if only she could have seen it! – and tramped along with the cold water having wicked up her skits and now completing the cycle by dribbling down her legs, into her socks and shoes, there to squish around uncomfortably.

Occasionally, another rush of splashes would sound, leaving her alone – as she had thought herself to be all along. Finally, she stopped, her feet ankle-deep in the water, resting on the slippery slime of mush-clay-"path". 'Who is around here?' she asked out loud. There was no answer. 'Where are you, Jasper', she called. Again, there was no answer. She called again, louder than before. She screamed her call, with a voice shaking in cold frustration. She waited. Slowly, she began to hear in the distance the sound of splashing feet. The sound approached, growing nearer and nearer until the ragged form of Jasper slid between the clumped marsh grass to face her.

'I heard you were looking for me'.

'I am. Or, rather, I was'.

'Why ever for? This is miserable weather for anyone at all to be out. You look wet'.

'I am soaked'.

'Your feet, too?'

'My feet especially'.

'You were foolish to come here. You know that, don't you?

'No. I needed to come here. I almost forgot the silence of the Fringe, the way the people here seem to evaporate from any visitor'.

'Except me'.

'Except for you, sometimes. You never fully settled into the Fringe. I think you are the only one from here that I ever see on the Fields. And your trips are rare'.

'They have to be rare. You know that'.

'Of course: there was a reason you came here. I remember that, too. My reason for being here is to find you in this mud'.

'You found me. Now what?'

'This water must have flooded all the places for campfires. That would make this a colder place than usual'.

These thaws used to be a problem. Or more of a problem. Last fall, I built up a segment so that there is a place to be dry and to create warmth. I keep some dryer grass elevated in the clumps. That has to serve us well'.

'That is new! I also had to relay Effie's concern for you out here'.

'She never cared much for me, not in the Hills, nor since. She was always afraid to see me at the Spinners' Shop'.

'There are lots of uncertain things about you. And she is most aware of those … from the past'.

'Always the past'.

'Not always. Sometimes we see things from the future'.

'The future? Yea: that does not sound too likely. But for the present, come with me. We need to dry out your feet'.

Obediently, Carymba followed Jasper as he wound his way through shallow puddles she had missed seeing since she entered the Fringe. Finally, they entered a raised mound, out of the water. In the middle burned a low fire. Several faces looked on from the marsh clumps toward which they had splashed. A stone lay there; Jasper waved toward it. She sat down by the low smoldering fire. She dumped her shoes and squeezed some water out of her stockings. 'Put your feet by the fire to steam dry. Afterwards, looking from the future, we'll get you out … dry'.

16 March 1986

CCXXXIII

The hour of mid-morning came upon Hyperbia. With dutiful resignation, Geoffrey moaned and stretched and grumbled beneath his breath, for the habitual hour of waking had come for him. Everybody else was up and busy and had long ago gotten over the daily trauma of emerging from bed. Geoffrey knew that he was usually the last to rise; but he didn't much care. He also imagined that everyone had as hard a time as he did, just dragging the body out of bed, from under the friendly pile of blankets and, unwillingly, into an awake state. He lay there, half thinking about getting up, half dreading the leaving of his neat little bed. But, being mid-morning, the competing interest in eating began to disturb his cuddled comfort and to lure him out from the covers. Blinking blearily then, he decided to rise.

With care, Geoffrey inched his way out from under his mounded pile of blankets, still high for Winter's days kept his room cool; he needn't worry yet about getting overly warm. Almost off the end of the bed, he turned himself over to sit on his pillow. Thence he pulled his legs up to his chest and shivered, for he was now emerged from those covers, and the cold greeted him unpleasantly. He frowned deeply and twisted himself around. He flopped his feet to the floor, from which the quickly bounced up again. 'Brr ... rr': he rolled the sound off his tongue with Scottish flair. He considered returning to the warm, cozy safety of his covers; he even yawned and drew up his feet, ready to reverse his squirm *out* of those covers. But just then his stomach growled and grumbled and, in general complaint, forced him in this ill-resolve to proceed with getting up. Timidly, he re-set his feet upon the floor; he grimaced and stood himself upright.

After such initial agony, Geoffrey fumbled his way along. He dressed himself and shaved. He arranged his waistcoat and aligned the creases in his grey-striped trousers. The spats lay correctly, leaving the gleaming toe of his shoes to brighten the day. He checked himself with care, then nodded and proceeded to his door in stately pace. This was certainly an ordinary, an every-day in Geoffrey's drudgery, and dread bore such a customary tint that he too readily recognized it for what it was, or appeared to be.

With such staid satisfaction, Geoffrey ambled into the dining room, his hat in his hand. The room was nearly empty as it always was this time of day. He meandered through the customary turns and twists to find his own accustomed seat, back in the corner, with the table dimly lit by low-burning lamps nearby, upon the wall. Placing his hat upon the table, inching to his seat and sitting down to wait, Geoffrey fulfilled his morning – or, rather, mid-morning ritual. Shortly, Thyruid emerged from behind the swinging door, a teapot and cup in his hand. Geoffrey smiled as the gentle innkeeper drew near. 'Good morning, Thyruid' he offered through the silence in the room. Geoffrey paid no attention and so did not observe Thyruid's taciturn preoccupation. The silence did not affect the gentleman's gentleman one whit. Instead, he poured his cup full of tea and watched the aromatic steam curl upwards to him. The oils in the tea left swirls upon the top; he watched them dizzily turn and curl before he raised his cup to snip and sip – being careful to blow the steam away and cool his sip first.

Thyruid returned, this time bearing the basket of biscuits, the butter and the jelly. Geoffrey watched him with anticipated glee. His mouth watered; and he swallowed hard. And then he swallowed again behind his growing grin. This day indeed lay now fulfilling the habits and long expectations of many, many days. They all looked so alike that now they lay cluttered in his mind, combining one on another to form a random collage of intertwining vignettes, melded together to make the expectable whole. He smiled in ready waiting. Item after item unfolded for him. He was content, so content he forgot to notice his strangely silent host.

Breakfast was ending. Geoffrey retrieved the buttered crumbs which, as usual, collected in the corners of his mouth. He savored them with visions of their hot, steaming, buttered, jellied and fragrant parent in his mind's eye. His cooling tea he sipped more vigorously, to finish and enjoy before the cool turned cold and unsuggestive to his taste. Finished, he wiped his face and fingers and began to plot the day: 'What should I do today?' he mused, out loud.

The sound of his own voice startled his ears. He suddenly realized that things had been very quiet. Thyruid had not spoken. And Geoffrey was not sure whether he had spoken himself, or not. He felt his brow furrow and his whole face contract, drawing down tightly on him, even into a scowl which distorted his appearance. He half-whispered to himself: 'Did I think to say anything? If so, why did my voice sound so loud to me now? I simply don't remember!' He sat there, worried. With time, his face relaxed, turning blank as he stared across the room, first trying to remember all that had happened, and then giving up on that and becoming blank against the day.

Thyruid came and collected the dishes, wiping off the table but leaving Geoffrey's hat. He looked at Geoffrey, blankly staring right past, or through him. He just shook his head and turned to go to his chores, leaving Geoffrey to examine the wall, or whatever it was that absorbed him so.

Geoffrey continued in blank un-awareness as the luncheon customers began to arrive. They chatted and laughed until they noticed Geoffrey sitting in his corner, pale and ghost-like, as if he were ensnared in a trance. Mahara stared at him, supposing his glance to be toward her. He sat and gazed, unseeing. She flushed and almost raged before she noted the utter distractedness of his glance. At that realization, she dropped her rage and looked with pity, then dropped the pity in a shudder which quivered her whole body. Turning to Guerric, she scowled: 'That is odd' she whispered. Indeed, everybody's chatter turned to whisper and then faded out, wondering about poor Geoffrey, but not at all wishing to interrupt him, nor to bother him.

Mary came in, some flowers in her basket. She entered with her cheeks on fire, tingled and red-tinged by the brisk air, for the wind was sharp and the moist, cold air nipped at her. She shivered as she set aside her coat, hanging it politely on the rack. Looking around the room, she saw Geoffrey sitting alone while almost everyone else had company. So she smiled and decided she would join him. Some time had gone by since last she saw him, and this would give her an opportunity to bring herself up-to-date with her friend. She had not noticed Geoffrey much, failing to glimpse his trance-like posture and blank gaze. She was too preoccupied with lunch and enjoying the rich and savory odors which permeated the air. She simply wove her way through the silent tables to his. Mahara watched her go, and took upon herself a worried look, then glanced away so as not to see. Unseeing, she would be innocent of it all.

Mary took the seat next to Geoffrey, out of the direct line of his glassed gaze. She set her basket on the table, toward the distant side; the flowers softly shone in the lamplight, offering their best to whomever might look with appreciation. Mary spoke lightly, over everyone's vanished whispers. There was no response. She looked at Geoffrey, then touched his arm (Mahara gasped silently across the room): 'Geoffrey, what should we have for lunch?'

Geoffrey felt the touch and his eyes twitched, then twitched again, gaining momentum to blink and thence to see. He smiled: 'Hello, Mary. I guess I was out to lunch; I didn't see you come. But I'm glad you're here. In for lunch, eh?' "Yes. What shall we have?' 'Marthuida's special is always right'. 'I'll go along with that choice'.

Slowly, the silence melted into whispers, and whispers grew into chatter. Thyruid came out to take orders, with a smile. Mary laughed, and no one seemed to mind, least of all the smiling Geoffrey.

23 March 1986

CCXXIV

'Clyde! You know this is not a good time for me to leave. There is so much work to do here in Apopar. The Borders folk have been asking for me. They really are in need over here. Clyde! I need to stay. I will not go. I simply will not go! And that is final!'

'Come along, Missus Carney. You have to understand that it is important. It is even important *enough* to draw me back across the Great River. Now *that* is something you never thought I would do. I certainly never expected to be back here. I would rather send any sneaking envoy than to risk my hide here. But I came because we need you. No one else will do. We need you for dinner. And if we don't leave soon, we won't make it in time'.

'Why is that?'

'We need … *I* need to travel in the dark here. So I need to get to the Great River and across the Great River before sunup. Or after sundown, if I don't get there before daybreak. And that would be too late. I would have failed my mission! You don't want that to happen, do you?'

'I need to stay here. You go on. There is ample time, before sunup. You can make the River and get across. You said the Boatman expected you'.

'No. The Boatman expects us. I need to leave, but I can't leave alone'.

'Are you afraid of the dark?'

'Perhaps. You had best lead me to the Great River. Here: I'll help you with your cloak'.

'Clyde, you are as sneaky and sly as ever. Who do we see, *if* I go?'

'Marthuida and Thyruid, Vlad, Yev and the rest: I'll be there, and Carymba and others. Those are the main ones. It is time for dinner. We planned a party to remember. What we need is you. I'll bring you back by morning, if you want'.

'There is no other way to get rid of you, is there?'

'No. But I could just throw you over my shoulder ...'

'You wouldn't dare!'

Quickly the fire was stacked and the cloak pulled over her shoulders. She threw the hood over her head so as to mask her pale features and her wispy white hair. Secluded in her wrap, she led Clyde on the way. The door closed silently behind them. The frosted edges of the path gave witness to their way, leaving the path a streak of brown sandwiched between the white of the frost coating on the lighter stuff beside the beaten path. They moved silently, avoiding the fragile white as they swept swiftly along their path. They left no trace as they came to the Great River and saw it dark and mysterious, a silent but broad streak between the frost-tinted branches and briars which poked the air on either shore.

Arrived beneath the overhanging undergrowth to stand at the place where the slightly swollen Great River moved in silent swiftness by the shore, Clyde gave forth a low, howling whistle, holding it long and low until an echoing snort replied. Then, content, they huddled and waited. Few minutes passed until a boat came speeding toward the landing place at their feet. Deftly, the steersman brought it to rest before them. Clyde held her arm; Missus Carney grasped her skirts and stepped into the boat, dropping quickly to her knelt position, sitting on her heels for the ride across. Clyde followed, shoving off with his trailing leg and then flopping into the boat somewhat less gently than did she. The Boatman hushed him: 'Hold still!' he whispered hoarsely as the boat slid out into the current.

Clyde lay in the bottom, awkwardly but still. There was nothing to see except the shadows of the Boatman as he worked with the soaring current of the eager Great River. The low, faint light barely let him see the bulging arms bend the rudder into the River to shove the boat across to the other side. His eyes searched the shadows to see as he could feel the river rush upon them, and hear the low, light gurgle of the current upon and about the boat. A light flashed: Missus Carney turned her head away; the boat rocked slightly. Clyde watched the Boatman's shadow as he felt himself stiffen. 'Shh. Be still' came the low commands. 'That River is icy tonight; we need no wet company. Soon we will be on the other side'. Lantern light held for a few moments. Clyde imagined eyes were studying their movement across that Great River.

Finally, the boat turned in lighter current and bumped the shore. Missus Carney sprung out of the boat, onto the shore. Clyde scrambled to find his feet and thence to move. 'We're even!' 'Even'. The Boatman began to turn his boat to shove upstream along this, the more friendly shore. Clyde and Missus Carney found a path and climbed up toward the Plain to continue their journey. The sky was just beginning to lighten. 'See, we didn't leave any too soon!' 'You could have gone without me?' 'No: I couldn't'.

Day came. They moved to the City on the Plain where they paused for a simple, quick breakfast, even as the day marched onward. Osburn, far above, watched the dark pair move across the melting frost, wondering at the omen of the day; he wrung his hands and shook his frowning, scowling head. 'I don't like the looks of it', he said to no one at all. Shortly, the pair emerged and moved on down the Plain, away from the City, toward the Inn-by-the-Bye and the Commons, or – beyond – the Fields. 'At least they moved on. But I still don't like the omen of travelers so huddled and dark on a frosty morning. They move with a step to change. That always is ill; I know. I know. How bitterly I know'. With that, the unnoticed Osburn walked away from his window and ceased to watch.

Afternoon was advanced as Clyde hurried Missus Carney along toward the Inn. 'An old woman get tired, Clyde'. 'I'm sorry. We will be there soon. You can rest in warmth then. We can arrange an opportunity for you to freshen yourself'. 'Hah! Let's go'. And Clyde hastened to keep up with her steps toward the Inn. Panting, he opened the door for her; Missus Carney stepped inside, throwing her hand back as she did so. He followed her in and watched her as she slowly turned her head to survey the provision of the dining room. Normally erect, she drew herself yet more so, then loosened her cloak and hung it on the rack. Looking to Clyde, she asked: 'Where do you sit, usually?' 'By the hearth.' 'Ah! You like the hot seat!' 'I always thought of it as warm'. 'Certainly warmer than a boat over a cold River'. 'Yes … yes'.

Twisting on her toes, Missus Carney took off toward Clyde's table. He hastened to join her. As if by pure instinct, she left him his usual chair and sat herself nearby. Clyde took his seat. No one came to wait on them. 'We are early, I take it'. 'We must be'. 'And you were in such a hurry!' 'I thought it would take longer. … And you might have wanted to freshen up some'. 'Me? Why? We must be to work'. 'We must?' 'Of course! Why else would I have left my work today, to come here?' The swinging door opened behind her; Missus Carney ignored it. Clyde lifted a hand; the door closed. 'He will be back shortly'. 'With water, I hope'. Thyruid brought coffee instead; Missus Carney thanked him anyway.

Dinner came. They ate and talked. Some tried to make her a guest of honor, a step she refused with a laugh. Instead, she waved to an empty chair: 'There is our guest of honor' she said. Everybody frowned: 'Why?' they asked, nearly in unison. 'Why? you ask! Can you forget so soon that this is a meal of release? That is the seat of the one coming to release. You all – most of you – came from Apopar. That is the seat of honor – empty to remind us of who we are and who we are become. Eat hardy. I must go'. Standing, she walked to her cloak, threw it around herself, and left.

Somewhere, Osburn shuddered, and wondered why.

27 March 1986

CCXXXV

Morning's reflected brilliance crept down the far wall of Uiston, moving along the jagged line of shadow left from the eastern edge of the cup-like Valley. Vlad watched from the front of the root-clung home he and his companions had dug and fashioned there, on the East wall. The diving line of light swept his eyes along its path, down toward the Valley floor. The light gleamed against the dark rough trees, and more against the waxen, bulging buds which pressed themselves nearly to bursting. The times were changing, but emergence of the signs of Spring lay off a ways, he thought as he watched.

The morning Sun began its march across the floor of Uiston, approaching Vlad from afar. The flooding light of day fell upon the drab and mottled land. There was some green here and there, but it was the muddled green and mingled brown of last year's excess. Long had it been pressed to sod by snow. Then it had been thatched to earth by rain and drizzle and the lifeless grip of icy cold. It all lay flat now, unresponsive to the teasing of Spring. In fact, the sod looked dingier, deader now than before. There was no glitter in the Sun's embrace. Rather, the cold sod lay there, longing for the soaking warmth which would come yet. Vlad frowned over the view, peering into the revealing light, seeking a hint of promise. He thought he saw a glimpse of tender green, the yellow-green of the first and tender shoots of grass, *this* year's grass. But no: the whole faded in a flourish, revealing but a fancied hope of Spring. Vlad felt his face fade, too.

Then his eyes caught, over by the edge of the Crossed Hills – the back side, of course – a flash of color. The color caught his eye as a blob, newly emerged and low, by the roots of a mammoth tree just up the slope from Uiston's base. He squinted and concentrated on it until he decided a crocus was about to bloom there. A smile shoved the frown and squint off his face. Softness inched about his features while he gazed. His face transformed with the eager greeting of Spring's surer signs. He nodded to himself; he had seen what he came out to see. Besides, he found himself shivering in the shadows of the barely Spring weather.

Returning inside, Vlad moved to the stove and rubbed his arms for warmth. 'Is it cold out there, Vlad?' 'It's cool: not really cold anymore, but cooler than shirt-sleeve weather'. 'I figured it might be'. 'I should have. But the sky was so bright that it invited me. And I went'. 'What did you see?' 'I watched the Sun's light come down the hill on the other side of Uiston. Then I watched it probe the dingy soil and last year's plastered grasses. But them, off to the side, by the base of the Crossed Hills, I saw a crocus coming out. It is not yet in bloom, but the green and the bud are unmistakable'. 'Do you know what color it is?' 'No. It is not that far along. … Say, let's have some breakfast, and then we can go over and see that flower close-up'. 'That sounds tasty, and pleasant – both'.

The two joined some others and talked over breakfast, thrown together as planned from the bready leftovers of the night before. Yev grunted over the spare offerings: 'Our problem lies in the bare fact that none of us likes to cook, least of all in the morning'. 'That is why we began to savor the leftovers from yesterday'. 'True enough, but it all serves to scrunch all appetite for breakfast!' 'Maybe that is why we do it'. 'Why? So we lose our appetites?' 'Only for breakfast! After that, we get hungry enough, and supply ourselves with fresher food'. 'I remember when we had fresh breakfasts'. 'Yes: and that was the only good thing we had, then'. 'True enough'. 'We escaped from breakfasts, and end up here, comfortable except at meal times'. 'I suppose our mistake was not bringing a cook with us'. 'Some have been wiser than we'. 'And some learn to cook, or not to complain'. 'Were you outside already, Vlad?' 'Umm … yes … I was. Now that I have swallowed, I can even answer'. 'What's it like out there?' Dum and I thought we would go and investigate a crocus after breakfast'. 'A crocus?!' 'Yes. I finally saw one, over by a big tree along the edge where the Crossed Hills rise on their back side'. 'What color?' 'I couldn't tell, for the bud had not opened yet. And you can't tell what it will look like until it does open'. 'True enough'. 'Sort of like breakfast'. 'Only prettier'. 'No one calls this breakfast a pretty sight'. 'Quit your belly-aching!' 'Yea. It beats hunger'. 'And you didn't have to make it'. 'I hear no volunteer cooks!' 'Dum, are you ready to go seek a quiet crocus?' 'I certainly am. Let's go'.

Dum and Vlad grabbed jackets, for it was too cool for shirt sleeves. The door opened for them, closed behind them, and the dust swirled behind, where they had swooped their way. The other six watched them go with a shrug. 'What's wrong with them?' 'I don't have any idea?' 'Yeah, all we did was complain about breakfast'. 'I thought that was the regular entertainment;. 'The mark of morning: a lousy breakfast and a complaining contest.'. 'Most days, that is true. Only on the days we have something to do, something important – then we don't complain so much'. 'That's right: we have something else to do – and so we don't *have* to complain. You know what I mean'. The six all nodded agreement on this final note, sure that any of them could have said any of the comments; authorship was merely accidental ... except for Vlad and Dum, who stomped out of the place, grumpy over breakfast chatter and with flowers (of all things!) on the mind. Yev frowned a bit, then pursed his lips in a knowing, frowning pucker: 'maybe they wanted to get out of clean-up today'. 'No problem there; today it is *your* turn, Yev'. 'I should have thought of that earlier! Maybe flower checking isn't such a bad idea, after all'. 'After clean-up, you can do whatever you like. *Afterward*: not now'.

While their friends debated morning chores, Vlad and Dum ambled across Uiston, their hands stuffed into their pockets, their jackets wrapped about them, for there was a damp crispness in the air, in spite of the deceptive glow of the morning Sun. Vlad shivered a bit, then wondered to himself how much was cold, how much was excitement. Dum yanked his hand out of the pocket and pointed with exaggeration: 'Look! I think that flower is opening already. Come! Let's hurry. I want to see it!' He began to trot and then, fumbling his other hand free at last, he pumped his arms and ran ahead. Vlad, slow to respond, finally got his hands free and yelled 'Wait for me' as he, too, broke into a run.

Panting, Vlad pulled up next to Dum at the opening crocus. Each stood very erect in order to peep over the edge of the upward pointed bloom, to see down inside and to enjoy first-hand the beauty. Dum was stretched as far as he could go; Vlad dropped off and climbed the root a ways back. 'Look, Dum. I'm not so near, but I have a better angle here. I can see quite well, even over your head!' 'That's always a choice, isn't it?'

'What?' 'Being close or seeing well'. 'With head-high crocuses, it is'. 'Not only that, but breakfast, too. We get so close we lose perspective'. 'You mean you can't see the stamen for the pistil?' 'No. You can't see the color for the angle'. 'Look, it is a lemon-yellow ...' '... with purple streaks'. 'Doesn't it shine in the sunlight?' 'Yes, it does'. 'I can smell it from here, now'. 'Me too'. 'Too bad the others didn't want to come'.

Some time later, the two still looking, each still pointing out one more observation to the other, Yev ambled by. 'Is that flower really that interesting?' 'Yes. Come up here. We'll show you the beauty everyone is missing today'. 'This is silly: but ... OK'. Climbing up, and having two arms wave his attention all through the flower, he ended with the admission: 'You are right. We complain too much about breakfast.

30 March 1986

CCXXXVI

Up, and only mildly frazzled, Mary scurried around her Shop, watering her plants and talking to them. Somewhere she had heard that talking to plants helped them, made them feel at home. So, as long as she had no customers, she chatted pleasantly to them. She only half remembered now how silly she had felt at first. But now, they did seem to be responding to her. They did seem to be more content and her ears had become accustomed to hearing her own voice talking to them. Her embarrassment at such foolishness was going away, and she was nearly at ease with herself as she jabbered about her Shop.

Time passed quickly, she found, as she chattered. The whole action kept her alert and attentive. The flowers responded; she was sure the chatter was the cause of the response, for she was not aware of any other change in her Shop. The temperature was about the same. Spring was coming, and with it more sunshine; but then, the flowers were in better shape than they had been in other Springs. Humidity was about the same. Yes: the only change was the talking. Such thoughts came to her mind, encouraging her. She smiled and dabbled some more over plants, taking care to explain what she was doing, so that any reasonable plant would understand her kind intent.

With such a morning quickly rushing toward an unsuspected noon, Mary happily puttered around and around her Shop, more at ease with her plants than ever. Only later, as noon had passed by, did her stomach begin to complain. She scowled at herself, and more at her stomach for the untimely ruckus – for she had no idea of the time. She scowled, and her stomach growled in return. She felt her stomach; it burbled insistently. She looked out the window to see all the shadows far advanced of where she thought they ought to be. She snorted to herself; 'the morning must have gone faster than I realized' she confessed and set down her watering can and meandered upstairs to her rooms and little kitchen. Eating, she found her mind wandering from the food which was aimed at immediate necessities to the plants in the back corners. 'I ought to arrange those better' she said out loud. 'They like shade, but they seem to be a bit too shaded now. Or, maybe, I don't talk to them enough!'

Mary fumed over her musing. The food sat in front of her as her mind escaped her barely-confronted hunger to dally over the plants in that back corner. She became absorbed in them. Her face wadded in concentration; her lips were all constricted, tightly pulled in on themselves and bunched into a prunish, picklish lump. The food sat there; her stomach burbled in acute dissatisfaction. Absentmindedly, she stuffed something in her mouth and chewed it for a while. Again absentmindedly, she swallowed the dry lump; it stuck and with disgust over the natural interruption, she grabbed her glass of water to soak the lump and ease its passage into her over-eager stomach. Again, she fell into distraction; again, her stomach raised a fuss; again she began the barely satisfying routine of quelling the riot. After a few rounds, it seemed her stomach took its leaden load and sat there, full enough but so disgusted with the whole process as to sit there in an inactive pout.

Deciding that lunch, such as it was, was ended, Mary shoved the excess away where it belonged and shuffled off to her work. Her stomach lay there like an angry lump, or rather a distended pouch, overstrained with a motionless, inert blob of matter. She grimaced and passed her hand over her abdomen, to feel the swell of flesh. A hasty sigh shoved the hands away, to take up her chores, and her chatter again. She looked to those plants in the thickest shade and slowly began to pull aside the excess. Her stomach all the while tried its utmost to get in her way, to inconvenience her. She spoke more sharply to her plants, then worried that somehow she had hurt their feelings. 'There, there: I'm sorry. I shouldn't have spoken so harshly to you. Do forgive me, and enjoy this space. It is a bit lighter for you now, but not too light, I do believe'.

Mary hadn't heard her Shop-door open. She was too preoccupied with her plants, on the one hand, and her lumped stomach on the other, to notice. She scowled at her stomach and chattered to her plants. She tried so hard to keep up a happy chatter about whatever she was doing that she sounded rather silly. 'There, there, little flower: you need some water … just a little … and oh, I wish that lump would soften in my stomach! Don't you think that would be nice? …' And on, and on, and on she went in the sweetest lilting tones, talking to her plants about her stomach. While she pasted the tones over her barely disguised dis-ease, her hands slopped water and splattered dirt and even upset plants. She shoved them into awkward places, with either too much or too little water. She didn't even notice at all, for the lump in her stomach decided to roll over. She grimaced and began to scold a shy, timid bud almost ready to bloom. Then she simply burped. 'Yuck!' she said in utter disgust at herself.

Her still unnoticed guest had closed the door with a gentle hand, and politely waited on the obviously-busy and preoccupied Mary. She – for it was Carymba – stood quietly, half-leaning against the archway inside the entryway, right at the bottom of the stairs. She had quietly listened to Mary's somewhat forced chatter with amusement. Repeatedly, she had fought the hurried waves of smiles which barely contained giggling; repeatedly, she had come to the brink only to hold back on sound with difficulty. Tears came to her eyes, the result of contained laughter; she had to dab them away discreetly. As she once again returned her handkerchief to a pocket, Mary saw her out of the corner of her eye, and started, catching her breath and forgetting entirely about the obnoxious lump which was her wadded lunch.

'Carymba! I didn't know you were here! How long?' 'Oh, no long, Mary: you were busy. I could wait'. 'Not too busy for customers'. 'Ah, but your plants were needing you'. 'To tell you the truth, since lunch I have hardly seen them'. 'You were so busy'. 'We all learn to make appearance, Carymba. Even to ourselves'. 'You've learned that, too. You *have* been busy!' 'What does that mean?' 'You never gave me the hint of duplicity. That's all'. 'Such is not my best of traits, I suppose'. 'Not for any of us'. 'No'. 'You look a mite frazzled'. 'Only since lunch, I think'. 'Did you put your slippers on then?' 'What?! Oh, my: no. I must have been preoccupied even earlier. This morning went so well'. 'I believe you worked on that side of the room this morning'. 'Yes, and this side … my! what a mess I made! And this lunch of mine sits like a lump on my stomach'. 'Now, Mary, what I needed when I came here was a cup of tea. Do you suppose I could interrupt you long enough to share some tea?' 'Why not?' Mary answered with a sigh. 'Yes: come on upstairs. There is tea enough, once I heat some water'. 'Good: thanks'.

Shortly, the tea was ready and the two were seated at Mary's little kitchen table. They talked of plants and Mary spoke of how the idea of talking to her plants had really perked them up this last while. 'Until this afternoon, of course'. 'Of course: what was the difference, do you suppose?' 'I think I had a bellyache'. 'That might make a difference. How is your bellyache now?' 'Why, it is a lot better. It must be the tea'. 'Either that, or you were paying your stomach some attention'. 'Yes. I had forgotten that'. 'And, of course, you had laughed and relaxed'. 'Do you think that helped?' 'Maybe so'. 'Tell me, Carymba: do you think talking to plants in nutty?' 'The one side of your Shop, where you really talked to them today, was lovely'. 'And the other side …': Carymba just winced. Mary laughed, almost spilling her tea.

6 April 1986

CCXXXVII

Prematurely warm and therefore more uncomfortable than usual for a temperature such as enwrapped that morning, Clyde leaned back in his seat and stretched, yawning widely over a lazier than desired day. He felt warm, almost sweaty. Activity more strenuous than a yawn would, he was certain, wring sweat out of him. And so he sat back and pondered the prospects of the day with mixed feelings. The hearth next to his seat lay cold; he missed the dancing flames he had enjoyed all Winter long, which had warmed him in the Winter's cold. But he also was glad the fire was not lit, for it would have made him most uncomfortable. He became restless as the chair seemed to become harder under him. He squirmed to one side. That lasted a few seconds before he shifted himself the other way. Again, the squirm came as renewed response to the prodding discomfort of his chair.

Irritated with himself, Clyde stood up and stretched again. He leaned over, trying to touch his toes without bending his knees; he almost made it. He bounced on his belt a few times, but to no avail: the ankles, he could reach, but not the toes. Standing erect again, he twisted himself around, loosening his waist. He breathed deeply and felt a spring of sweat break out and trickle through his beard. 'It is too much. I *can't* sit still. What am I going to do with today?' His words burst out of his mouth, surprising him but eliciting no answer. The walls looked on as glumly as before. The brass shone in unblinking stare. The steady lamps burned low, uncaring at his malaise. 'Bah at you!' he exclaimed at the empty room.

Clyde drew himself up in defiance at his day, so uncooperative was he finding his fitting with the day. He felt a certain rage inside, which confused him. Responding or reacting to his inner itch today, Clyde furrowed his brow and twitched his beard in an enfolding scowl. With a heavy, forceful sigh, he took off and paced to the stairs, then clamored upward, two steps at a time with a heavy, stomping foot. The whole Inn-by-the-Bye echoed with his step. But Clyde was preoccupied with himself today, and the noise never rattled his restless consciousness. He plowed into his room, grappled for his shawm, found it and spun to leave his room. His door slammed behind him, closing on a tousled mess.

Clyde impatiently pushed himself down the stairs, taking two or three at a time, barely allowing enough care to keep from hurtling headlong into a heap on down the stairs. With a rattle-bang, Clyde found himself on the foyer. Righting himself, but barely enough, he grasped the door, turned the handle and ripped it open. Ejecting himself, he heaved the door shut. The Inn quivered as the dust filtered from secret crevices; then the Inn itself seemed to sigh in relief that Clyde's energy had escaped the unwilling cage.

Clyde took his long strides and drove himself across the Commons and around the Great Rock. He had no place to go, but was most eager to get there. At the 'Y', for no real reason, he rushed blindly down the Valley Road. He saw no one, for there was no one to be seen. Of course, he wasn't looking, either. Rather, he was rushing, pumping his arms furiously, his shawm held firmly in his right fist. By the time he reached the Sea Road, with the waves lapping at the beach below, he was breathing heavily and his sweat was soaking into his shirt in damp-looking blotches. At the turn, with the bluff of the Hills riding out to the Sea on his left and the Sea Road and beach stretching out to his right, with the Sun climbing higher in the deep blue sky, he stopped, waiting for his breath to catch up with him. His face glistened; his beard channeled the run-off sweat. His chest heaved and his pulse pounded within him. He felt the exultation of effort on a day like today.

Gradually, his eye scanning the gentle waves on the Sea, Clyde felt himself settle down. He held his stance, legs apart, hands on hips until his chest stopped its heaving and assumed a gentle rhythm. His restlessness, however, rose to make him feel the itch again. He squirmed inside himself and scowled at the world. He was hot and sweaty and sticky; he didn't like that, ever, and certainly not now, for it was all too early for such things. He shifted around, scratching himself with his shirt – or thinking he did. The trees hanging over from the Hills were just sprouting green, a frail and lacy, timid fan upon the branches. He watched them sway very lightly in the almost-breeze which whispered off the Sea. The little stuff was more ready, more anxious for Spring; it was poking out all fresh-green and leaning eagerly after the still un-veiled Sun. Clyde looked at that probing green, and nodded. His steps took him over to where a layered shale gave seat under the fanning umbrella of some Spring-eager brush. Shaded like an Turkish pasha, he sat down, then drew his feet up into a seated position. He took out his shawm and began to play. All he was missing was a turban, a hookah and the flowing pants.

Music drew out his restless venom and soothed him. Had he not been so wrapped in melodious notes, he might have realized the facts – but quite likely would not, for then the music would not be working rightly. The plaintive tones pushed into the breeze and charmed the waves in time to the lapping on the beach. A strange rhythm consumed him as he pushed his breath, his soul through the double reed and quivered the tune upon the air.

The Sun had come behind him now, and the shade of the Hills stretched over the water, the lacy leaves leaving their furtive shadow at the very edge of the shade. Clyde felt a certain comfort in it all, as he continued on and on with his penetrating modal melodies. He lost the sense of time beyond the regular beat he gave. The growing shadow stretched widely, unacknowledged. The hour grew late; the world came to rest as his legs went sound asleep, unfeeling. Out of those lengthening shadows came a voice: 'Clyde!'; the call came. Clyde heard and did not hear; the shawm kept on in its wail. 'Clyde!'; louder came the call. Clyde paused and looked aside, fracturing his spell. Over on the Sea Road stood Geoffrey, with Carymba. Geoffrey had called. 'What do you want?' answered Clyde with a voice still given to the curt raspiness of the restless morning. Indeed, without his self-charming tune, he found the old restlessness churning in his body. 'Well?!' he bellowed. Geoffrey, timid now, offered answer: 'Can you come?' 'Where!?!' 'To the Inn'. 'Why?!? I just left there'. 'Oh? You were gone before I arose. I believe I heard you before I crawled out of bed early; but then you were gone'. 'What do you want?' 'Don't you remember?' 'Remember what?' 'The Party'.

Clyde grew quiet. 'The party!' he thought to himself with a questioning frown. The party! 'Oh! I forgot! I'll come!' Clyde shoved his feet out in front of him; they flopped helplessly over the ledge of shale, dangling, asleep. 'Oh oh!' he offered as he waited for blood to stir his forgotten legs again. They hung limply, but he could feel the pressure build in them. They ached; and then they tingled. Gritting his teeth, he stood down, leaning on the shale shelf for support. His knees finally held. He moved free from the shelf and came toward his friends. 'I had forgotten'. 'We had looked for you, until we finally heard you and came. The others are expecting you, and your shawm'. Clyde grinned as he hobbled along to them. 'We can't have that. Here, give me a hand, Geoffrey. These legs fell asleep and are grossly uncooperative!'

13 April 1986

CCXXXVIII

Finding herself wrapped into a little ball, Effie twisted her way halfway out of sleep – just enough to realize that she was cold and thence to reach down and pull up another blanket, her comforter in which she had snuggled away many a Winter's night. Having nestled herself, Effie gradually warmed. And, as she warmed, she loosened tightened muscles. Her joints grew limp. Her flesh soothed in comfort. Her body melted into her bed and her head into her pillow. Slowly, slowly she slithered into sleep, melting into dreamless slumber. The warmth enfolded her and the night passed on uneventfully.

Morning came with Spring brightness bursting eagerly into her room. The little eastward window glimmered in brightness. All the leftover Winter smudges on the windows refracted a dusty light and gave the appearance of a blazing pane. Thus morning prodded the warm and cozy Effie. The sunlight warmed the room and perspiration began to emerge on her, and sometimes trickle down until the covers or her bed soaked it up from her now-dampening body. Her coziness was becoming musty, a discomfort of swinging temperatures and the dominance of a newly bold sunshine. She found herself groggily rousing. She did not want to move. Her body felt heavy and bloated, hot even, and sweaty. The stickiness on her was new again; Winter had intervened against her former memories, now hurrying back upon her grogginess. She lay spread on her stomach. She squirmed slightly, and moaned. She lifted her head a bit, then let it fall again – kerfluff – into her pillow. Her hair flopped damply against her cheek. Questioning, she ran her hand up to feel her hair; damp and set in clumpish curls. 'Ugh', she grunted unbecomingly.

The warmth under her comforter had made her sleepy, almost like a drug. She awoke in her own displeasure, ill-at-ease and not very aware of what was going on. The memory, or half a memory of the early pre-dawn chill rumbled over her mind: 'Oh' was all she said, and that in the dullest of tones. She shoved her elbows under her, raising her shoulders and droopy head. Her eyes were open, technically, although they were puffy and uncooperative. She pouted at the ideas of getting up, ideas which needed to be fulfilled regardless of her own predisposition. That fact slowly came to mind, too, adding to the puffy pant. Nevertheless, she rolled onto one elbow and, with flailing coordination, heaved the covers away.

The room proved cooler than she expected. Her sweaty-moist skin and nightgown cooled rapidly. 'Brrr ...': she rolled the r-s in Highland fashion, simply to please her ear. The pout turned into a handlebar grin, her chin a wadded ball underneath. She shivered and lunged upward to begin the day. At the end of her lunge, her body came more or less erect, her feet fumbling on the floor, staggering to find a balance for herself. After a moment or two, she managed to stand still. Her head spun a bit; she held it in her hands, ringlets still damp, curling around her fingers. Morning finally had broken her slumber, as much as she hated to admit it.

An extra splashing wash that morning added to the time for preparation. Effie wondered, after a while, what might be the time. She hastened to finish her dressing and to correct the sleep- and sweat-fussed hair. Grumbling over the distressful locks, she drew them tight and fastened them down with force, unnaturally. From rumpled look, she soon assumed a stark, severe form. She pulled herself straight, tidied her room, then hurried out to the kitchen they shared above the Spinners' Shop. All was empty. All was quiet. Puzzled, Effie hurried down the stairs. All was empty. All was quiet. She wadded her face in puzzlement, straining her fresh, severe hair, making a few stray strands escape their bondage into frayed disarray.

More quietly and less severely neat, she climbed the stairs again, her hitched skirts in hand. The empty kitchen and sitting room were flanked by closed doors. She listened carefully, holding her breath for silence' sake ... and silence smiled back at her. She sighed. 'I must be early, then' she muttered softly to herself. 'I am too awake to go to sleep. And it is too late to go to bed ... or should I say too early? Oh well, my stomach suggests a breakfast might soon do well. Hmmm: I wonder if I should prepare for one or for four? The time is *so* jumbled in my mind!' And on and on she reasoned to herself in the very best logic she could muster. 'I'll presume the day will soon begin. Breakfast here is for four'.

And so she began to fix breakfast for four, in quiet inefficiency. She plodded around the kitchen carefully, aware that almost everything there was really Martha's setting. Martha had been there long before Effie came. And, coming as she did, under Gilbert's care, Martha was always a bit reserved with her. 'How will Martha take to this?' she thought in mid-labor. And she paused with only a tinge of dread. 'Martha is so careful; I mustn't spill' she said, and watched her hands assume a clumsy trembling for the very first time. The kitchen became warm, she thought, as she strained in tense attention so as not to spill anything in her tense-preparing mode. She held and poured with careful touch and amazed herself at just how sloppy she could be. Warmer yet she grew. Her neck felt hot. Her brow grew moist. Her hair eased free into new damp curls, tugging free from unnatural severity, then hanging down upon her cheek, and dangling daringly toward her eyes. She blew it back with a burst of air and flip of her head. The hair bounced back, then dribbled slowly forward as she studied her untidy cooking. 'What will Martha think?' she gasped to herself in desperation.

'Old Martha thinks you will do better if you relax a tad. This is only breakfast. I don't feel like cooling. You picked a good recipe. Now, just do it. And ... you needn't slop *so* much'. Effie looked up to see Martha lean against the doorjamb of her room, arms folded across her chest, hair hanging free, bare feet crossed as they emerged from the bottom of her gown. Effie swallowed hard. 'Uh ... good ... uh ... uh ... morning, Martha' she stammered out. Martha would not smile; a smile now just would not do. Instead, she sputtered 'I'll be back. Just continue for now'. And into her room Martha disappeared.

Effie's hair sprung free. Her last restraining pieces clattered to the floor. Resigned to utter failure, she felt a trickle down her cheek, one which tickled clear to her chin. There, the drip dropped off somewhere, she knew not where. She sighed and felt her flush sinking slowly, leaving first her brow, then her cheeks, her chin, her throat to mellow softly into more natural, unhastened tones. She cooled, but still her hair clumped down in wayward spirals on her cheeks, and dangled to her nape. She swallowed hard; the gulp was heard, she was certain, at least by Martha and likely by Marthuida at the Inn-by-the-Bye as well. At least she knew that glottal echo in her head. But she did continue.

Breakfast neared completion before Martha ventured out again. 'Have you called the others – Gilbert and Chert?' 'Oh! No!' 'Never mind: I'll do that'. 'Oh, never mind: I can complete my chores'. 'No. No. I'll end your rounds. Defend your hair'. 'No, Martha' interrupted terse Chert. 'The hair needs no defense ... just care to avoid being spun into someone else's yarn. Now, tell me, Effie: is this your breakfast?' Collecting herself in spite of freshened flush, Effie responded 'Yes ... and yours, if you will'. 'I will' he answered. 'And so will I' answered Gilbert. Martha, in reserve, winked her way and agreed to condescend with secret glee, ignoring for now Effie's residual mess.

20 April 1986

CCXXXIX

All around, the world became bright, poking into every window and infiltrating every crack which exposed itself to the eager brightness. Hiding was difficult, even for Missus Duns, whose sod house lies snuggled into a corner of the Hills, in the shade of the Hills every morning, and now disguised further by the sprouting green on the branches all about. The blue sky sill poked into her little hollow. The daylight, even in the shadows, spread in a bright, diffuse visibility to her house. The daylight spread through Missus Duns' little house by every little window. The light shone all around her and roused her from her night's sleep. For morning found Missus Duns stretched in her bed. Her covers were snuggled into her neck. Her night-cap was pulled half-off. The weather had been good for sleeping: cool but not too cold, nor too damp. So she had slept well and, by the time daylight surrounded her, she was about ready to wake from the slumbering-off of yesterday.

Waking into the early brightness, Missus Duns rolled to her back and stared at the ceiling overhead. She brought her arms – all covered in her long-sleeved nightgown – up, and twined her fingers together beneath her head. And she blinked. She blinked at the brightness and also at the new need to bring her eyes into focus. With a gradual sense of accomplishment, she succeeded. Her eyes focused first on the ceiling and then began to shift about with, at first, meandering glances, and then a more and more perceptive inspection of her home. She cleared her throat and swallowed, then observed out loud to herself: 'Yes: Spring is here. I ought to straighten things a bit'. Having spoken, she set her jaw and lay there, gathering the resolution to perform the next stray act of morning – rousing herself from her bed.

More gradually, with greater deliberation than for her reclining inspection, she stirred herself. First, she moved her hands from behind her head. Then she stretched, and wiggled her toes. Her arms flopped on top of her covers as she blew out her breath in a great sigh. That marked a first exercise and she was none too eager to attack the second. There is, after all, more ease in thinking about doing things than in getting up. And so today, like almost every day, she scrambled herself against an urgent resistance to getting up. Both, she knew full well, worked inside herself. Daily she watched herself debate, then stir and stop, stir and stop, until she finally shoved herself up, to sit and then to turn and dangle her toes into the uncovered space alongside her bed. Once again, she followed the usual scenario with, she thought she noticed, a little more reticence than normal. She wondered, in a quick little flash, if her determination of need to clean had anything to do with the extra-fondness for her bed and covers this morning. But then she would fuss at herself and say no, she must do her work and not give in to her unnatural laziness. Then she would lie there some more and review her earlier study of needs once more.

Eventually, her stomach growls and the needs she suspected in herself conspire to overcome the comfort of the covers and, inertia altered, he rises. So it happened today. And so she roused herself and set herself upon the edge of her bed. She liked it as little as usual. But she did stay up; she did *not* flop back onto the bed, no matter how attractive that idea was as it fluttered through her mind. Shaking her head, she wedged herself erect and smiled with satisfaction. Before dressing, she decided, she would take care of breakfast. So, barefoot, she padded to her kitchen, rubbing her arms – for the chill was still in her little house. There, in the kitchen space, she stoked her stove first and sputtered over it until she got a flame going and a bit of warmth emerging into her house. She stood near the stove, the door to the firebox closed, and felt the quick warmth come to her. She smiled, ending the grin in an irrepressible yawn, and a grumble in her stomach, as if she were warning herself not to forget breakfast!

As the stove warmed the kitchen and, moreover, Missus Duns and her whole home, she busied herself with breakfast preparation … and scones for lunch. She liked to plan ahead that way. She ate her breakfast and plotted her cleaning day, for Spring had come and (she was once told) almost everyone cleans in Spring. Now, she decided, she ought to join the almost everyone. She looked about her place as she slowly chewed her breakfast. The more she looked, the slower she chewed. But chew she did, if even in a dawdling fashion. Today, she dawdled just a little bit more as she pondered the size of her task she had taken for herself this day.

All dawdling comes to an end eventually, for even the bestest of dawdlers. So, with a sigh over the inevitable, Missus Duns finished her dishes and moved to find and assemble her necessary gadgets for cleaning – brooms and dust pans and rags: things like that. She set them all together against a chair in the middle of her kitchen, right across from her stove. And she stood there and looked at them, her hands upon her hips and a defiant glance in her eyes. She watched them do nothing and the defiance seeped from her eyes, leaving a timid sadness in its place. Then her hands sagged and the wrists flopped, leaving the shoulders to sag. Her posture dipped in dismay as those tools just sat there. One hand fell to her side, and then the other. She felt so very, very old. The notion of going back to bed crossed her mind temptingly. 'No' she declared out loud, standing almost erect once more. She looked around; no one heard her and she gave a sigh of relief.

Missus Duns stepped toward her tools and stopped short; she suddenly remembered she had forgotten to get dressed! She smiled at herself for her foolish forgetfulness, and for the obvious delay in cleaning with the circumstance prescribed. She walked on past the broom and plodded, barefoot to her dressing corner. There she set about making her bed and dressing herself. She puttered happily with her hair and dawdled some more over such details of feminine arrangement. Again, dawdling could only dawdle *so* long. Then she was ready. And the broom remained standing at a jaunty angle, waiting for her to come visiting. She frowned at the broom, then shrugged and shuffled over to the broom, taking it in her hands. With a deep breath, she entertained the thought that she really, truly *liked* the house the way it had been all winter.

Under such an awful influence, Missus Duns began her chore of transforming her house into a new form or fashion. By no means was she energetic or enthused. No; rather was she slow and belligerent with herself. In fact, she had hardly begun when there came a knock at her door. Grateful, she leaned on her broom wearily, and called out 'Yes?!' The knock returned again. So she went to the door, using her broom as a walking stick, not sweeping a pathway to the door. The knock repeated as she neared: 'I'm coming. I'm coming' she muttered and sputtered under her breath. By now, dawdling had become her way of meeting this day-to-be-put-off. Opening the door, she saw Carymba and Geoffrey waiting for her.

Missus Duns smiled a warm greeting. They entered. 'My, Missus Duns, we are not disturbing you, are we?' suggested Geoffrey. 'This is nothing that cannot be delayed, I assure you' she replied with a significant grin. 'Perhaps we could help you?' offered Carymba, softly. 'Oh, I couldn't …'. 'No, no: we mean help. We could clean, perhaps while you mix up some scones for lunch'. 'Well …'. 'What do you say?' 'Well, I'll say: good enough'.

27 April 1986

CCXL

With sprightly step, Geoffrey crossed the Plain under a late morning Sun. He had risen, just about on time for him, and slowly prepared himself to gather for the day. His tea and biscuit had surpassed all fond and fair anticipation, pleasing him in all the lasting, subtle ways. He had carefully daubed his face, removing every wayward crumb, every smear of excess butter, or of currant jelly. He had expressed appreciation and taken his hat and set out for a stroll. Overhead, the skies were a deep and brilliant blue, punctuated by balls of puffy white. The leaves were fast-emerging on the trees and a warmth unusual this early gave the day an air of serenity. Geoffrey grinned pleasantly as he started out; the grin had not faded as he walked around the Commons, and thence decided to head out back, to see where the day might take him after that.

Geoffrey had no fixed agenda, no well-wrought plan to mold his day. Instead, a mute and futile curiosity brought him out calmly to investigate the day. he came with broad and quiet interests, intriguing him with all the vast surprises Spring rushes into view. He came with an appreciative eye for all the beauties of the place and time. Carymba had taught him well, if slowly, to observe what is there. And so his sprightly step still left him leisure to examine very carefully the wide expanse about him. The grass was shading into deep rich hues of green, the lengthening blades thrusting bright and toward the favoring Sun. Within that thickening carpet stirred a rich array of colors as the tiny flowerets of the field peeped out, and hinted to the larger cousins Geoffrey could see towering over his head in clumps of brightness. His grin grew broader as he savored all the good and fine contentments he enjoyed.

The chosen, meandering path led his steps onward into subtle surprises. The growing world erupted sweet and heady fragrances which made his head swim. The earth itself exhaled a musky-scented breath into his twitching nostrils. He sneezed a time or two, and scratched his nose with the back of his hand – then sneezed again in good measure. The rising Sun beat down on him with warmth that became hot. The rich and fragrant grasses arched over his head and swallowed all the breeze from off his brow. The moist and spongy soil steamed all about as the haughty Sun enticed it all from high overhead. His grin began to fade a bit in spite of all the earthiness of Spring, a whole event encompassing him in itself, as part of it. His step as well became more docile, not so ready as before to settle into a lively pace. He began, in short, to fade in the day's mid-day warmth.

At such a slower pace, Geoffrey ambled over the Plain with no more direction, but with far less attention. He noticed his sneezes and his sweat, but failed to appreciate the peeping blossoms; their mute greeting fell unobserved by eyes grown fuzzy in the mid-day heat. His path had far bypassed the City on the Plain. Instead, he had gone over by the Leaferites' Hill, on past the cut back to Uiston, along the hilly, wooded land from whence came Guerric. Now, he was bending into Gypsie Land. The heat continued to enfold him, leaving him increasingly grumpy and out of sorts with himself – there being as yet no one else around.

By now, the afternoon had become well spent. The grass was shorter and patchy here. The soil became drier, sandier, sliding under his step. A breeze began to blow, and some clouds gathered overhead to soften the Sun. Geoffrey half-way smiled to himself as the day gave new relief for his wearied head. As the cooler tones gave respite unto him, his pace became more sprightly once again. He began to notice things again. The scrubby grasses sprouted in a dingy green. The loose and sandy soil gave way under his steps, almost like walking on a beach. The sky, once blue and high, dropped lower in weighing grey. The air grew cooler and the breeze freshened, nipping at his nose. Geoffrey huddled in his coat which earlier had been too warm. He frowned again. The sand, he noticed, tumbled along the ground. At times, a gust of wind picked up some sand and threw it in his face with stinging force. He winced and turned his back, raising his collar in spite of himself. 'There is no shelter here', he thought out loud as the lowering clouds burst out in great bombarding drops of wind-directed rain.

Geoffrey kept going: the directory of pride. He felt the raindrops fall on him, at first in great balls and then in smaller, quicker darts. They were grown cold. And they soaked his clothes, once their fury had been spent. The sand underfoot grew wet as well and clung to his shoes and spats. He was convinced he did not like these Spring storms. He thought rememberingly of a sheltered place, and moved toward where he recalled it, back into the hilly area Guerric once called home. The overarching trees gave some shelter as the leaves broke up the hardest of the rain. That left Geoffrey, wet already, cold and shivery in the unwarranted day. He looked at himself, all wet now. He scowled and pitied his steps. He felt his every tired muscle contract against the chill the rain was leaving in his body. Once more, he noticed only himself.

Then, out of the woods chased a pair of laughing lads, hurrying from mischief unto mischief. Poor Geoffrey, paying no attention to anything but himself, proved to be once more in the wrong place – their path. In eagerness, the first collided with him: they sprawled upon the moistened ground, Geoffrey underneath. Against his sputtering defense, his attacker scrambled free and rushed away as the second crashed upon the scene and fell over Geoffrey, sprawled again unwillingly, upon the loose, rich woodland soil. The second, too, spoke harshly, rose and raced after his neighbor. Geoffrey sat upon the ground, examining his wounded pride. He found, as well, his clothes were soiled in streaks of rich black dirt. The crumbled remnants of last year's leaves clung on his coat indignantly. He snorted, shivered, at his worst.

'There is no good in sitting here, I guess' spoke Geoffrey as he twisted to help himself up again. Erect, he straightened out his mussed clothes, to cover over the accidents of the day with a façade of regulation dignity … 'just as Sir James would always have insisted'. Then and there, Geoffrey decided to go back to his own room, now. There were dry clothes. There he could repair himself. There a hot cup of tea could be found. And all could be handled in one order or another.

So he moved on through the wooded path until he found an entrance to the ways which crisscrossed over all the Plain. The grass was high and served him well to soften all the wind. The rain, however, beat on him, unimpeded. He hurried over land until, a wet and shivering mass, alone and nearly as grey as the now-leaden sky, he splashed through the last long muddy yellow yards to gain the porch of the Inn-by-the-Bye. As he approached, he noticed only where he was, and that Thyruid had planted a fire in the fireplace of the dining room of the Inn-by-the-Bye. He almost smiled over that: *almost*, but not quite.

He reached the door and opened it. The Inn resounded with company. Puzzled but cold, Geoffrey stepped right in and closed the door upon the unruly elements outside. The fire danced boldly; he watched it with enchantment. He thought to go to it, then decided some dry clothes would be a better start. He looked around: the room was full, and only his corner chair remained unused; he smiled in timid appreciation of the remembrance thus implied. Two steps toward the stairs brought interruption – 'Geoffrey! Come and join us. Have some tea. … Oh! He's wet clear through! – No matter! Move his chair beside the hearth. Clyde won't mind'. 'For now, I'll even trade … but not for always!' 'Come on, Geoffrey: the tea is ready. We've awaited you'. Sheepishly, Geoffrey doffed his hat and dripped. Then, smiling, he waddled in to take a seat beside the fire. He smiled at a sort of warmth he had not known today.

4 May 1986

CCXLI

Wilbur, the faithful boatman whose skill provides the only safe passage from Apopar to the Plain, across the Great River, sat quietly in his cottage. This cottage perched above the River, above the River's boldest floodplain, granting him a dry, secure refuge for all the hours his service is not needed. His window grants him a view of all the signal spots from which he may be called. Each Spring, he must trim the brush to keep that scan of sight clear. His work comes only on demand, and yet he had to keep an eye attuned for signaled call. The only way to learn of need was visual. The River was too wide to yell, and no other means of getting news across was readily available.

The knack of watching across the River while he did some other chore was one that Wilbur long ago had mastered. His eye had trained itself to see the changes in the scenery, beyond all change of seasons. When he had noticed the sign, he would swing his sign around and catch the time and place in code the underground knew well. Then, usually by night, he would take his boat upstream – how far depended on his reading of the current and just where his touching land across the way was needed.

This day was quiet. His skill had not been needed lately, and Wilbur had begun to think of going boating just for the fun of it. He always had the worry that he would be gone when someone needed him. And he would not even have the excuse that he was already on a run of mercy. He worried about those kinds of things, and thus stayed home and waited. He waited today, too, keeping his alertness keyed to the opposite bank.

While Wilbur thus amused himself and wiled away the day, waiting, he did not notice the near-by movement. He had no urgent need to keep track of *his* side of the Great River. This was his home-side. He knew peace and security here. Trips to his house by anyone were rare. Few on this side even knew where he lived, or that he was; the exceptions were those possessed of longish memories, or those whose lives had once been swept across the Great River by his boat-handling skill. They had known were to find him from the other side. But time and needs and the quite different terrain on his side left him obscure. Only those who went, sometimes, across the other way had learned to find him right at home. They knew that, if his boat were tied along the River, he would be at home. If the boat were gone, he would return as soon as his trip was completed safely.

Along the winding trail which wound from the Plains and along the Great River, the high-ranging cliffs rising on the right hand side of the path, there moved the limping gait of young Carymba. She long ago had learned to make and keep a syncopated rhythm in her walk. With daily determination she plodded along. This day her plodding carried her beside the River, toward the secluded cottage Wilbur called home. The path, after the initial windings into the brambles which led to the River edge, grew thin from rare and unaccustomed use. In fact, if one were not aware that the path existed, eyes would not presume that anything more than accidental partings in the underbrush were there. Yes, since she knew the way, the path unfolded for her, upon dry land, overlooking the Great River.

Wilbur was sitting back, his feet up, gazing somewhat blankly, yet attentively, across the River. His thoughts were growing restless, even with his grave resistance against all wandering. He sought to keep his concentration sharp enough to see a sign if one should happen to be flashed. In such a state, the knock upon his door came upon him, disturbing him. 'Oh!?' he said with animation, his eyebrows rising into puzzled arches, his forehead wrinkling into ladder form, asking ascent up further on his balding head. His mouth was temporarily stuck into a tight 'o' form. And his mind raced through all forgotten possibilities before it settled at last upon a visitor, knocking now again upon his door. 'One moment, please' he called out loud with his shrill voice as one more scan was passed along the places signs might come.

Wilbur scrambled to his feet and flexed his knees, then moved with clumsy step through all his accumulated clutter in order to reach his door. Opening, he exclaimed: 'Well, well: come in, my little friend. How long has it been since you came by to visit me?' 'Too long, I'm sure. And from the looks of the trail back there not many have come this way since then'. 'Not many: that is true. I'm trying to remember whether anyone has probed that none-too-obvious path betwixt the River and the Cliff. I think that. as of just a moment ago, you were both the last and next visitor to this door'.

Peeking past him, Carymba commented: 'I see your skills at housekeeping have hardly improved'. 'Oh no: I heartily disapprove of time and energy spent in rearranging clutter. My mother used to think it was important. But I always had something better to do. I have no problem at all, except when I try to get to the door quickly. But you see how often anyone comes to visit'. 'I see'. 'Oh … I suppose it would be more polite to ask you in. And then I could go back to keeping watch over the possible calls for boating skills. I'm not much of a housekeeper. But there's no one else around today who can compete with me in boating'. 'Thank you. I will come in, and let you watch again'. 'Good enough. Come in. And … uh … close the door behind you as you come. This path, you see, is also single file'. 'Adorned for visitors about as well as the one I followed through the brush'. 'Precisely: … now, have a seat and tell me why you've come'.

'I came to visit and, if opportunity should come, find transit over the Great River tonight'. 'Why didn't you say so?! I've had so little business lately that I've grown concerned. My eyesight, or my concentration may be failing, understand. And that would not be good. Besides, I've itched to take a ride, but have been worried lest I miss a call while out to take a joyride'. 'How long has it been quiet over there?' 'Let me think: … about two weeks now – far too long for ordinary goings. I have never been in the house this long. 'There is always the chance that life has eased'. 'How likely is that?' 'Not very'. 'As I thought, too'.

The pair dropped into silence, pondering the view. Then, all at once, Wilbur's eyes flew open and he threw himself forward to watch a wave. He yanked his rope to acknowledge that he saw. The arms waved back to give a time and place. Wilbur yanked the rope again. And then the figure slid from view. 'Tonight, I'll drop you off, then slide on further to collect my latest passenger. Perhaps we'll learn eventually what has disturbed the commerce so'.

Afternoon slid away as Wilbur chatted widely, learning all he could of news which does not come his way too easily. He laughed more easily than he had earlier. He gathered up some simple food, arranged without once losing sight of the waving places across the River. The two of them ate and shared a meal. They smiled, at ease with one another and waited for the night's dark descent.

At last the last of lights above gave way. The stars were splattered everywhere on a clear and moonless night. 'This is the kind of night which is at best for crossings. The darkness covers all, and only well-familiarized eyes can tell the way they've gone, and have to go. Come along. By the time I move the boat upstream, it will be time to go. We'll be quiet once we go. When you see her, tell Missus Carney hello from Wilbur'.

The trip upstream was slow. Then came the swift sweep from shore to shore. Carymba scrambled out. Wilbur pushed along, then swung to shore. A timid girl climbed in, afraid. Wilbur pushed off to safety on the Great River's current. 'Thank you' she whispered softly. 'I will be safe now?' Wilbur smiled and nodded: 'Yes'.

11 May 1986

CCXLII

Heavy-eyed, Thyruid fumbled into his morning routine. He grasped, more or less, the polish pot in hand, and set out, yawning, to refresh his favored brassware's shine. He knew the hour was right for rising and for polishing this brass. But his eyes were loathe to open and his legs felt heavy, as if they were encased in lead. He shuffled across the dining room far more clumsily than usual. He felt stiff, and shrugged himself within his heaving scowl. The polish rag rubbed slowly on the brass. He had, it seems, no spirit for the chore. He grumbled at himself and jammed the rag back into the pot, set the pot upon the nearest table and reached to pull back the curtain. He wondered if he had been fooled; if this were not, really still, the middle of the night, if beneath those all-consuming yawns there might not be a realistic call to sleep again.

Outside the day was grey, not black. The clouds hung low and gently dropped their heaviness in drippy mist. The window was all coated with the drops of mist; a few trickles rumbled down the panes in silence. More drops accumulated as he mutely watched. He yawned: alas, it is indeed the time to rise, preparing his dining room for the coming, dreary day. He yawned again and shook his head as he stretched as high and wide as he could, hoping to shake away the clotting weight of his reluctant entrance to this day. The shaking had no effect as such. And so, he dropped the curtain and resumed his chores, prodding himself in hopes of becoming somewhat more lively.

The hour was still early, Thyruid was still yawning over his polish pot, and the breakfast had not come out from Marthuida's kitchen when the door opened. Thyruid listened; he heard no more that the pattering of the heavier drips of mist. He scowled and began to bump his way toward the door, perturbed that the cool damp was penetrating his Inn so quickly and so thoroughly. Stumbling up the step to the foyer, he sputtered. Then raising his eyes he saw a timid girl at the door. 'Oh!' he said, exclaiming at his surprise. She stood her ground although she looked frightened and ready to rush away. ''I wondered why my door came open. Why not come in?' 'I wondered if I should' she squeaked, forcing her voice to face, with what brazen boldness she could muster, the anticipated inquisition. Thyruid swallowed another yawn, then stepped back: 'Of course you should' he said with warmth, and even the first half-smile of the day. 'That weather is cold and damp. I think I'll need to build a fire to keep it away from us in here. Does that sound inviting?' 'Oh, yes sir' she blurted out, then winced over her uncontrolled eagerness. 'Then, come on in. Marthuida will have some breakfast ready soon'.

She entered by tiny, creeping steps, for uncertainty had deeply influenced her. The room seemed open, if dim. She jumped a little when Thyruid closed the door behind her; she glanced back quickly, but there were no extra latches to be seen. She swallowed hard and moved herself forward tentatively. 'Go on in, and take 'most any seat. I'll start a fire and warm this room up for us all'. She nodded obediently and took a seat as near the door as she could manage. 'Marthuida should be out soon' he reassured her.

As Thyruid organized the fireplace and then began to light the fire upon the hearth, she watched him closely. As the fire began to dance, Thyruid stood up, satisfied. 'That will warm us promptly. You'll warm faster over here, if you would like'. He wiped his hands on his stretched apron, and returned to his polishing, more awake now than before. He thought to himself that the work of keeping an Inn like this came easier when a guest was near, or at least expected soon.

Thyruid polished, starting and keeping up a line of casual banter, hoping to relax the girl who sat so huddled, her hood still on her head, her cloak still wrapped around her – even though they both were wet. Finally, in answer to her muffled one word answers, he invited her to hang her cloak over a chair near the fire so that it could dry out more readily. She grew quiet then, and Thyruid wondered if she were more frightened or more thoughtful now. He kept his polishing rag working away, listening carefully but not watching her; he suspected she feared being watched most of all.

Indeed, she watched him work as she sat in silence. She studied his arms and shoulders, his benevolent spread about the waist. She watched the brass respond to his work. Then her eyes looked over at the fire. The flame danced brightly, inviting her to its warmth. She realized, watching the glowing brass and then the dancing flame that she grew cold. She had been cold all along; she knew that much. Now, however, the temptation to taste the warmth directly, and dry herself as well as her cloak pressed upon her. It was best, she felt, to be wary, to be very cautious. One could ill afford to be too trusting, she believed. The only exception she had ever known was Missus Carney. Even trusting Wilbur, the boatman, was hard for her to do; necessity forced her trust, and land felt good beneath her feet when he had set her there, on this safe shore. She studied Thyruid, then the fire, then back again, uncertain what she ought to do.

Marthuida brought breakfast into the dining room for Thyruid and herself. Setting it out upon the counter, she looked up and noticed their early guest. Smiling suddenly, she spoke: 'Good Morning! I didn't realize you were here. I'll bring you some breakfast, too. Would like tea or coffee? I can get some milk, too, if you wish'. 'Milk sounds good to me' came the soft reply. 'Give me a minute'. Then Marthuida stepped back through the swinging doors. The girl sat there in disbelief. Nothing she had known worked quite this way.

Soon Marthuida entered again with another plate, high mounded, and a mug of milk. 'Would you like to join us at the counter? or would a table be more comfortable for you?' 'Here is fine'. Marthuida drew near. 'Why! you're all wet and shivery. Let me sit you near the fire. There's no need to shiver like that'. So she moved the plate and mug to the table by the hearth. The poor girl looked confused and almost ready to panic before Marthuida's steady tones interfered. 'Come here. And slip your cloak off. You'll be warm and safe. The girl squirmed and shivered, thinking of running away, but looking again at the fire and feeling cold and wet all over – and at the breakfast and feeling hunger gnaw at her. 'OK' she said as firmly as she could. Then, gritting her teeth, she repeated: 'OK'.

Warmer, fuller and drying by the hearth, she finally leaned back and looked around the room. Marthuida was still sitting at the counter. The girl asked: 'What kind of place is this, anyway?' 'An Inn. We call it the Inn-by-the-Bye'. 'You seem nice'. 'We try to be'. 'I mean, I haven't found your secret yet'. 'Our secret?' 'Yes: there is always a reason for being nice. At least that's how I've always found things. If someone gives you food or drink or warmth, they want something back'. 'Are you full, and warm?' 'Yes. I guess I am'. 'Then the return is there'. 'I can't pay for this, you know'. 'You haven't received a bill, have you?' 'No. I guess I haven't. But I can't do very much'. 'Can you smile?' Surprised, the girl smiled. Then she laughed, or half-laughed, half-cried. 'I guess I can. Is that all you want? What kind of place is this, anyway?' Thyruid answered: 'It's the Inn-by-the-Bye. We have a place and a way of life. You're part of it now, you know'. 'I am?' 'Yes. You most certainly are'. 'I belong here?' 'Why not?' 'Who are you?' 'I'm Thyruid and she's Marthuida'. 'Hi'. 'Hi'. 'My name – I guess I should tell you – is Eliza'.

18 May 1986

CCXLIII

Cold drizzle swathed Hyperbia once again today. The grass was slick and wet; long ago the beads of water ran together, leaving only wet and clinging blades of green to bow beneath the rain. The green looks darker than usual under low and angry skies. The pathways, in which the laden blades of grass were bowing low, lay streaked with yellow-mud, a slimy swath, or set of swaths cut along the wee folks' customary tracks. Harder rain may fall again; for now, it seems the clouds are satisfied to cast a heavy mist, condensed into substantial drops only occasionally.

The day conspires to encourage private, lonesome ways. Without sound reason, no one would be likely to emerge from under all that protection homes provide against the sort of day this one had become. Within each shop, the shop-keeper puttered at the chores, fairly certain that no customer would come today. The weather was too cold and wet, the paths too slimy and slippery for any but the most necessary business. Mary tended her plants. Martha slowly spun her wool. The tinker sat at home. Missus Duns stoked her stove for warmth and dryness. Father John rocked creakily by his stove. Thyruid rubbed his polish on the brassware a second time today. Geoffrey slept beneath a modest (for him) pile of blankets. Mahara readied herself for extra baking while Guerric snorted occasionally in his sleep. The others likewise huddled safe inside their homes, staying warm and dry, putting off their business for another, better day.

Down over the gully, in the Great Dome, stood Yves. He grew restless – any observer could tell that! To no one in particular, he muttered: 'This is one day of rain too many for me. I want to do *something*!' Betsy, none-too-excited herself, responded: 'Then go ahead, do something. You're a big boy, I guess'. 'Bigger than anyone else around here'. 'I was not referring to

169

size, but to maturity'. 'La-di-da!' 'Oh go outside and get wet: see if I care. … And the mud make you miserable!'

Yves swallowed hard: this challenge reached to his very self esteem. He must respond. 'I think I will' he declared and threw the door wide open – and out he charged, leaving the door wide open. Of course, he gave no thought to Betsy. Not now, certainly. That the cold rushed down their hall to laugh at her as goose bumps rose and shivers quaked her body – that was no concern for Yves who now has run into the mist and through the clinging mud. Betsy, in a rage, bellowed after him: 'Yves, you fool! At least you could close the door!' But Yves was up the hill then, leaving Betsy to adjust. She stumbled to her feet, then hobbled as she learned her feet had both gone to sleep, and now must rouse from their numb and hollow slumber. 'Ouch' she yelled at the empty room. Shivering, she slammed the door, then stumbled to the stove to warm herself again.

Yves, at the top of the hill, looked around. What to do for fun was the pressing question in his mind. All too many days had come and gone in showers, cold and just plain indoor weather. 'I'll run' he said and began to sprint toward the Plain. The grass became matted beneath his steps and gave a slick surface to his feet. He went to turn, but had no traction; so down he went and slid along the grass. The mud and torn wet grass ground into him. He thought he was wet before; but now a more thorough drenching has soaked into his clothes and attacked his skin. He shivered and decided it was colder than he thought. 'Maybe I ought to go back home, having had my run. Hmmm. No. Not yet. I'll not give her that satisfaction'. Climbing to his feet again, he muttered under his breath: 'I'll need to be a bit more careful. That grass is slippery!'

The run was clipped to a jog. Yves panted as the wind picked up and needled his flesh with water drops. The drops collected, then formed themselves into river that cascaded down his cheeks. 'It can't be sweat; I'm too cold for that!' Yves talked to himself while he ran, if there was no one else with whom to talk. 'Even Betsy will answer. That's better than talk with no answer at all!' But no one came out to play and Yves continued, clear to the Great River – which is Great and a River even for Yves: he has never had a way to get across to the other side. He could only watch. So watch he did that day.

Across the Great River, he could see, there was nearly as little business as here. A shawled and huddled, wet-looking figure slipped along a muddy path. Yves could see the trailing skirts, that they had wicked up yellow-mud, and it had caked, and was streaked now by all the mist which soaked the droopy, darkened dark clothes. Yves watched carefully the steps she took – presuming the skirted figure to be a woman – with all her garments clinging to her closely. He rubbed his chilled, wet arms, imagining her chill. 'She should be inside on a day like this': the words pop out of his boyish mouth as he shakes the water from his stringy hair.

The figure across the Great River paused while Yves' voice boomed brightly to her ears. She watched him: he felt her eyes. So he smiled and he waved with a great, wide swinging wave, clear from the shoulder. She saw his smiles and smiled in return, waving slightly. He thought he saw her wave; 'is that a smile?' he asked himself. He waves again, more boldly. He thought to yell, but then remembered all the tales the wee-folk tell of life across the River.

The thought twisted round and round his mind – how odd it is that all the wee-folk can, and many had, crossed this Great River boat by boat, yet he, who is so large compared to them, had never been across the way. The current swept quickly there: his eyes could see it well. 'I'd never swim … and all the boats around are far too small. I'm stuck right here' he heard himself say.

More quietly, he thought his thoughts, his hands now set upon his hips. 'I wonder where she's going now? Her pace is quicker than before. She's turned upstream and nears the riverbank. Where is she now? Oh, there she is, beyond those bushes, looking up the stream. She's waving. Who lives down there? I don't know. There really is not room enough for me: those paths are made for the wee-folk: they go places I can't go … but I go faster!' His chest heaved out in the momentary flurry of a young lad's pride.

'What's that?' He spoke almost out loud, but held back sound because he somehow felt it would not be completely right to shout. 'A Boat! He moves quite swiftly, up to the shore. She's in! And off they go again. He's pulling hard across that current. Look at how the water churns about the boat! I wish *I* had a boat. Perhaps I'll make one someday, just to cross that

River. He handles that boat neatly. Here they come right up near me …
but overshot a bit. Oh, well: I'll move to them … to her, for there she is
on shore again … *this* shore.'

The tiny black-draped, wet old woman stood before him, looking up
so high into his eyes. 'You must have wanted something. This isn't a good
day for anyone to be out. You are soaking wet and chilled. It must be
important'. 'Well, … um … I'm Yves'. 'I'm Missus Carney'. 'And I was out
for play. Why are you out today?' 'I'm out, just going home from helping a
neighbor who is sick'. 'You can get sick in weather like this'. 'So can you'.
'Yea … I guess that's right'. 'Do you want to know …?' Yves was smiling
then, through all the cold and washing rain. It came a little harder just
then. Missus Carney smiled, and nodded before the two parted their ways.

25 May 1986

CCXLIV

Carymba stirred. Her eyes opened into the dark. She had not realized that she had fallen asleep and thus concerned herself. The memories came back: she had spent the evening with Mother Hougarry. Having no urgency to go, she sat and visited, she even shared a yawn or two with her hostess. She must have dozed sometime: 'Mother Hougarry must have been pleased' she murmured quietly. She stirred her hand, finding a light blanket laid over her, to keep her warm against the cool dampness of the Spring night. She pulled the blanket to her cheeks: it nuzzled softly, a flannel piece with plenty of flannelling left for her. A soft grin crept across her face, appreciating the kindness represented there. Listening, she heard the slowly regular breathing of sleep. The hour was unknown; such things are hard to grab together in the darkness which pervades. For Mother Hougarry, it is an hour of sleep. For Carymba, it has become an hour of freshness, for rising.

Slipping the flannel blanket to the side, and savoring its softness to the last, Carymba stirred herself from the chair, and rose. Her feet were unsteady, and her limpy hip was uncertain of any cooperation. Yet she mastered herself and stood. For balance, she jostled around and squeaked the floor. She held her breath as Mother Hougarry tossed in the bed. She slept though, and Carymba thought of being more careful. Having folded the flannel blanket and set it on the seat of her snoozing-chair, she quietly hobbled to the door. She folded her shawl – a light one now – about her shoulders and slipped out the door. The latch clunked softly as the door went closed. Carymba waited: all was silent with the Hidden Cabin.

Familiar paths greeted her feet as she stepped from the porch. Long habit carried her along of necessity, for the night was dark and her eyes could not penetrate the low-hung overcast and the night's sealing away any light. Foot-worn care brought her down the Crossed Hills, to the root-steps above the Valley Road. Her hands felt the tree, large and rough, with cragged bark absorbing night's darkness into its deep grey crevices. Her stretched fingers grasped a deep-grooved ripple of bark, a handle made convenient for these gnarled steps. For stability, she backed down, as down a ladder, groping first the bark and then the upper roots. At last, her feet found sound security upon the hard packed hearth – hard packed because the leaves which fell last Fall have long since been ground to dust.

Upon that Valley Road, Carymba paused, and then decided to go to the Fields. The path was easily followed now. She had to wind her steps along the blackened yet well-known route. She knew by "feel" when she had drawn near the 'Y'. She slowed herself and felt the path with her feet until she found the growing grass. She leaned over to feel it with her hands, to verify for herself just where she was. The blades of grass felt long and plump; a rich dew coated each blade with drops which washed her fingers in chilled brilliance. She smiled, and knew that, should she lose the path, her skirts – and more – would all be quickly soaked.

With care, then, she moved herself along the Fields, taking the path which traced along the edge of the Hills. She paused at the Way Down. Nodding, she turned uphill, and then back around to sit upon the rock which guarded the edge of that main artery into the Hills. Sitting high above all wee-folks' height, she drew her knees up under her chin; her flowing skirts draped her. With her arms about her shins and her chin between her knees, she sat and waited through the darkened night.

Beneath the shadow of the Hills which loomed over her shoulders, Carymba watched the sky begin to soften. The black grew fuzzy, and only then sighed away into a charcoal grey. Watching, she decided that it was far too much to say that the day had dawned: 'The night just gave up'. The Fields hardly noticed. The black was gone, and at the edge of weighty grey, barely alight, clung the homes and shops about the Fields. The grass itself lay bowed beneath the heavy dew. There was no sparkle; only the deep-bending blades gave witness to the globs of water dew had left. Otherwise, the dark rich greens lay waiting for the release of day, which may not come today. 'The grass can be so patient. I tend to be more ready for the light of day than the grass seems to be. Those plump green blades seem quite content to wait a day or two, or even more for the spark of sunlight and warmth to bathe them'.

With the Sun's supposed rising, the deep greys became more agitated; the wind began to stir and whip the land with moisture-laden air. Carymba shivered and pulled her shawl more snugly about herself. The image of that flannel blanket peeped into her mind and danced for her. She watched the blanket all unfold, offering her a flannel receptivity. She smiled and even wondered why, or how she had come to leave that snuggling chair. Mother Hougarry's kindnesses were nestled in her mind; she savored them, then shrugged. For she had left for all the inner reasons which she knew too well. She'd left, and now she is content to sit and wait to find her reasonings revealed to her.

From far across the Fields she spied some movement. She looked more carefully to see the Spinners – Chert and Martha, Effie and Gilbert – leaving the Shop and walking around by the Flower Shop. She mused on them. They passed Mary's place. But there came Mary in a hurry, out her door; she stopped, then climbed back up her steps and disappeared inside. Not long afterwards, Mary re-emerged and, slamming her door impatiently, she rushed after the Spinners. Carymba smiled: 'the grass is so patient for Sun. But we are not so given to patience. We prefer not to wait, nor be detained'. Mary caught up with the Spinners at the Big Rock, then disappeared with them onto the Commons.

Carymba thought to follow and almost moved to join them, but chose instead to pause. A silent troop moved stealthily from her right. She leaned over to see Jasper in the lead and a straggling crew of very uncertain, nervous faces trailing behind. They were all from the Fringe, and they bore the appearance of cold and wet, a lean hunger which marked them deeply. These, too, straggled around the Big Rock, onto the Commons, with deep determination.

A rumbling came down the Way Down. Carymba turned her head to see Walter rush down the slope and then stumble past the path and into the soaking grass of the Fields. He sputtered and displayed his anger at the dew and the chill. Surprisingly, however, the burst of outrage passed quickly and he shook himself and stormed toward the Big Rock, and beyond.

The Tinker clamored by, and John and Peder and the laborers; many came and stumbled along beneath her, hurrying onward, beyond the Big Rock.

All these in succession drew Carymba down from her perch. She went carefully, slowly, at her customarily insistent syncopated pace. She rounded the Big Rock and crossed the Commons, being careful on the slick yellow-clay-mud path. At the door, she reached and opened for herself the entrance to the Inn-by-the-Bye. Entering, she saw a wide spectrum sitting there together, eating. The men from the Fringe were silent. Walter looked uncomfortable. Clyde was burrowed in his mug. Mahara smiled, brightening her olive face. Geoffrey in the corner waved; he had a seat there, just for her. She smiled and wove her way across the crowded room: 'This place is brighter. I can be patient here'.

1 June 1986

CCXLV

Crisp air hung over the sparkling dew. High blue skies suspended the whole. The morning Sun had leapt into the sky and the daily trek was advancing well. The shadow of the Leaferites' Hill still spread over the Commons and of the Hills on all of the Fields. The activity of the wee residents was hidden within their homes and shops. The wispish smoke from Marthuida's kitchen was about the only sign of activity a casual observer might find, for other kitchens and stoves were quiet still this morning.

Within that clear and clean, nearly pristine morning meandered one lone figure, young and little, timid and wrapped in her old, dark, hooded cloak. Eliza, so newly come, had not yet found herself a home. Being wary of almost everything, she moved among this friendly folk with careful disbelief. The way these people lived together seemed so open, so free; never before had she seen anything like it. She had met people almost everywhere, and many a table had spread to feed her. Missus Duns had given her space to sleep, any time she pleased. 'That was nice', Eliza thought. 'But my, that sod house was different!' And Mother Hougarry had lent her room – 'where Carymba used to sleep when she *would* stay the night'. Mary had some room, 'and the flowers were so lovely': Eliza smiled at the thought – one of those timid, blushing smiles which caused her hand to pull her hood more over her face.

She had stayed overnight with all of those; others had offered but she had declined. She worried over many things, and who she would decide to trust was first among her worries. 'I sometimes wonder if I were not better off beyond the Great River. Over there, I knew where I stood. Over here, … well, it's all confusing me'.

Her walking this bright morning led Eliza along the edge of the Hills. She was talking to herself in the quiet stillness of the morning. She suspected no one was around. And so she spoke to hear herself, and was surprised to hear another voice: 'Eliza!' She stopped, and felt the blood drain from her face. She touched her cheek: it was suddenly cold to her touch. Her head began to swim, and then to pound as blood raced through her veins. She felt her muscles tense and her eyes began to dart, to plot a plan of escape. 'Relax, Eliza: I'm Carymba. I'm up here, atop this rock. Come up and join me; it's peaceful up here'. Eliza heard the words and quickly glanced above; there shone Carymba's smiling face, looking down, her hair straggling forward along her cheeks. Eliza smiled. Relaxing, now the blood returned on a more normal trek, but with more force than usual. She flushed. Her face was fire, she thought, both red and hot. 'Come up the path, then swing around; a little climb will bring you here'.

Eliza paused and frowned a bit as she studied the steep Way Down. It seemed to her a ready path, one she had not as yet pursued. With a shrug, she turned and started up the climb. As everyone in long skirts climbing the Way Down, she soon hitched them up, to give her feet a place to step. Past the rock she churned, puffing along and anxious to succeed where hills abound although her step is more accustomed to the level ground of Apopar. She charged on past the subtle turn. Carymba called: 'Hold on! You've stepped a mite too far'. Eliza heard, but only slowly did the word engage her mind. She stopped as Carymba called again: 'Wait!' Eliza caught her breath: 'Wait? You said to climb, so climb I did'. 'Yes, but you climb too far, too fast. You lose sight of where you are when you go too fast. Step back a few paces. ... Yes, there, ... now look to your left. ... That's right; now, step through that slit in the brush ... and go around to the other side. You see how you climb, a little steeper now. ... Here: I'll give you hand for this last little bit'.

Eliza's hood fell off as she reached the top of the rock. Her long hair fell free and into her face. Unthinking, she shook her head and her hair flew free, then back to trail behind her neck. She looked around under the shade which hung above the rock in late Spring and Summer, even early Autumn. She whispered: 'The view is lovely here. And we are so very much secluded. That path is not easy, nor has it been heavily used'. 'No, not too many come here. The quiet here is my delight. Even the voices on the path seem far away. The Way Down, as we call it, runs right by this place, but no one stops to climb'. 'Except for you'. 'And you now, too'.

Watching the Fields, they saw the Sun begin to draw back the shadow which had lain all morning across those Fields. The grass, so richly green this time of year, became a blaze of glory as the sunlight danced across the dew. They squinted in the gleam which flashed at them in mirrored action from the field of gold. 'Is it always that bright?' 'On a day like this one, yes. Sometimes, however, they all lay dull – without a dew, on in the glum of an overcast sky'. 'Why do you think Missus Carney sent me here? She's the only one I ever learned to trust. She sent me to the boatman, Wilbur, and he carried me across the River. I was frightened half to death'. 'I can imagine that you were'. 'She told me to find the Inn-by-the-Bye; and I did. Thyruid is a strange man'. 'Oh?' 'Yes. He fits none of the patterns I ever knew'. 'What patterns did you know?' 'He wasn't afraid. And he wasn't pushy. He wasn't the boss. And he wasn't walked all over. I'm not real sure just what he was'. 'I see. Maybe that is why Missus Carney sent you here'. 'I don't know what you mean'.

Carymba grew quiet for a long time. Eliza was uncomfortable in the silence, but could not leave. At last, after her mind had tossed and fumed over all this silence when she expected explanation, she grew weary of the struggle and watched with squinted eyes as the Sun progressed toward them. The Fields remained a glaring blaze, a hand which hid the dimming green behind. Gradually, she realized that the whole did not remain fire, but only where the dew still lay in fresh witness of the blades of green. The fire the Sun ignited there drove the wet away and left a dry, un-flaming Field behind. Eliza broke the silence as the Sun stood overhead and all the beauty she had witness passed away. 'The morning's flash is gone' she said. 'Yes, the Fields are dry and business-laden now'.

'Is lunch-time over now?' 'Are you hungry?' 'I missed breakfast, too'. 'For a girl as young as you, so active learning what there is to learn, or beginning, I should say, the work must leave you starved'. 'My stomach growls. That much I know'. 'We could get lunch at the Inn-by-the-Bye. We should be going there'. 'You think so?' 'Certainly: there is hardly a better place to be. We might find Clyde'. 'Clyde?' 'Yes: he too was sent by Missus Carney'. 'Does she send many?' 'Occasionally, and for many reasons. Wilbur's her best accomplice'. 'Lunch does sound good'. Come on. We have to take the little path. You know it now. Just don't betray it to just anyone'. 'I won't'. Carymba winked and led the cautious trek down to the Way Down and to the Fields.

Together they went, at Carymba's stead pace. Eliza forgot to put up her hood, and the Sun danced warmly on her bouncing hair. 'Clyde plays the shawm. He makes it sing a plaintive song'. 'I heard a shawm once, long ago'. 'You'll like it. The music is the tale which tell us of the rich green growth which sprouts beyond the fiery glory'. 'You know Missus Carney, too?' 'Yes'. 'Does everybody?' 'Almost. You'll know her better once you see'.

8 June 1986

CCXLVI

Bright morning Sun illumined all the sky, a bright and endless blue, the type of sky which invites a pondered, peering gaze, pretending to investigate the whole while really soaking in the purity of the vaulted clarity, the cloudless sky. Beneath that blue, within the shadows cast by the Hills, moved Carymba. She had left her shawl at Mother Hougarry's Hidden Cabin, for the warmth this time of year precluded such a need. The morning crispness bid a brisker pace than normal. So, she hastened her limp along a bit more than usual, swinging her arms energetically. She smiled, admiring the alluring beauty of the day, breathing deeply the freshened air.

Her path had made a circuit of the Fields, beginning at the Big Rock, and moving down before Mary's still-quiet Flower Shop. She had glanced down the wash place where excess rain would slide down to the gully beneath, but kept on, around the corner. The Spinners were not active yet. Neither were the others: craftsmen, weavers, potters, blacksmith, coopers, ironworkers. Even John, at the Foundry, was not about – his furnace banked and burning, but not attended now. The unattended quiet of the Fields that morning, as so many mornings, gave a spacious peace, a freshened frame of mind to the briskly walking Carymba.

At the distant, northern corner of the Fields, she slowed and glanced around. She stopped and, hands upon her hips, she gazed into the scruffy land which makes the Fringe. What paths she could see were clear enough, and solid. The marshy spaces, through which the paths meandered, were wet and murky. Clumps of reedy grass stood stiffly erect, drinking the stagnant waters. There was no breeze, which meant the low stale odors clung to the Fringe, undisturbed; she could detect them as they gradually unfolded for her, spreading from the marsh. Wrinkling her nose in distaste, she thought of going on, quickly away to the far side of the Fields, or even to the Inn-by-the-Bye. She smiled at that prospect, then frowned and turned instead to trace the paths into the Fringe.

Inside the Fringe, the reeds closed behind her, leaving her in a stale, unmoving air. The bright blue sky still shone overhead; she merely needed to look straight up to see it. Closeness in the air came snugly about her as she walked. She knew the Sun, once overhead, would warm the place and make the muggy wrapping denser. And she walked along anyway, making progress into the Fringe's offerings. As usual, the reeds and winding paths left all the quiet faces hidden; she saw no one, and heard nothing. The wanderers of the Fringe learned long ago to walk in silence, unobserved and unobserving. Only when absolutely necessary did one of those secluded ones splash through the shallows. Otherwise, they moved and even Carymba was not able often to hear them, nor observe.

Eyes did see her, though, as she moved with slow care along the narrow trail between the wet and mucky ground on either side. They peeped from clumps of reeds, found by a short jump from some other part of the meandering set of paths. They watched her move, not knowing she saw them, too. They did not trust a newcomer; she knew that. Even one who had come before was not one of them, automatically … for she had come and gone. And that freedom was unaccustomed here. She knew that, too.

The curves and turns all look the same when only a bright blue sky is visible for landmark purposes. The clumps were all alike. Now, the rising Sun was poking into that marshy land, raising steam from all the extra water lying low. Carymba was not sure just where she was; losing direction was part of the mystique of the Fringe, and she once more succumbed. One curve, however, opened on an opening, not unexpected although the exact location of this inner meeting ground was not recalled. She nodded in contentment when she arrived within the space.

Slowing her step some more, Carymba ambled on around the circle, seemingly ignoring all the populated clumps surrounding her. At last, she found the entrances all fade from view, lost amid the sameness of the Fringe. Across the way, where she had passed during the circuit of the opening, Jasper stepped out and stood. Seeing him, Carymba stopped and turned toward him – directly across the circle – and smiled softly.

The Sun was high now, and the still air warmed and stank. Jasper felt his own sweat drip down his body, uncomfortably. He watched her; the Sun shone on her, dancing reddish and straw off her hair. He smiled, knowingly. Or, rather, he smiled as much as he could smile in such a place. In the light, her blue eyes flashed and a subtle pink emerged on her cheek. He thought he felt that brightness in her once again, and shuddered at the memories he wished he'd lost long ago. 'Hello'; he spoke in a soft low voice which boomed across the silent opening, shattering the all-pervasive echoless quiet. 'Hello', she returned, more softly, or so it seemed because the silence was already gone. 'What brings you here? My fellow wanderers are nervous, having you here'. 'They always are, and so are you'. 'The habit of silence and freedom from watchers comes quite easily to one. I've been here long enough to belong. But you just come and go, a fleeting touch we do not handle well'. 'Am I unwelcome then?' She bent her head to the side, causing the Sun's shimmer to quiver in their sight. 'No. Just give us time to trust'. 'I'm in no hurry'.

Near Jasper, another figure came out and stood and stared. Carymba glanced down, then back, and nodded her acknowledgment. He stood in frozen silence until Jasper poked him. 'Uh … h … he … he …'. 'Hello' she answer the stammered greeting gently.

Gradually, the faces came, from Jasper's side and then all around. She watched them come and crowd the circle's rim. Each face betrayed a fear in twitch or quiver at the corners. She nodded gently, smiled and, with her glance, comforted each one. The faces dripped with sweat, wrung out by nerves compounding heat and heavy humidity. The bodies slumped, curved over slightly, ready to retreat, or turn, or strike, uncertain of their place. Yet steady stood each one. Jasper spoke at last: 'Well, we are here; and so are you. What happens next?' 'I'm not sure'. 'You have, then, no agenda set for us'. 'No. I entered … on a whim, some would say. But really, I came because I needed to come'. 'And why is that?' 'I don't know. I wasn't curious: I've been here before. Neither was I drawn by the sweetness of the setting'. 'I can understand that'. 'I came, I suppose, to see the lot of you'. 'And here we are'. 'All of us. Is there a seat around? I'm … I'm tired'.

A splash sounded near her there, as one broke ranks and plunged into the marsh. The steps were heard tracing through the water, then no more. All the rest stood staring at her, accepting slowly her look back.

The splashes sounded once again, coming louder, toward them. Finally, with panting breath, the one who broke the ranks returned, carrying a crude stool. He set it on the ground, beside her. 'Thank you' she said, smiling especially for him, and touching his cheek: he blushed. She sat, and sighed. The blushing man sat before her. Others slowly came and did the same. Jasper alone stood, at the rear of the group. Carymba looked at him; he smiled. 'I've rarely been so warmly welcomed'. Jasper nodded, then sat down, too.

15 June 1986

CCXLVII

Strong wind blew heavy rain in nearly horizontal sheets across the plains of Apopar. With wild abandon the beating bombs of driven water crashed into the huts in which were huddled the fearful many wee folk there. This was a day for staying home, with the door closed, and hoping that they all survived the arrogant blast of the storm. As evening drew near, the fading of the faded light of day left slate-black driven clouds to lurk more menacingly. Outside the huts, the rain assaulted unseen. Inside, the huddled groups sustained a timid light which flickered off their faces, casting deeply the shadows of worry and concern. The faces sat in whitened silence, listening to the countless beating of the rain, the moan and whine of wind. They sat, carved with anxious waiting till this natural storm should pass.

The huts groaned, too, for they were stressed by the restless haunt of wind. The whole atmosphere was that of heavy oppression. Apopar shuddered, altogether, under the rage of wind and beating bite of rain. Among those battered huts and deeply bowing shrubs, and under straining branches which cast spare leaves into the wind, staggered Missus Carney. Her long black clothes were drenched, and clung to her skinny frame. White wispy hair was soaked and clung to her head in plastered swirls. She walked by leaning all her strength into the wind and keeping herself from blowing along like so much shredded tumbleweed.

No one inside those huts imagined anyone would be out, unless, of course, their hut had collapsed under the wind and storm. No one inside those huts dared entertain the thought of collapse; such calamity would render them helpless at the last.

No one outside those huts thought to find anyone wandering about on a day like this, if they had no need, nor order to be out. And only the unlucky Guards were out to witness authority's stand this day turned night, when only wind was heard, and fierce rain was felt, and nothing was to be seen. Indeed, most Guards, even the unluckiest, had taken refuge. Only one remained to walk around, inspecting and enforcing the reign of rulers long unseen. That one attempted to make his rounds, seeking out calamity's signs on pretense of inspection. He too was wet; he too leaned into the wind, trusting memory to find his way around. He was not as wet as Missus Carney, however, for he had taken time to use the slicker given out by those in authority.

The meandering Guard watched carefully, seeing nothing in the lightless night. He heard instead the creaking of branches and the groaning of huts. The wind whined and the rain slapped against him, against almost everything. The weather made him wonder if he could hear himself think. Musing over that odd thought, he took to muttering out loud; his voice was swallowed by a moan the wind inspired. The voice was unheard, so he spoke again, louder. That, too, was masked by riveting rain. So he shouted, and heard the sound of his voice. A grin swept across his face, reflecting an enjoyment over that civilized sound, the croaking roar of his own voice. He roared again, just to hear himself against the haughty hastening wind. He heard, and laughed, assured that he was not merely his own fantasy.

Out of that howling wind, into his ears, a different voice appeared. He started: 'Who's there?!' he bellowed officially. 'Who's fool enough to lean into that wet old wind?' came the shrill reply. 'A question for a question, eh?' he boomed as loud as he could. 'Yes. And are you the only Guard out tonight?' 'The rest decided only fools would stay this storm outside'. 'Wise thought'. 'But are you?' 'This night is as black as any night has been'. 'None blacker: I find you only by your voice. Here's mine: Aoo … oo' she howled.

Groping, he found her drenched and laughing. 'It's not cold, this rain. But the wind drives awfully hard'. 'You should be inside'. 'And where? I've not been home all day. And getting there now is more than I can muster'. 'Commandeer a rest inside a hut, most anywhere'. 'Fine for you to say'. 'Ha! You'd be more welcome than I in any of these bleak huts'. 'True enough, in weather better than this. But now those doors are barred, and only resentment will open them'. 'And I, I assume, am the master of resentment'.

'Tonight, at least, yes, you are'. 'Then resentment's master must make a move; for you are drenched, I fear'. 'You could wring me out, and make a lake, or could if there were more of me'. Grabbing her arm by luck, he dragged her after him: 'Come along: we cannot have such truancy tonight'. 'Truancy?' 'The term will do in the midst of a storm'. 'Indigence, perhaps'. 'Give whatever name you like. Just come along'.

Inside one hut, not far away, three huddled figures guarded the candle which lit their home, free from the storm. They felt fortunate, in a way, for this storm did not meet their door. As a result, they did not have the door leaking rain and creaking and groaning and being a constant threat to forsake its latch and have the storm assault their hearth. They watched that flame dance in the drafts, the inevitable drafts on a stormy night. They watched the candle light their meal as they ate their porridge in silence. The hut overhead seemed to lean in the wind, and then relax as a gust passed on, before the next gust came to shove some more, and then lean the hut a little. The old woman felt herself leaning with the hut in which she'd lived so long, and then relaxing. Having realized at last her antic, she chuckled to herself. The candle flickered, and she leaned once more with her wind-pressed hut.

That trio felt secure, alone, at peace in spite of the wind, until a rap beat on their door. Each found their breath held tight, and all their blood go racing round as their hearts pounded wildly in the night. The rap repeated, louder now. They looked at one another, questioning. Again, the rap beat insistently. With a shrug, the old woman rose. It was her hut longer than the others had been alive. And she, alone, toddled to the door. The others sat, hushed. She creaked her old, old voice: 'Yes?' 'Let us in!' 'Why?' 'Because it is wet out here'. 'Oh'. That's all she said, and then lifted the latch and creaked open the door. The light flickered wildly behind her, and yet threw illumination out the door. The official slicker shone. She hid a sneer. At the extension of the arm, a thin, wet, dripping figure stood, pale and plastered with white hair twisted in the wind. The deep eyes glanced about. The old woman grinned at her old woman guest. 'Come in. Come in. You're wet as a rag'. 'And nearly as limp'. 'There's a fire and some porridge, if you'd like'. 'I'd like'. The Guard shoved her slightly, in through the door. The old woman glanced at him, before he turned away. She began to close the door, then stopped and, on impulse cackled into the lee of the storm: 'There's porridge enough for you, too'.

He paused, then turned again and entered. 'Thank you. The night is dark, even for such as I may be, or appear to be. 'Yes. Appearances are more than they ought to be. Porridge on a stormy night: now *that* is real'.

22 June 1986

CCXLVIII

Evening had folded all around the Inn-by-the-Bye. And Hyperbia was nestling into sleep – the whole land, or nearly so. Within the Inn, Thyruid had but one lamp left on, the one beside the doorway into his – and Marthuida's room. That lamp was low, and flickered slightly in imagined breezes. Each flicker of the lamp sent long, diffuse shadows dancing over all the room. If those shadows were not so quickly dancing, their very heaviness would suggest the lumbering, lazy shuffling of sleeping giants. They made the sultry room remain lively, until the lamp go out and darkness fully pervade the room.

Within that room, Thyruid lumbered slowly about, yawning and pausing to stretch and bend himself while mumbling through the last few chores before concluding in informality the day begun near dawn. In such a time, he wearily finished things. Marthuida had finished in her kitchen and had gone to bed. He too must follow soon; but first he had to finish straightening his dining room. 'I like it better when it's all ready for morning' he mumbled through another yawn as he shoved another chair into place.

One last glance around the room convinced Thyruid that all was done. He turned and shuffled slowly around the room, aiming more or less directly toward the last lamp and thence the door into his room. His eyes grew glassy after a long, long yawn; he had to pause and blink them clear with a battery of flickers of his lids. Cleared once more, the eyes then guided his hand to reach the light. Just then, the front door opened; Thyruid paused, and glanced toward the foyer. The wall blocked his view of the door, and so he waited. Heavy steps pounded across the foyer and brought to sight the burly figure of Clyde. Thyruid watched as Clyde stopped atop the step, his hands upon his waist. The heavy beard twitched as Clyde shook his jaw and pursed his lips, and frowned. 'Good evening' spoke Thyruid, in spite of himself.

Clyde glanced over: 'Oh, you're up yet. Good'. 'Barely up, but up: that is true. What can I do for you?" 'The kitchen is closed'. 'Correct: Marthuida has it all shut down until morning'. 'Well, that's what I get for being late'. 'True enough'. Thyruid yawned massively, not even trying to disguise it. If, however, Clyde saw the yawn (and he *must* have seen it), he chose to ignore it. For, stepping into the dining room, he strode to the cold hearth, pulled out his customary seat and plopped himself into it. 'This has been a long day' he said, his forehead furrowed. 'Yes, it has' replied Thyruid, slumping slightly by his still-lit lamp.

Clyde sat slumping, his arms folded on his stomach, his feet stretched out straight from the edge of his hair to the floor. His eyes studied the vacant shadows, dancing still. Thyruid watched him through weighted eyes, pondering the lumbering evening tide. He wanted to shut off the light and go to bed. He wanted to end all hospitality tonight. He wanted to pretend that Clyde was not there. In fact, as Clyde sat submerged in silence, he almost convinced himself that he was dreaming, and the proper conclusion of *this* dream would be to go, recline within his room, leaving everything dark until morning came. He even nodded to himself and reached again to dim the lamp.

But then Clyde's voice destroyed illusion by proclaiming right out loud: 'You're not too tired to sit a minute, are you, Thyruid?' The question hung upon the shadowed air, or so it seemed to Thyruid. The Innkeeper blinked his eyes some more and tried to guess what words should chase that brash request. He watched the shadows dance more lively now; 'what breeze disturbs the light?' he wondered in his mind. 'Perhaps I'm breathing far too hard. … No. … Well, I don't know. … Now, how do I answer?" Bed is so attractive! But I am the host; he is my guest. …' Silence lasted quite some time, and Thyruid began to wonder if this weren't a bad, bad dream. His eyes weighed heavily and he needed to get off his feet. He reached for the lamp, again, to bring to an end these lengthy dreams. Besides, his legs throbbed.

Clyde's voice interrupted once again. 'Do sit down'. Thyruid squeaked a chair, the one nearest the lamp, and flopped himself into its waiting lap.

'What's the problem tonight?' 'Oh, no problem: I had just been pondering all the silly, deeper things in life'. 'Oh, like what?' 'Like the changes I have found in my aging'. .You are not aging much, as yet. At least I can tell I am far older. My legs feel that tonight'. 'Am I keeping you up?' The note of unthought anxiety wavered in Clyde's voice. Thyruid noticed and almost played the tone for release to slumber. Yet somewhere in those ponderous shadows lurked the hint that kept him seated. 'Oh, I'm doing alright'. That's all he said, although he hoped Clyde would not be *too* long.

'Good. I spent today walking. And my legs are tired. Not too tired: but the last ways to the Inn – they really did not want to lift my feet. My shins hurt sharply, like a cramp. Only sitting down relieves that pain. And, better yet, I ought to raise my feet. And bed would feel so good right now'. Thyruid's droopy eyes pried open a bit further. He half-smiled in his round-faced way, and nodded agreement over the notion of lying down for a good night's sleep. 'But first I have to put together my day'. Thyruid sighed as quietly as he could. 'Where did you go?'

'First, I walked around the Fields. That was early, after I left this morning. I watched the Tradesman, all of them at work in peace. I smiled and meandered around. I went up into the Crossed Hills and said hello to Mother Hougarry. Then went on through Uiston, saw Father John, and moved along, to Guerric's strange city with the market square. The Gypsies and some hidden lands nearer the Great River were my next discoveries. I sat with some of those in hiding, sharing whispers over news and thoughts'.

'I take it you found them important'.

'Important? I hadn't thought in quite those terms; but, yes, important they were. I spent all afternoon with them. They had moved by night to the coast, then along the brush near the seashore until they reached the Great River. They said they did not dare turn back. And just as bad was staying there. So they took a log, held on, and swam. Of course the current shoved them out into the Sea. They clung the tighter and tried to swim their tiny raft to shore. Once past the River's thrust, they found they could take advantage of some back-currents and eddies. And so they made it to the briar-ridden part of the Shore and came up this bank of the Great River, seeking food and shelter. What they had was not much. And they still were afraid. They had no long roots here, like Father John or Mother Hougarry. They were not at home like the Tradesmen on the Fields. They were not arranged, like the people in Guerric's old territory. But they breathed easier. I sat and watched the Great River and told them of the Inn-by-the-Bye, and all. They wouldn't believe me, but snuck away to leave me watching the Great River swirling by in front of me.

Thyruid had tried to listen, but his eyes were very heavy, and he snored. Clyde heard him when he paused in his tale. 'It *is* too late, I guess'. He rose and went to turn off the lamp, and go to bed. 'Sorry I kept you up. But what can I do now?' Thyruid merely snorted in his dreams. 'Good night, good host'.

29 June 1986

CCXLIX

Drizzle dripped, and every leaf and twig was duly laden with dripping drizzle, stored until a vagrant breeze disturbed and sent an additional, secondary shower onto any who may have been kept largely dry before. As with drizzly days, the sky hung low and dark. There was no anger in the skies, but only a lazy melancholy weeping greyly upon the earth.

Those great drips which fall from weighted leaves and the corners of twigs, where water collects on drizzly days, came down irregularly and therefore unpredictably, to splatter noisily upon the Hidden Cabin. At least it was noisy inside, with the drumbeat crashing on the roof and the excess splatter washing quickly over the edges and walls. Mother Hougarry did not notice anymore. But her young visitor, Eliza, had not lived in the woods before. Where she grew up, there were no overhanging trees, and therefore no random drips which came so unexpectedly. Each drop surprised her, and she would jump.

'Would you like some tea?' asked Mother Hougarry, believing that the beverage would help calm her obviously nervous guest. 'Oh, not just now, thank you'. 'I thought you might relax with a cup. And I wanted one anyway'. 'Just go ahead. I really don't see how you stay so calm. Those drips, as you call them, sound like they are going to break through the roof and destroy your house'. 'Oh, is that what is bothering you! I'm sorry. They come so often; and I have lived her so long that I barely notice them anymore. Honest: not one of those drips has ever come through the roof. In fact, once I stopped shaking, I noticed the rafters didn't shake either'. 'Amazing! To me, it looks like everything shakes'. 'Usually that means that either everything does shake, or you shake in fright'. 'Silly me! It must be me who shakes!' 'Would you like some tea now? I can't stop the drops, but with some care we might hold down the damage from slopped tea'. 'I'll try. Thank you'.

Mother Hougarry toddled to her stove, took the hot kettle and poured two cups of tea. As she poured, an unusually large spat of water crashed on the roof overhead. Eliza leaped to her feet, her eyes wide and her blood draining from her face. Mother Hougarry neither spilled a drop nor was visibly (nor invisibly) ruffled. 'That one was bigger than usual' stammered Eliza. 'Yes, it was a significant drop. Those leaves sometimes gather a large glob of water before dropping it down on us'. As she finished preparing the tea, Mother Hougarry brought the cups to her table. 'Considering all the unaccustomed racket this morning, perhaps we would do better if we sipped our tea at the table'. 'That ... yes, that sounds quite ... quite reasonable' replied Eliza.

The pair moved to the table and sat down. Eliza looked at her tea, afraid to pick it up. Mother Hougarry noticed the blank gaze. 'Isn't it marvelous how that steam swirls and curls upward? I always enjoy watching the twists and turns it makes before it simply disappears into thin air'. 'I had never noticed before'. 'Living alone in quiet like this does give a body leisure to observe. Besides all that, there is nothing else to do to break the tedium between visitors ... except chores, of course'. 'Of course'. 'And even folk like I find myself to be are not inclined to re-do chores all day'. 'So you watch the steam curl up from your tea'. 'Yes, that and the oily swirls on the surface of the tea, which spin around in slow company with the steam's outpouring'. 'Now that you mention it, I do see those things. They are surprising to observe. Really they are'. 'People say I am silly, or bored, or both. But they don't see half of what I see, for all their eager looking'. 'I believe that. But maybe they see different things'. 'They are in different places. But they tell me of seeing dreadful things; they are so afraid! Somehow, I may see more in my dust-kitties and tea-steam than they do in their nervous fright'.

Another large glob flopped upon the roof. Eliza was watching her steam at the time, and started a bit. The jump, however, was minor, hardly ruffling her at all. She smiled at herself afterward, when she realized how steady she was all of a sudden. She noticed the light playing off the oily swirls atop her cup of tea. Another splat landed overhead; she heard it but did not jump at all. Her breathing continued as normal. Her pulse was soft, relaxed. She smiled at her sudden control, and began to become a little bit cocky.

Mother Hougarry sipped at her tea, still piping hot. 'Ahh ...' she said; 'I've grown fond of my tea over the years. Do you like it, too, Eliza?' 'Oh yes. I mean, I do imagine I will. ... Where I lived ... before ... tea was rare. The young ones had to wait until later to try some'. 'I see. So this is your first cup of tea?' 'Yes. Really it is'. 'Sip it slowly, then; do savor it'. 'Thank you for the advice'.

With nervous bravery, Eliza lifted the cup. The handle seemed slippery in her fingers, so she touched the rim on the other side with her fingertips on her other hand. The fine cup had become quite hot, although the handle was comfortable; she was surprised. Drawing the cup to her lips, as she had seen Mother Hougarry do, she sniffed. The odor was strange, with a sharpness she had not anticipated. She wiggled her nose, and wrinkled it at the pungent aroma, then quickly blew the steam away, lifted the cup to her lips (it was hot!) and sipped softly. The liquid rolled into her mouth – not a lot, but enough. She sat up, surprised. She cocked her head and frowned, thinking: 'did I burn my mouth? No. But there is an oily feel now. Is that the oil I saw on the surface? And the taste ... well, the taste is ... is ... is ... I don't know how to describe it'. Setting her cup down, she heard Mother Hougarry's quiet tones: 'How is the tea, Eliza?'

'Oh! Fine, just fine, thank you'. She blushed; then added 'but hot'. Another great glob of water crashed onto the roof. Eliza looked about and saw nothing shake, except the water-rippled view through the window. 'The taste, I take it, was rather new'. 'Very new! I've never tasted anything like that before. I used to wonder what my grandmother liked, but I was never old enough to try'. 'Tea really is not that bad!' 'I meant, only the old folks had tea, because we had a hard time getting tea in Apopar'. 'Well, it may have helped you ease yourself'. 'Oh, but that was you more than the tea. You got my mind off that terrible crash and now I've sort of got a perspective – I think that's the word – on it'.

A rapping came at the door. Eliza stiffened and her breath grew light. Her fingers clutched the tea cup snugly, in spite of the heat. Mother Hougarry patted her shoulder: 'I'll get that, Eliza'. The old woman tottered to the door, and opened it to greet Carymba. 'My dear, I am always glad to have you come. But you should have come before the drizzle dripped all over us. Here you would be warm and dry. Look at you now! Come in, and let's find you some dry clothes. And then some tea. … You know Eliza, don't you?' 'Yes. Hello, Eliza'. 'Hello'. Mother Hougarry dragged the dripping Carymba to the corner where some clothes were found. While waiting, Eliza thought about Carymba, and that drizzle, and those large globs from the leaves which fall on roofs, and maybe on others, too. The tea: she sipped it again, now more temperate in feel. The taste was smoother, too.

Another splat hit the Hidden Cabin. Eliza chuckled at the memory of her own fears.

6 July 1986

CCL

Night hung low and dark in the sky, moonless but spangled with uncounted stars, each competing for space to spot the velvet black. Along the Beach blew a steady wind, hot and drenched with water. Everything clung close to people in their attempted sleep, and in their heat-drugged stupors which passed for sleep that night. One, at least, had given up: Carymba. She walked along the lapping Sea, allowing the warming waters to slosh about her toes. She had hitched her skirts from the top, rolling some distance under the waist band, keeping the hem relatively dry – although the more restless waves had long since drenched the lowest bit. The Sea was lazy in the bay, where the wind rushed long across the waves, stirring water but not in company with lapping of the earth-heaved waters on the Beach. Thus, she walked along and felt wet sand and trickling salt water between her toes. That much, at least, was cooled for now; the rest of her was wet and sticky in the muggy wind.

Day was coming soon; she knew that as the stars began to dim before her eyes began to notice the gradual light in the distant east. Then, along the Sea's horizon slowly lightened the black of night. A slow grey band emerged, and brightened into white along the edge. Then all did race into the sky, chasing black night hastily away and pulling upward a low red bulge. The haze which hung within the wind caused the bulging blob to quiver in the sight, and hang as half an egg upon the horizon's fuzzied edge. Slowly now, it stretched up, seeming in the sight to lift the Sea as well, to moisten further the coming day. Carymba snorted: 'more of that is quite unneeded now!'

The Sun, once separated from the watery horizon, rose as a lazy old red ball, poking its fresh heat into the still relentless wind. The world grew more oppressive, and the Sea appeared more lazy still. The sand began to warm again, even where the Sea attempted to bathe the edges of the Beach. Carymba kept her feet within that gently-washed fringe until she neared the end of the Valley Road. There, she re-applied her sandals and started out over the baked Beach sand, climbing toward the Sea Road, and, over that, to enter the Valley Road.

Once Carymba had made that change, exertion added to the rising temperature of the soggy air to make her sweat more heavily. She felt her hair plaster along unruly rivulets, down her cheek, over her chin, along her neck. The hair ended in continuous drips, which then ran on and on, down her body, growing ever stronger, to her waist band. That band soaked and became a soggy clump about her middle. Even the Sea-wetted hem grew warm and slapped her shins with sticky goo, then cling unwelcomely. The Valley Road soon brought the hot wind to a stop as she entered the lee of the Crossed Hills. The wind had become far too hot and moist to cool anymore. But now the earth itself seemed to exhale steam as well, and the familiar choking heat of Summer's worst days came upon her, remembered in the re-presencing of discomfort.

The Beach was growing hotter; she knew. And wee folk know enough to leave the Sea alone; so, that coolant was not really available to her. None of the wee folk were comfortable today. She thought of Mother Hougarry: on the porch by now, rocking and fanning herself until night fall. Missus Duns will stay inside, trusting her sod house and the Hills to keep her as comfortable as may be possible. Marthuida may not cook today; but that can't last too many days before the cool substitutes need replenishing at the stove. Yves will wade in the stream, and so will Betsy. Their size makes that safe. The Fringe will seethe more closely than the rest. Uiston will bake; 'poor Father John' she said out loud to no one at all. 'Mary: yes, I'll go see Mary in her hot house Flower Shop today'.

With new direction, then, Carymba trudged through the Valley, past the Narrows and on to the 'Y'. There she took the path which leads along the Fields, toward the corner and past Mary's Shop. Inland here, the breeze was softer, moister, just as hot as it had been on the Beach. And the Sun was not even yet over the Crossed Hills, leaving the Fields, or most of them, in a dull shadow. Thus Carymba padded her way to Mary's Shop.

Knocking at the door, Carymba waited. Inside, Mary stirred, but slowly. She had not yet pulled herself from bed. Instead, she had lain there dripping, her night clothes clinging to her body in wet splotches. Her sheets were all damp. Her body was limp and weary from the off and on pretending sleep, always disturbed by another river of sweat. Now she heard the door and uttered weakly: 'Just a minute, please'. Of course, Carymba did not hear but rapped again, and took to whistling softly. Mary heard the whistle, and the rap, and sighed. One leg flopped across the edge of her bed and slapped a foot upon the floor: she moaned. Carymba tapped again. 'She must be sleeping, and sleeping-in. That is not like her'. So she tapped again as Mary shoved herself half-erect, sitting in a growing puddle, on her bed.

Before Carymba rapped again, Mary had changed her gown for something dryer and less clingy. She had even wiped the past accumulations off, although she moistened over all more quickly than she dried. Then, barefoot, with hair awry and plastered every which way onto her head, she sputtered to the door. Opening, she saw her friend: 'I'm glad it's you! I must look awful. And just a minute ago, I looked even worse'. 'I'm not so neat myself this morning'. 'True enough: come in. I'll find some water; I'm not in the mood for making tea'. 'A glass will fit me fine'.

Mary's windows were open; everybody's were, in hopes of catching a lighter breeze, to ease the weight of the spell which was cast by the rising Sun and the hot, hot wind. They had no luck, except that moving air gave fond illusion of relief. Mary and Carymba, sitting near the window by the Fields, began to sip their glass of coolish water. Suddenly, there splattered in the window cold water, muddy water. At the same time there was a rushing sound all around the house. The two enjoyed the surprising muddy splash, but were startled nonetheless. They spun about to look outside. The Sun was shining over on the corner of the Fields, and yet the dirty water dribbled down the window panes. 'I'll have to wash them, now' Mary said with a perplexed tone. 'But from where did it all come?' 'I don't know. It's dirty: not rain'. 'True enough'.

The pair grew curious and, setting down their emptied glasses, went out the door. The Fields were just beginning to be bathed in sunlight. The steam rose from the sod; they could almost see it rising there. The opened door met the rising temperature upon the Fields. They did not like that omen. But at their feet lay a splatter of muddy water, considerable water for such a time as this. The sky above was rich and blue; not a cloud at all was there. The face of the Flower Shop dripped with dirty water; the streaks were plainly seen. 'What kind of relief is this?' they said to one another, and looked about while standing on the stoop.

Suddenly, once more, there crashed from overhead a mass of water, rushing down and soaking them. The water felt cold, and once they regained their balance (they managed not to fall from the stoop), they looked around. 'What is going on?' yelled Mary. A giggle from behind the shop told her quickly. Another splash: another giggle, and the two went out behind the shop to laugh in the cool water gathered there, with Yves and Betsy peeking in with giggles from the Commons, back behind, beyond the rough.

13 July 1986

Appendix
Texts For The Stories

CCI	Mark 6:7-13	CCXXVI	Jeremiah 1:4-10
CCII	Ephesians 5:15-20	CCXXVII	2 Corinthians 3:12 – 4:2
CCIII	John 6:60-69	CCXXVIII	Luke 4:1-13
CCIV	Deuteronomy 4:1-8	CCXXIX	Genesis 15:5-18
CCV	James 2:1-5	CCXXX	1 Corinthians 10:1-13
CCVI	Mark 8:27-38	CCXXXI	Luke 15:11-32
CCVII	Jeremiah 11:18-20	CCXXXII	Isaiah 43:16-21
CCVIII	James 5:1-6	CCXXXIII	Philippians 2:5-11
CCIX	Mark 10:2-16	CCXXXIV	Luke 22:7-20
CCX	Proverbs 3:13-20	CCXXXV	Exodus 15:1-18
CCXI	Hebrews 4:12-16	CCXXXVI	Revelation 1:9-19
CCXII	Mark 10:46-52	CCXXXVII	John 21:1-19
CCXIII	Deuteronomy 6:1-9	CCXXXVIII	Acts 13: 14, 43-52
CCXIV	Hebrews 9:24-28	CCXXXIX	Revelation 21:1-5
CCXV	John 18:33-37	CCXL	John 14:23-29
CCXVI	Galatians 6:6-10	CCXLI	Acts 7:55-60
CCXVII	Jeremiah 33:14-16	CCXLII	Acts 2:1-21
CCXVIII	Philippians 1:3-11	CCXLIII	John 3:1-16
CCXIX	Luke 3:7-18	CCXLIV	1 Kings 8:38-43
CCXX	Micah 5:1-5a	CCXLV	Galatians 1:11-24
CCXXI	Galatians 4:4-7	CCXLVI	Luke 7:36 – 8:3
CCXXII	Luke 2:36-40	CCXLVII	Zechariah 12:7-10
CCXXIII	Isaiah 42:1-7	CCXLVIII	Galatians 4:31 – 5:1, 13-18
CCXXIV	1 Corinthians 12:3-11	CCXLIX	Luke 10:1-12, 17-20
CCXXV	Luke 1:1-4; 4:14-21	CCXLIX	Deuteronomy 30:9-14

About the Author

I am a retired minister from the Christian Church (Disciples of Christ) living in the hills of the Northern Panhandle of West Virginia. I began writing these stories as a part of my background reflection for sermon preparation in August 1981; I continued the discipline for nearly twenty-five years. The changes in my circumstances twenty-two years into the process eventually brought the series to an end. I came to refer to my stories as fairy-tale exegesis of the text from which I would be preaching the following service. I now live in retirement with my wife of forty-seven years, two dogs, and several cats.

Printed in the United States
By Bookmasters